# Divinely Dramatic

## by

# Sandra L. Young

**Divinely Dramatic**

Cover Art by *The Wild Rose Press, Inc.*

The Wild Rose Press, Inc.
PO Box 708
Adams Basin, NY 14410-0708
Visit us at www.thewildrosepress.com

Publishing History
First Edition, 2023
Trade Paperback ISBN 978-1-5092-5187-2
Digital ISBN 978-1-5092-5188-9

Published in the United States of America

When compared to Divine Vintage's pristine order, the room reflected a surreal mashup. How in the world would she find anything she needed up here? Her attention flitted around, seeking a semblance of anything Victorian, and she felt her stomach tighten. She'd have to dig through the disarray, with little hope of unearthing any suitable pieces. Super-organized Justine must not have been up here since her last costuming gig a year prior.

"This is a jungle. I don't think—" Marcy halted and did a double-take. A faint white glow had started to pulse in the far corner. Lindsay faced the same direction and didn't seem to notice as she offered vague words of guidance.

She couldn't force herself to tune in. Her focus stayed riveted on the brightening cloud. The glow resembled...an aura. White, for a bright, intuitive believer. Marcy frowned and stepped nearer. The light fluttered into waves as she approached, spooking her heart rate into a pounding drumbeat. The illumination intensified when she reached out a tentative hand, sending her reeling back as it dimmed and disappeared. She grabbed a dozen heavy, hanging costumes and shoved them away, exposing a bare wall. No lightbulb. No lamp. No person. A chill ran through her, and she whirled toward her companion, who appeared rightly confused.

After extensive research over the past three years, she'd finally become comfortable with seeing and categorizing auras. But in relation to people, not hovering in the air in a disconnected, ghostly fashion.

## Praise for Sandra L. Young

**DIVINE VINTAGE:**

"What an amazing transcendent historical romance…A phenomenal tale that is truly a delight!"

*~ InD'Tale Magazine*

**DIVINELY DRAMATIC:**

"…Young immerses us in the chaos and camaraderie of community theater, complete with a resident ghost, weaves in a romance, and ties it all up in a mystery that can only be solved when Marcy taps into a power she's long tried to conceal. A heart-warming romance with a touch of magic."

*~ Kerry Anne King, author of Improbably Yours*

"Cuddle into your favorite cozy chair with this clever, entertaining ghostly novel with a bit of spice and heat. Sandra L. Young does it so well."

*~ Linda Rosen, author of The Emerald Necklace*

"…a great job of weaving romantic threads and a strong dose of the paranormal…makes for an intriguing read in this new, lively work."

*~ Nancy Nau Sullivan, Author of The Blanche Murninghan Mysteries*

# Acknowledgement

One of my great joys through the publishing journey has been meeting other authors. Both in-person and online, I've gathered a wealth of wisdom and support. The strongest connections have come through The Wild Rose Press (especially The Terrific Ten and editor Kaycee John), the Writer Support Group hosted by Lainey Cameron and Charlotte Dane, Women's Fiction Writers Association, WF Critique Group, and 2022 Debuts. Much gratitude to them all, and to my local support system of family, friends and fiancé Rick Swanson.

For this sequel, I received plot line guidance from a friend in Juvenile Services and Lisa Faustino, Director, Hollins University Graduate Programs in Children's Literature. Finally, thanks to LaPorte Little Theatre for allowing me to take liberties with small details. I've performed in several wonderful shows there through the years. The costume loft truly isn't disorganized!

"We are all in the gutter. But some of us are looking at the stars." – Oscar Wilde

Chapter One

*September 2016*

To Marcy Alexander, agreeing to costume a community theater production—for the first time—called for an ultra-special splurge. She'd savor an easy day and enjoy her friends' company instead of juggling two part-time jobs. Her lips curved as she imagined a swanky spa visit with mani-pedis and a full-body massage which hopefully would ease muscles strained from hefting platters of food and piles of vintage garments.

The fantasy bubble burst.

First, she had to figure out how to costume a cast of eight strangers in Victorian finery. She booted up her laptop on the kitchen table in the modernized log cabin, backed by '80s dance tunes and the savory scent of her mom's cooking. "*The Importance of Being Earnest*," she muttered. "What a wacky, old-fashioned name."

"By the great Oscar Wilde," her mom chimed in from the fifties-era stove, where she'd refused help to create a vegetarian chili. "When you read the script, you'll appreciate his sarcastic wit."

Surrounded by the fragrance of chopped peppers and tomatoes, Pat Alexander seemed thrilled at her daughter's new project. *Too thrilled*. "About time you got out and loosened up. You know what they say: all work and no play." She snorted a chuckle and waved the paring knife in her gnarled hand. "No *play*. Get it? Anyway, I can't wait for your dramatic interpretation. I'm betting on Steampunk."

"I imagine they'll prefer traditional." Marcy regarded her bestie's costume suggestions, handwritten in neat, cursive rows, and drawn from years of expertise in managing fashion displays at the local museum. Yet this afternoon, Justine had begged *her* to take on full responsibility for providing costumes for an exacting period show.

"Personally, I'm all for combat boots, bustiers, and bustles." She twisted an auburn curl around her finger and looked up to catch her mom's smirky expression transform into a wince. The knife clattered onto the cutting board.

At least she'd kept some control of the sharp implement. Two pottery dinner plates had smashed at their feet the week before. Both were irreplaceable; her mom couldn't create replacements. Marcy's heart twinged. "Hey. My eyes are tired from reading all those notes. Let me finish chop-chopping." She jumped to her feet and strode toward the stove.

"With blurred eyes? You want to lose a finger?" Her mother eyed the knife with a scowl, as if it had chosen to leap out of her grasp. "Fine. Take over. You cook every night, and I wanted to give you a break." She stepped aside and rubbed the ridge of bumpy nodules on her left hand. Yet she continued to hover at the poured concrete counter.

*Oh no.* Marcy stiffened, trapped in the corner. She'd have to shove past and run to avoid their next inevitable topic. She could almost hear the words rolling their way up her mom's throat. Their conversations featured a variation of hints, nudges, discussion, disagreement toward pursuing her master's degree.

"Listen, when you're back on the computer, check the next entry deadline for the campus in Virginia. You don't want to miss out again in January."

Marcy's assured slicing rhythm misfired. She gasped as a dot of blood bloomed on the end of her index finger. "Damn it."

"Sorry. Didn't mean to distract you." Her mom grimaced. "I'll get a bandage."

"Paper towels work fine." She ripped a piece from the nearby roll. "Sit down and relax. *Please*." The tone came out harsher than intended.

Lips thinned, her mother limped out of the room, favoring her swollen knees, feet, and ankles. A yellow-gold aura flared around her body, the sunbeam color in direct opposition to her apparent mood. Marcy squeezed her eyes shut and clutched the ribbon of paper around her finger. Sometimes she missed the oblivious days when facial and body cues alone had illuminated a person's heightened emotions. Now, the presence of an aura reinforced the growing intensity of their skirmishes about when she should attain advanced education to support her dream career of illustrating children's books.

Not *if*, but when. An important distinction. To her, anyway.

Over the past week, her mom's non-verbal cues had been especially easy to read. Early September damp and chill aggravated every nasty rheumatoid arthritis symptom. Yet instead of taking advantage of her live-in helper, she'd intensified the urging for her to move out and move on.

3

"Nope." She kept her voice low, buried under the thumping music. "I won't leave you while the pain rages unchecked." They'd supported each other for years since her dad had flounced off to New Mexico. She wouldn't abandon her now.

Her eyes welled, and she blinked several times and blamed the pile of slivered onions. Though darn it, Justine's unexpected costuming request and the dust-up with her mom had thrown her off-kilter. After dinner, she'd tackle the massive new challenge by visiting the theater. She shuddered at the reminder and pulled off the makeshift bandage, noting the bleeding had stopped. She washed her hands and finished dicing the squash before scooping the rest of the vegetables into the pot.

Her eyes drifted closed for a few centering moments, and she inhaled the rich, tangy aroma through controlled breaths. Unfortunately, a full-on meditation would have to wait. If she had time, she'd sit cross-legged on the Hello Kitty rug in her room to generate positivity toward her goals, but she'd barely skimmed the stack of notes to prep for the evening.

While the soup simmered, she went through them and also searched the website of a nearby costume shop in South Bend, Indiana her friend had recommended. In between jotting ideas, she glanced at the door, in nervous anticipation of her mother's return. They were both creative people, and neither liked conflict. But they also shared a dominant stubborn gene and somehow had become locked in a no-win showdown.

Banishing the unacceptable thought, Marcy leaped up to stir the chili, releasing a blast of spice into the room. She tasted the broth, added a dash of salt and pepper, and resumed the research. Within a half hour her own notes filled additional pages, as the initial scatter of words transitioned into costume sketches. Women posed in long, sweeping gowns with huge, ridiculous sleeves. Men strutted in dandy-ish slim suits and towering top hats. The costumes, she decided, would reflect the exaggeration of the parody.

Engrossed in the whimsy of the work, she opened the script and started to skim through the descriptions and dialogue. The first paragraphs left her smiling. By the second page, she'd giggled at the wry comments about marriage and class distinctions. Snarky, witty humor, her favorite type.

Her mom slipped inside the room and, without a word, popped breadsticks into the oven. A buttery-yeasty scent mingled with the chili powder tang. Marcy peeked up, thankful for the pop music filling the awkward silence that lingered between them.

She pushed the computer aside and stood. "I'll fill our bowls and the water glasses." Usually, she would have completed all the dinner-related tasks by now, but she'd gotten caught up in the research.

"Thank you." Her mom's voice retained an edge of reserve as she headed to the silverware drawer.

They executed a polite dance around each other to set the table. Marcy began to sing along to the tunes to lighten the mood. She raised her voice and mimicked dance moves to "Walk Like an Egyptian" and earned the ghost of a smile. To her relief, after they sat and dished up the food, their usual warmth seeped back into the room. They fell into conversation, avoiding touchy topics in favor of the upcoming costuming adventure.

"My goal is to have fun with the concept and also stay true to the Gay Nineties era." Marcy gestured with a breadstick toward her sketches, pleased with the work. At first, the pencil had felt a little foreign in her hand, after two years of consciously squelching her artistry. Yet the creative flow had reemerged, awakening the familiar, immersive buzz of pleasure. "When I started at Divine Vintage, I realized how hinky some of the community theater costumes were. But in three years of gathering basic knowledge at the boutique, I've never even assisted Justine with a show." She bit off a chunk of bread, chewed, and talked around it. "Geez, I wish they weren't doing a period piece."

Her mom stretched to snag a napkin from the ceramic rooster holder. "Can you blame her for wanting to go to California with her handsome hubby for a few weeks to consult on his screenwriting project?"

"No, of course not. I'd have preferred to ease into this, though." She sighed and opened the oversized, glossy research book her friend had passed along. "At least 1895 fashion is iconic. They called these 'leg of mutton' or balloon sleeves." She indicated a fashion plate illustration. The fabric on the gown billowed out a whopping eight inches between the shoulder and elbow.

Her mom's gaze roamed over the sketch. "Balloon is a fitting description. She could take flight in that getup."

"My lady, you are cleared for take-off." Marcy attempted a plummy British accent then returned to her Midwestern drawl. "Hopefully I'll find something similar at the theater or be able to supplement with rental pieces." She slapped the book closed and collected their emptied bowls. "You may not believe it after my moaning and venting, but I'm actually getting kind of excited about this new challenge. Onward to the theater."

\*\*\*\*

With multiple ideas fluttering in her head, ten minutes later she squeezed into her vintage lemon-yellow Bug to travel the rural highway to LaPorte Little Theatre. Best to tackle the beast immediately and bolster her confidence, as rehearsals had started the night before, on Tuesday. Perhaps the new outlet would also satisfy her creative energies until she could commit to the intensive, two-year, on-campus illustration program.

A semi zoomed by on the four-lane road, shaking the frame of the car in the looming dusk. She gripped the wheel and slowed to enter the outskirts of LaPorte. The dreary industrial zone was lined with factories, but soon she'd reached the reviving, antique store-focused downtown. The storefronts were mostly closed in the evenings, yet the brick planters continued to burst with blooms on every block. At the edge of the historic district, she parked and strode into the church-turned-theater before the seven o'clock start time.

The whitewashed brick building had stood on the corner lot for nearly a century. She'd attended several productions over the past years, and noted they'd since updated and painted the compact entryway. The box office and refreshment areas were encased in a soothing Lake Michigan blue, the walls lined with photos from plays and musicals.

Her stomach jittered at a burst of laughter filtering from the attached performing space. She peeked through the velvet divider curtain but didn't glimpse anyone before entering between the rows of chairs, set up in three sections. The basic cream walls were accented by small, lead-glass windows, and any aspects of a church had been eliminated. Pews had been replaced by cushioned metal chairs at some point. Ahead, a wide front stage spanned, with five steps leading up from ground level.

Her eyes adjusted to the dim interior, and she spied a figure seated at a table. Most likely the director, Mike something. She glided toward him in her high-tops, smoothed her hands over her geometric-patterned tunic, and uttered a cheery hello.

The man's broad shoulders jerked before he glared up, with flashing eyes matching coal black hair above a rugged face. She pressed a hand to her racing heart. "Uhh, I—"

"Can I help you?" he grated in an irritated baritone.

She tried to reply, appalled when her lips quivered. "Marcy Alexander. I'm here to help costume the show." Justine's soothing voice echoed in her head: *The director's a sweetie.*

His frown deepened, far from exuding sweetness and light. The folding chair squeaked as he crossed tanned arms over a broad chest, straining the plaid shirt over his biceps. "You're here to help Justine?"

"No. I'm taking over for her." Apprehension stirred butterflies in her chest as his expression remained dark. "Didn't she tell you she's heading out of town to consult on Jackson's project?" The image of her friend's Oscar-worthy begging flitted through her mind as the man shoved a hand through his cropped hair.

He stared at her for several piercing seconds and huffed out an audible breath. "I didn't get around to returning her call yesterday. So, Marcy Alexander, you ever handle costuming before?"

"No." Her voice pitched high, landing as a question. "But I've learned a ton working at the Divine Vintage boutique, and Justine left me a research book, and lots of notes."

To her dismay, his aura flared crimson. *Down-to-earth, honest, passionate.* She categorized the basic traits automatically and considered turning on her heel and leaving him speechless. Or else he'd curse her all the way down the aisle.

He bumped back the chair to stand; his height towered beyond her own six feet. "Great. Not only do I have to direct a chick comedy, I have to deal with the frickin' costuming." He practically growled the words as he pivoted in a red haze and paced a few steps—away from her.

Wait, she was doing the fool a favor. "Just because I haven't done it doesn't mean I *can't*," she fumed, anger erupting through the rapid tapping of her right foot. "I'm fully prepped to be true to Gay Nineties style."

He swung around, emitting annoyance and another hot rush of color. Apparently, he didn't tune into the warm-fuzzy side of his aura, either.

"Hey, Mike." A male voice sliced through the tension hovering between them. "Whassup?"

She whirled toward a trio of young people, thankful for the interruption. They swarmed past her to surround him. The director returned the greetings, and his tint calmed and disappeared. She again pondered slinking away, but he jabbed a thumb in her direction. "Guys, meet Marcy. Justine's been called out of town and can't costume, so she recruited help."

*From the second string.* She could almost hear the unvoiced criticism. The group shifted focus, no doubt recognizing costumers can enhance or hinder onstage sex appeal. She halted in tapping her foot and pasted a pleasant expression onto her face.

"Hi, I'm Will." Medium-height and lanky, with brown hair, glasses, and a thin, angular face.

"Chase. Playing the role of Algernon." This one was tall, blond, drop-dead cute, and sported a killer smile with a dimple. Hmm, cool flirt vibes.

"I'm Lindsay. Thanks for jumping in to help." The girl beamed. She was petite and pretty with light brown skin. Waving dark hair fell below her slim shoulders.

They all appeared to be in their early twenties, compared to her twenty-six, the director even older. But grump could be adding to his perceived years. "Happy to meet you." And she was. "I'll take sizes and measurements later."

"*All* of our measurements?" Chase sent her a sexy grin. Yep, a flirt.

She lifted a brow at the innuendo, but before she could respond, the director assumed the role of "adult." "Keep it in your pants, hotshot. Here come the others." He pointed across the room and rattled off names she immediately forgot. The four older cast members waved and uttered hellos before he continued, all business. "We have a lot of ground to cover. Let's start where the ladies enter the sitting room."

Five actors headed toward the stage. The others took seats. Apparently dismissed, Marcy did the same, slumping to indulge a sulk. What the heck was with his attitude? She didn't deserve a brush off and had agreed to donate her precious time to volunteer. She'd stay only because she didn't want to damage her friend's reputation with the theater.

Plus, she'd definitely enjoy rubbing her costuming competence in his annoying, scowling mug.

Chapter Two

Mike Figueroa tried to shake off his feisty mood to give full concentration to the play. Damn, he hoped the girl would prove semi-competent. Period shows were tricky, and expensive. *Justine's a pro*, he told himself with forced calm. Surely, she wouldn't hand the production off to the first available goofball.

She'd caught him off guard, sneaking up in those neon orange sneakers, while the rest of her outfit shouted a crazy statement. Bright yellow tights under a multi-colored mini dress. Or a long top? Wasn't sure, didn't care. Though he couldn't miss the long, shapely legs. Her face could be referred to as "gamine," an old word, but hey, it fit. Wide blue eyes, a mane of red, bouncy curls. Cute, but kooky. The unexpected fire spitting into those striking eyes intrigued him, reminding him of the cornflowers his mom grew every year. Now, he was mildly sorry at going off on her.

He tuned in to the absolute silence around him. His head jerked up. Onstage, the cast loitered and tossed questioning looks in his direction. He cleared his throat roughly. "Go ahead." They'd blocked the scene the day before, and the actors fell into formation and read from their scripts with varying degrees of British accents.

They'd have to polish those up. He jotted a note on his pad as a well-delivered punchline drew a giggle from behind him. The new girl. He ignored the urge to look and trained forward. He let the scenes flow, interrupting a few times to correct the blocking. At the end of the first act, the players shifted. Maria Torres sat alone onstage, prepared to read the governess role, and peered at him from under her fringe of dark bangs.

He surveyed the depths of the room behind him. "Where's Nicki?" Couldn't she have taken a bathroom break earlier? "Hold on, is she here?" His lips twisted with annoyance. The girl playing Cecily was known to be a handful, not malicious but demanding. "She called off yesterday, but did she tell anyone she wasn't coming tonight?" he called, loud enough to draw everyone's attention.

Offstage, cast members shrugged or shook their heads.

"Great." He didn't hide the disapproval, his engineering project management compulsions coming to the fore. Setting expectations mattered with a tight timeframe. You had to construct a strong foundation with a play, same as a building complex. "Hopefully, she'll get here soon. Thanks to the rest of you for being on time. Let's start again at the top of Act Two." Without conscious thought, he zeroed in on the new costumer. "Can you hold book?"

She peered at the empty seats around her before regarding him with a wrinkled brow. "Me?"

He swallowed a groan, already regretting the request. "Hold book means to sit onstage and read Cecily's lines. Please." He added the afterthought. "To give Maria somebody to relate to. You don't have to act or attempt the movements."

"I know what it means to hold book." Marcy's lips pinched, and she lurched out of the seat, script in hand, to stride toward the stage.

He didn't reply. Best not to come off as a bigger dick. He blinked hard as she mounted the final step. Man, those yellow tights were blinding under the lights. But the legs…

The girl settled at the folding table standing in for a garden tableau. Maria smiled a welcome and opened her script. "Your German grammar is on the table. Pray, open it at page fifteen. We will repeat yesterday's lesson."

"But I don't like German. It isn't at all a becoming language. I know perfectly well that I look quite plain after my German lesson."

The newcomer's strong British accent and appropriate deadpan expression surprised him. He'd expected a flat, uninspired rendition. When Chase's character swept in to open a volley of flirtation, she continued to hold her own.

More important, however, could she handle the costumes? He tapped his pen on the tablet and willed her to deliver a stellar statement with the clothing, to help raise the show above the joking bet which'd landed him, protesting, at the helm of the play. He planned to rub the pranksters' noses in their success. Plus, he'd worked hard to earn a rep as an exacting, excellent director. No way would he jeopardize the cred with a shoddy production.

The act wrapped, catching him off guard again. He pulled himself together from the unusual fretting to give them a break. They were doing fine for a second-night rehearsal. He'd guide them to improve the piece over six weeks, rehearsing Mondays through Thursdays…*with an MIA cast member and a newbie handling a critical crew role.* His neck spasmed as the fill-in costumer ambled up, reminding him of a firecracker, overloaded with color and excess energy.

She rocked on her toes in the high-tops. "Should I take measurements now?"

He flexed his shoulder and gritted his teeth as the neck pain shifted lower. "You can start, but you'll have to come back another night to catch Nicki. She's in the role you just read."

The girl flapped a hand, displaying short, orange-tipped nails at him. "I'll need to spend time in the costume area anyway. Which is where?"

He raised his arm, grimaced at the twinge, and pointed to the upper left-hand side of the stage. "Up there, accessible by the back staircase." Chase approached, with his eyes trained on the girl. Never took him long to hit on a fresh female.

Mike wondered if any of the cast had a pain reliever. Lindsay lingered a few feet away, but he asked another favor instead. "Lins, why don't you show her the costume loft before we start."

****

The jerk wouldn't even use her name. Marcy crinkled her nose at the slight but followed as ordered. They wound past the chatting older cast members into "the green room"—where the walls were a dingy white. In the long, rectangular space, lighted mirrors topped a yards-long countertop fronted with benches. A scatter of makeup containers tumbled at one end, and metal shelving held random items she supposed might be prop pieces. The mirror reflected their progress. She towered above her guide, trying to keep up as the girl zipped through the room. "Have you done many shows here?"

"A half dozen, plus all the high school performances. I had the lead in Cinderella." Lindsay flipped a grin over her shoulder and slowed to enter a narrow, dark hallway. "Theater gets in your blood, and the friends become family. "

"I'm just hoping I'll survive doing this favor for my best friend. I sure wasn't prepared to go onstage tonight. But actually, I enjoyed myself."

"You read the lines well. Have you ever done a part?" Dark hair bounced as she flipped light switches and mounted a set of narrow wooden stairs, hidden behind a wall.

Marcy followed more slowly. "Some small roles in high school. The accent's courtesy of *The Best of British Baking* on public television."

"I love that freakin' show. Wish I could actually bake."

"Luckily, I'm able to do quite a bit in my second job at Northside Deli."

The old steps creaked as they advanced to enter a doorway at the top. Her words sputtered to a stop. The area equaled the size of a large bedroom, with a half wall opening to the stage below. She turned in a slow circle, numb and overwhelmed by the explosion of clutter. A forlorn, naked mannequin posed with a straw hat on her bald head. Costumes of all shapes, sizes, colors, and eras jammed onto racks and overflowed out of boxes and bags. A pile of shoes and boots was shoved against a wall, as if the actors had kicked them off and run.

When compared to Divine Vintage's pristine order, the room reflected a surreal mashup. How in the world would she find anything she needed up here? Her attention flitted around, seeking a semblance of anything

Victorian, and she felt her stomach tighten. She'd have to dig through the disarray, with little hope to unearth any suitable pieces. Super-organized Justine must not have been up here since her last costuming gig a year prior.

"This is a jungle. I don't think—" Marcy halted and did a double-take. A faint white glow started to pulse in the far corner. Lindsay faced the same direction and didn't seem to notice as she offered vague guidance.

She couldn't force herself to tune in. Her focus stayed riveted on the brightening cloud. The glow resembled…an aura. White, for a bright, intuitive believer. Marcy frowned and stepped nearer. The light fluttered into waves, spooking her heart rate into a pounding drumbeat. The illumination intensified when she reached out a tentative hand, sending her reeling back as it dimmed and disappeared. She grabbed a dozen heavy, hanging costumes and shoved them away, exposing a bare wall. No lightbulb. No lamp. No person. A chill ran through her, and she whirled toward her companion, who appeared rightly confused.

After extensive research over the past three years, she'd finally become comfortable with seeing and categorizing auras. But in relation to people, not hovering in the air in a disconnected, ghostly fashion. She must look like a freak with the overreaction. "I thought I saw some Victorian gowns," she improvised. "There's plenty of time to check them out later. We'd better scoot for Act Three, or Mike'll kick our butts."

No way she'd stay in the room alone. Once outside, she raced down the stairs, bracing her hands on the walls to avoid skidding, and barely registered the footsteps descending behind her.

Chapter Three

The wild theater intro rambled around Marcy's mind the next morning at Divine Vintage while she prepared online purchases for shipping. Surrounded by packing boxes and tissue paper in the open, brick-walled storage area, she listened to jazz tunes for ambience. The windowless room had never bothered her before, but today she wished for sunlight to dispel the reminder of the eerie floating light.

Goose bumps prickled on her arms, and she rubbed them, thinking she should have commented, casually and carefully, to Lindsay. Maybe she'd seen the glow, too, and could've confirmed a brief reflection from a spotlight or something.

She hadn't dared. While she and her closest friends leaned creative and "gifted," other people might mock and distance themselves. The emergence of the weird ability had stretched her own levels of rationality but been somewhat acceptable on the heels of an even more fantastical occurrence.

Had it really been three years since she'd linked with two friends to immerse herself into a vision from the past? She could hardly believe they'd witnessed the haunting resolution of a murderer's confession and that the explosive images had awakened her own talent. Yet she'd watched her mom and the director both push the intensity of their dominant aura colors the day before, their annoyance with her flaring in bold, primary tones.

She shoved away the disturbing thoughts and dragged her attention back to the list of outgoing items, with her ears attuned for the front doorbell. Her boss and good friend Tess Dunmore had taken the day off, and traffic likely would pick up on a cloudless, early September day in Michigan City's Uptown Arts District.

Marcy pivoted to the hanging rack for the next garment, a ruby-red, 1940s dressing gown headed to a New Orleans address. Slick satin caressed her fingertips as she rolled it in paper and tucked in the puffed, gathered sleeves, which reminded her of the 1890s glamour in the show. Would this slinky gown be worn as an enticing come-on, unzipped to show cleavage?

The flirty thought recalled Chase's attempts to play with her, on and offstage. Though some might be offended, she didn't take the interaction seriously. Obviously, he'd been born to charm. She sealed the box with packing tape and realized Justine had been right. She enjoyed meeting such interesting new people.

Most of them, anyway. As an upbeat and positive person, she regretted that the gloomy director had fired her up. If the cast hadn't arrived, they would've clashed in a no-holds-barred shouting match. Not her style at all. From now on she'd remain controlled and aloof, no matter how he growled and grumbled. She slapped on an address label, the sharp sound emphasizing her resolve.

\*\*\*\*

When she arrived at the theater before the evening rehearsal, she found the cast members chatting together in the audience seating area.

Lindsay spied her and beelined over. "Hi there. Do you want to take my measurements before we start? I'm five-five and usually wear a size four."

Marcy jotted notes. "Great. What shoe size?"

"Seven. Oh, those are rad." She tilted her head to admire the rainbow platform sandals complementing lime green capris.

"Thanks. Eighty percent off. I love a bargain."

"Me, too. I've worked at a shoe store in the outlet mall every summer during college, mainly for the employee discount." Lindsay stuck out a slim leg and flexed the foot in a bejeweled flipflop. "Five-dollar bargains. The store's cut me slack with the show and being my senior year in college."

"Super cute."

Marcy started to ask about her chosen degree field, but saw Mike enter from a side door, his face and body posture relaxed. He glanced up, caught her eye, and held it. Something brief and indefinable shimmered between them, and her stomach skittered. The easygoing look slid from his face, and a faint red glow outlined his form. He gave a brief nod, and the color dissolved when he broke the contact to talk to Will.

He must still be unsure of her abilities, which rankled. She tried not to fume and turned toward Lindsay, but she'd drifted away. Flustered, she consulted her notes and wondered when she'd be able to measure the other lead actress. Her head whipped up as the director's raised voice commanded attention.

"Did anyone connect with Nicki? She didn't return my calls or texts." With no response, he stalked toward his card table and chair, crimson again edging his body. "Let's start from the opening, and hopefully she'll sweep in before her entrance."

Marcy had intended to return to the costume area,

but thoughts of the strange aura in that room kept her rooted a tad longer. Plus, the more familiar she became with the play, the better she could interpret the needs. She found a seat and watched, enthused that the actors had retained their blocking and begun to flesh out the characters. The end of the act caught her by surprise as Maria took the stage, alone, to read the governess role.

Mike swiveled toward the back of the house. A flare of red rimmed around him as he vaulted to his feet. She held her breath when he crossed the aisle to loom in front of her. Frustration etched across his clenched jaw. "Could you read again tonight?"

"Sure." *Yep, she was an in-control team player.* She followed him with her script, but he stopped to exchange the copy with his own. "Cecily's blocking is written in. If you don't understand or can't read the notes, ask."

A burst of anticipation sparked as she trotted up the steps—until her sandal caught on the top one. She caught her balance, arms flailing, embarrassment replacing expectation. With a muttered, "sorry," she sat across from the governess, and the scene wobbled forward.

After a couple of pages, concentrating on the accent and moving according to the blocking instructions helped her awkwardness melt away. She felt ready when Chase / Algernon swept on to engage her / Cecily in flirtatious repartee.

"…You are the prettiest girl I ever saw…"

"Miss Prism says that all good looks are a snare."

"They are a snare that every sensible man would like to be caught in."

"Oh, I don't think I would care to catch a sensible man. I shouldn't know what to talk to him about." The quip drew a deep chuckle from below. She almost shaded her eyes to look beyond the lights to catch Mike's reaction. No, she definitely didn't want to meet his eyes again or appear overeager and needy. But she'd made Director Grump laugh.

****

Despite his displeasure with Nicki's absence, Mike appreciated the lively interaction onstage. He even snickered a few times, including at the costumer's delivery. The chit wasn't bad, he thought, smirking at his use of Victorian slang. He called a break at the close of the second act, more mellow, but determined to track down his absent lead actress.

He approached the stage, watching the others scatter. The new girl headed to the steps and paused when she saw him. Damn, those legs. He shifted his gaze away from the length of granny-apple green fabric, unable to meet her eyes. The earlier connection when he entered the theater and saw her across the room had unnerved him. Best to keep it all business.

"Red, Lindsay said she didn't show you all the costume areas." He stared past her toward the loft. "Follow me up." She'd been gracious to fill in onstage, but he wanted to ensure she stayed on-task. Without waiting for an answer, he strode toward the side door.

He expected her to protest the flip nickname—an attempt to distance himself, not belittle her. To his minor disappointment, she didn't respond. Her footsteps sounded behind him as he passed through the green room, mirrors reflecting his jean-clad image and her quirky color combo. Did the girl own any neutrals? Above the eye-popping pants, a psychedelic, tie-dye blouse hugged close at the chest to flow out in a looser sheer fabric. Hopefully she could override her wild

21

fashion sense when it came to depicting the Victorian era.

Stray tubes and pots of makeup lay in a heap as he passed the countertop. They'd have a cleanup day before the opening. Maybe sooner. After growing up with a mom who rarely cleaned, he couldn't handle mess. Or messy people. Damn Nicki for blowing them off again tonight. He'd left her a half dozen messages through text, email, and phone. No answer. Unless she was in the hospital or had another urgent excuse, he'd have to replace her.

He sighed at the hitch in his careful plans and trooped up the narrow staircase, turning right at the top into the smaller, second room. The flipped switch illuminated a dozen stacked plastic tubs, plus an unsorted mass of hats, shoes, wigs, and other accessories. She joined him inside, her eyes wide.

"The collection's been growing for decades." He tamped down the urge to begin sorting and straightening, as he'd often done to help his two younger, slob brothers. Not his problem here, though he'd *chosen* to assume a responsible role at the theater, rather than having it thrust on him by two busy working parents. "You'll have to dig and find as much as you can, and we'll rent the rest."

"Sure." She looked as unsure as a kitten facing a slobbering puppy.

He brushed past her to enter the larger main room, noticing her spicy fragrance, something like cinnamon. His stomach rumbled in response, reminding him he hadn't grabbed dinner before coming to the theater. Chafing to return to the cast and the final scene so they could all leave, he added, "We'll probably run another half hour. Bring down anything workable, and they can try them on next week."

She followed him in. "Justine told me about the South Bend shop. I can't wait to go. My mom suggested a Steampunk theme."

"What? No. Absolutely not." He rubbed a fist across his chest as it tightened, all his fears materializing. He'd have to find her a level-headed assistant or boot her, too.

"Umm, kidding." Her lilting voice mocked him. "We'll play it straight."

Relief surged through him, enough to ignore her snide tone. "Well, good." He retreated toward the door with purposeful steps and stopped cold as she uttered a whooping shriek. His blood chilled, and the hairs on his neck stood on end. He flipped around to register a small black blur whip past his head.

"Aaaahhhhh!" She wailed again at ferocious volume, running blindly toward him in a blur of color. He stumbled into the wall as she slammed against his body full force, cracking his head and knocking the air from his lungs.

Arms flew around his waist in a squeezing vise. Her face pressed against his chest. "Baaattt," she bleated, nearly incoherent.

He registered the word and had to draw on every manly instinct to keep from ducking and pulling them both to the floor. *Bats. He hated bats.* Please, please let the bugger whiz out of the building or into an unused chimney to fly away in the night. His heart pumped at a marathon pace, matching hers, and they clung together, panting, as he dared to sneak a look around the room. Quiet, thank God.

When he could muster a voice above a squeak, he chided, "Are you trying to give me a stroke? They have to live somewhere, too."

"Baaattt," she murmured again, as her body trembled against his. Her fear gave him courage. "Hey, hey. Everything's okay." He patted her back with three small thumps. She didn't move, buried face-first in his chest. He wondered if she'd leave bruises where her tense fingers gripped his back. In fact, her firm body pressed against his in every intimate way possible. Breasts, thighs…everywhere. His body began to warm and respond.

*Nooope, not happening.* He put his hands on her shoulders to forcibly disengage as footsteps pounded up the staircase. "Ah, crap." He'd ignored the concerned shouts from the cast members on the floor below, and they were coming to investigate.

She loosened her fingers and peeled away from his chest, standing a hand's breadth away. Her lips shook, and she cupped her cheeks with quivering hands. "I am so, so sorry. I majorly freaked." She whispered the words. Afraid the bat would hear and return?

He fought the compulsion to look around for the winged invader. "Obviously." He glared to keep her from guessing his own fear. The wide eyes held his, and he felt his expression soften at her obvious distress. An urge to comfort, to erase the fear, caught him. "Calm down. We're safe." He placed his hands on her shoulders to anchor her, and the same sparky feeling from earlier jolted between them.

Will and Chase burst into the room and almost ran them over, their raised voices merging. "What happened?" "Is everything okay?" They stopped short and stared as Marcy took two big steps away from him, her cheeks flushed pink.

The situation had to look sketchy. He squeezed his eyes shut.

Chase tilted his head. "Dude?"

He wasn't an actor, but he could act, aiming toward nonchalance. "Marcy stirred up a bat and ripped a few years off my life with those screams."

She held up both hands, palms out, and shivered. "I really don't dig bats," she offered, in a monumental understatement.

The younger guys began to snicker, and Chase slapped his hands against his thighs. "Man, we were afraid maybe he put the moves on you." He choked off the laughter as he caught Mike's thin-lipped expression.

With more couth, Will slung an arm around Marcy's shoulders. "Next time you want to come up here, I'll check the room out for you."

Mike's adrenaline slumped after the intense moments, sapping his patience and energy. "Such a prince. You'll be screaming next." He leaned over the open balcony to address the cast. "You heard the story. Let's call it a night."

"Adult night," Chase hooted and took Marcy's hand. "During rehearsal runs, those of us of legal age go out for drinks on Thursdays. I bet you can use a little somethin' somethin'."

"I'll take your bet and double it."

She let him lead her to the door. Before she passed through, she checked over her shoulder and stiffened. Mike followed her gaze, pulse quickening, but the bat didn't hover nearby. Her vivid imagination probably had conjured the whir of wings. He rolled his eyes, flipped off the light, and followed them down the stairs, berating himself for losing control with her. Again.

Chapter Four

On the short drive to a local sports bar, Marcy almost decided to head for home as she replayed the mortifying incident with the bat. Not only had she screamed so loudly her throat continued to burn, but she'd practically mown Mike down in her derangement. She'd clung to him so tightly the poor guy could hardly breathe. He'd been surprisingly chill, trying to comfort her, but she'd glimpsed a trace of fright in his own face when she finally disengaged from the hard body.

*Criminy, the man had muscles.* Taut arms, sculpted chest. He must lift weights. Even his thighs were whip-tight against hers. Ugh. Handsome, but irritating. Though at the end, she'd sensed another unexpected tingle between them before they'd separated. Shifting beyond the shared mania to a hint of recognition. Maybe the incident had broken the ice, and they could get to trust…and like…each other.

She drummed her fingers on the steering wheel and waited for a red light. As if she'd needed more drama, on the way out, she'd seen the eerie light pop up again. Yet he'd showed no reaction. If the glow came from a reflection or a light source, he should've noticed a sudden bright flash.

The answer would emerge soon enough, she told herself, attempting positivity. Or it wouldn't, and the image would disappear, and she'd forget and move on.

Her humor semi-restored, she swung into the parking lot and entered the bar, to join the others seated at a long central table. Television sets hoisted around the noisy room reflected sports from golf to horse racing.

Chase pulled out the seat next to him, across from Will and Lindsay. "Hey, bat girl," he teased. "Let's get you a drink."

Marcy sank into the chair. "I'll take the drink, but nix to the nickname."

"Fair enough." He winked and handed her a menu.

"Is everyone coming?" She flipped back to the specialty drinks.

Will shook his head. "The older cast members don't always join in. Something about getting up early and responsibilities." He chortled. "The rest of us don't see that as an impediment."

The outer door swung open. Correction—one of the "elders" had joined them. Mike hadn't expressed his intent either way when the rest of them trooped out, but apparently, he'd locked up and headed over. She felt a flush of color rise on her cheeks at their recent close entanglement and focused with intensity on the menu as he approached.

Actually, it wasn't fair to lump him in that age category, she thought. He probably was in his early thirties, but his height and serious demeanor added gravitas.

"Hey guys." He took the open seat at the head of the table and grimaced, rotating his shoulders a couple of times to relax them. "Tough night. What with bats and missing persons. Does anyone have a clue what's up with Nicki?" When no one offered an answer, his lip curled. "I hope she isn't sick, but she could at least respond. I

27

tried again on the way over here. We may be looking for a replacement, which would suck."

Lindsay frowned. "I tried texting her today, too, and she didn't answer. But she can be a ditz when things get crazy at work."

As the others commented, Marcy watched the entry door open again, and a tall, gorgeous brunette sauntered in. Overdressed for the casual surroundings, the woman rocked a pink minidress to expose an abundance of tanned limbs. Her dark-rimmed eyes searched the room and lit when she saw their group. She pranced forward and stopped behind Mike, placing beringed hands over his eyes.

Was this the MIA Nicki? Had she received the message and come to explain? Looking like that, she probably got away with misbehaving.

The director's face relaxed below her manicured fingers. "Hey, baby." He reached up to catch and kiss the palm. The sexy gesture tightened Marcy's chest. He must be super relieved she'd finally made an appearance.

The newcomer draped her arms around his neck. "Hi, everybody. How was rehearsal?" The sultry voice pitched low for effect.

Will snorted in amusement. "Rehearsal went great, until Marcy rousted a bat in the costume room and burst Mike's eardrums." He jumped up to grab the nearest empty chair and tugged it to the end, next to the director.

Huge brown eyes shifted toward her. "Marcy. The fill-in costumer." Not a question, or a particularly friendly comment.

"Yes. Hi." She offered a polite smile, surprised to be let down at her time filling-in onstage ending.

"I'm Tara. Mike's girlfriend." She emphasized the

last word—to lay claim?

*Director Grump had a girlfriend?* A flood of heat now flushed her chest, shifting upward. How embarrassing that the guys had imagined something between the two of them in the loft. The only "spark" had come from mutual irritation. She nodded without words, swallowed hard, and buried her face in the menu again.

From behind the laminated pages, she pondered the realization that the polished female wasn't the elusive Nicki, but his significant other. Careful makeup and the floating scent of expensive perfume didn't mesh with his brawny jeans and T-shirt appearance. But hey, opposites attract, and the wench had nothing to worry about from her end. *Nope, nada.* The waiter approached, and she concentrated on ordering a strawberry daiquiri and an appetizer to share, determined to erase the tension of the evening. Especially the close encounter in the loft.

While the couple murmured together, the other cast members began asking about Marcy's history. "I'm born local and attended New Prairie High School rather than LaPorte," she clarified. "My mom and I live west of there, in the country."

Tara leaned forward, her shaped brows arched high. "You live *at home*? Do you work?"

She and Mike had stopped their whispered conversation to listen in. Marcy grabbed her water glass, trying to appear unaffected and keep her cool. "I have two part-time jobs. At Northside Deli and Divine Vintage." She gulped half the glass and resisted fanning herself with the menu. Or swatting the woman with it.

"Hmmm. What a quaint little boutique. But I've never ventured in." She flipped long, silky hair back over her shoulders. "Don't tell me; you're into vintage and Goodwill."

*Yikes, the claws had flexed.*

Before she could answer, Lindsay reached across the table to clutch Marcy's hand with overdone enthusiasm. "I looove vintage and thrifting. We'll go bargain hunting soon."

She shot her a small smile in appreciation of the intervention. "That sounds great. Really, who wants to pay full price?" *Only social-climbing posers. Geez, was the girlfriend always so welcoming?*

Thankfully, the drinks arrived and diverted everyone's attention. Marcy sipped silently to avoid becoming a further target—or defending herself with a snarky slap back. She was missing something here. Some shared group knowledge. Lindsay had been kind to intervene, and she could see them becoming friends.

When they'd all been served, Chase lifted his beer for a toast. "To our fearless director and cast for ignoring the curse to perform Earnest at Little Theatre for the first time in fifty years."

Will clinked his mug against his friend's. "Only because he's a lousy bluffer."

The others drank, but Marcy left hers untouched, nerves jangling at the toast. Hopefully, they were kidding. "What's the curse?" she asked.

Beside her, Chase's face sobered. "Sorry, I didn't mean to be flip. An actress died backstage during the run of the play in '66. Nobody's around the theater anymore who knows the full story. There used to be a plaque in the entrance." He scrunched his face, as if searching his memory. "The board of directors must've moved it when they repainted. I don't recall her name, but people say the play's cursed, similar to MacBeth, and the place is haunted."

Her heart thumped so loud she feared they'd all hear it. "Has anyone researched old newspaper archives for the real story?" The others had stayed quiet to listen, and they joined in to mutter: "no," "not me," and "don't know."

The storyteller continued. "Maybe it wasn't an accident though. Get this, I do remember the plaque said the actress played Cecily, the part you've been reading." He wiggled his fingers in the air and mimicked a ghostly voice. "Woooooo."

A chill slithered through her. The white light assumed a more ominous possibility. She jerked visibly in her seat, and the others stopped smiling.

Chase rubbed her arm with his palm. "You okay?"

Mike cleared his throat. "She's jumpy after the bat launch. Cut her some slack."

She composed her face and tried to appear unaffected. Sharing the other occurrences up there now would brand her as a wacko. First, she'd prefer to dig for a natural cause.

The girlfriend rolled her eyes in slow exaggeration. "You guys are so juvenile. Nobody believes the place is haunted. Don't scare the poor girl, or you'll end up wearing ugly, funky costumes."

*The poor girl. Right.* Marcy bit the inside of her cheek and searched the room for the server. Where were her fried green beans? She needed a greasy veggie distraction. Relieved, she watched the young man approach with a tray of steaming food.

The conversation thankfully segued from hauntings to hot gossip—who'd hooked up, who'd been dumped.

She ate, listened, and learned. As usual, she didn't strive to be the center of attention, and preferred to observe others. With a group of dramatic thespians, the feat was not hard to accomplish.

When the waiter returned for drink orders, Mike passed. "Gotta go, boys and girls. Early day on the jobsite tomorrow. Have to keep the lakeside condos on schedule."

Tara nuzzled into him. "You're so important." She flipped a glance at Marcy. "He's the project engineer. For the biggest deal the company has handled." Her tone slid from flirty to flint as she stared across the table.

"Impressive." She held her eye, refusing to give in to an attempt to make her feel small. Again.

To his credit, Mike seemed sheepish about the praise. Rather than puff up, he peered down at the table. "Good employers give their people chances to learn, improve, and take on new challenges. But I do appreciate the cheerleading, hon." He squeezed Tara's hand. "The rest of you, have a fun weekend, but don't come in Monday with hangovers. We have too much ground to cover."

At the good-natured grumbling and denials, he dug out money and left it on the table with their bill. The duo left to a chorus of goodbyes. The brunette slid her arm around his waist. As they neared the door, she looked behind them to focus on Marcy and, with a pronounced gesture, dipped a hand to settle in his back jeans pocket.

Marcy dropped her eyes to the daiquiri and emptied the glass. Why did Tara feel she had to go all possessive and nasty? Did she regard all females as competition? Some women operated on that vibe, but she didn't think she'd thrown out any signals of interest. Because frankly, none existed. Her main goal was to do her job without stirring up controversy. Which meant staying mum about the aura.

"Don't worry about Princess Tara." Lindsay's voice interrupted her musings. "She's what I call ultra-high maintenance."

"He puts up with such bull?" She winced at the crass comment. "Sorry. Not my biz. Does she act?"

Will affected a dramatic air as if patting down an elaborate hairdo. "No, but she acts out." He waited till the burst of laughter subsided. "To be fair, she can be fun, and I've never had a problem with her. She and Mike seem to click. Maybe she had a bad day."

The comment induced more eye rolls from the women before the conversation switched to the other's jobs. Marcy was glad to move past the uncomfortable moment to learn that the two guys worked in information technology. To save money, they also shared a house, for now, with Will's partner.

Lindsay talked about finishing a business management degree at the local commuter college. "I live at home, too, but Tara never pays much attention to me," she added, with a conspiratorial smirk. "Do you have a degree, too?"

"I commuted up to Chicago for a Bachelor of Fine Arts and decided I wanted to work in watercolor illustration. Eventually, I'll pursue a certification program to focus on the specialty, but my mom has health issues." She hadn't wanted to divulge the personal information to the other two after the belittling treatment.

Chase wrinkled his brow. "You're an artist? They'll nab you for set work."

"I'd enjoy the challenge." The words tumbled

before she remembered she hadn't painted a canvas in almost two years. Yet with the encouraging response to learning about her art, she decided to reveal her passion. "I really want to portray the whimsy in children's books. Imagine them falling under the spell of the words and delighting in the fantastical worlds. Books provided some of my greatest escapes and friendships as an only child."

"Aww, sweet." Lindsay toyed with her glass. "Do you need to take advanced courses to excel in the field?"

"Those credentials and connections would definitely help me break in. During my senior year, we had a speaker from a two-year residency program in Virginia. I was super impressed at what they offer, including internship opportunities. Meanwhile, I ply my talents in artistic baked goods and vintage clothing." She stood to hide the stab of hurt and grabbed her bag off the back of the chair. Enough bleeding for the night. "I've had fun tonight, but I'd better head out, or I'll fall asleep at the deli tomorrow morning. Thanks bunches for the invite. Since I didn't pull any costumes, I guess I'll come by the theater again on Monday." She pointed a finger at Will. "You'd better believe I'll take you up on a bat sweep before I tackle the loft again."

He mocked a karate stance. "I'll protect you from the ghost, too."

The others joined in with his laughter. She waved and walked away to hide her dismay. If only they knew...

Chapter Five

The next morning at Divine Vintage, Tess shared highlights of the Wednesday date night with her hubby. After dinner in Chicago's Greektown and a musical, they'd luxuriated at a fancy hotel. "Trey splurged on a suite with a huge, jetted tub. We have to take advantage while I'm still limber." She cradled her growing stomach and pealed with laughter at her assistant's cringing, hear-no-evil hand gesture.

The cordless phone rang on the desk between them in the back office. Marcy made a shushing motion and answered on the speakerphone. "Hello. You've reached Divine Vintage, where retro is queen."

"Hey girl." Justine's cheerful voice rang out. "How's my costume diva?"

"I'm hanging in, and so glad you called." After the other two exchanged greetings, she updated them on being asked to read lines onstage, and the bat fiasco delaying her progress.

Her friend's snicker echoed from the speaker. "I probably would've jumped over the balcony. Mike's a looker, isn't he?"

Marcy recalled the steadying comfort of his palms bracing her shoulders in the loft, his face looming inches from hers. Yes, he had the type of strong, handsome features you'd imagine on a hot lumberjack. A prickly one, with a big axe. She shook herself, and the image dissolved into him kissing Tara's palm—an unexpectedly gentle, sexy move.

"He's okay, I guess. His girlfriend came to adult night afterward. She's a hot number, with an attitude." She snorted. "Toward me, anyway."

Tess dropped into a chair and kicked off her shoes. "Interesting. I've met her a couple of times, and she's always been cordial." She rubbed her feet, which had begun to swell recently when she reached her fifth month. Though they were still tiny at a size six. "I had the impression she and Mike had a fun, easy relationship."

The assessment echoed Will's kind comment at the bar. "You're probably on target, and I caught her on an off night." Maybe she'd been too quick to judge and take offense, but her intuition was pretty reliable. "Anyway, Justine, what's happening with you in lovely LA?"

"Besides catching up, one of the reasons I called is Jackson's project has bogged down in details. I'm super thankful you took the gig for me, and he kept his condo here, because we'll be staying a couple weeks longer. Otherwise, California is great, as usual, and I've been consulting with the producers. My parents are thrilled when I use my history degree."

The comment provided the perfect prompt to seek her friends' joint assistance. "For your sakes, I hope the project perks along soon. Speaking of expertise, I'm afraid I need some advice. On ghosts."

Tess stiffened to attention and planted her feet on the floor, her shoulder-length dark hair swinging. "What's going on?"

"Twice in the loft I've encountered a weird white glow in the corner. I'm wondering if—I'd better back up." Marcy paced the small room and rolled off the basics of the decades-old theater tragedy, concluding, "What if the light's tied to a ghost?" She halted to lean against the wall, anxious for them to weigh in.

Her boss tapped a finger on her chin, considering. "That's possible, I guess. I'm assuming you haven't told the others at the theater?"

"I barely know them. The bat incident already branded me a flake. The director has barely accepted me replacing his ace costumer." She'd been toying with an idea and proposed, "Would you be willing to go into the loft with me next week? Your sensory visions from vintage clothing have strengthened over the years, and I trust your perceptions."

"Of course, I will." Tess bent to put on her sandals. "You've got me thoroughly intrigued. Maybe I can convince Trey to join us if we think we need a male point of view."

Justine interjected from the phone. "When we get back, I'll be happy to assist, too. Sometimes I still marvel at how all of us have been drawn together with our unusual abilities. I felt kind of freakish until I met you, Tess. I'd only confessed to Jackson and Marcy that I'd conversed with a ghost. Then she began to see her auras after joining with you two in a vision at Carver House."

The doorbell tinkled, and voices began to trickle back to them. Tess smoothed her vintage maternity smock and headed toward the shop. "I've got to welcome some customers, Justine. Enjoy your brush with fame and give Jackson a hug from us." She paused at the door and lowered her voice. "About what you said. I've always believed power attracts power. I accepted and celebrated that long ago, and I'm stoked to tackle a little mystery again."

"Darn it," Justine wailed over the speaker. "I'm missing out."

\*\*\*\*

Following Will's "sweep" of the loft on Monday night, the two friends ventured in before the rehearsal started. With no signs of a bat buddy, Marcy indicated the far corner. "I saw the light there, twice."

Tess walked around her, casual in maternity jeans. "Over here?"

"Yes—" The words froze in her throat when a shimmer of white appeared, larger than she'd witnessed before. She covered her mouth with her hands to keep from squealing as the light pulsed and spread across the walls, resembling a dry ice fog. She bit into her finger, mesmerized at the display.

Her friend approached the corner and turned. Her eyes widened. "I don't see anything, but apparently you do. Stay calm, and I'll check the clothing." She selected an area of hanging gowns appropriate for the Victorian era and started to rifle through them. A peach-toned eyelet formal drew her attention, and she lifted it out, tilted her head to one side, and waited a few beats.

Marcy held her breath and ventured closer, watching for a physical response that would indicate a vision. When none came, Tess moved on to an ice-blue satin gown. She shook her head over that one and paused with her hands on her hips to stare at the rack. "This would be right in line for Earnest." She pointed at a blush-pink polished cotton with mushroomed sleeves, a narrow waist, and froths of lace draping the neck.

"Yes, the gown would've been a nice addition to our costume tableau, but the tiny size wouldn't fit someone even as slim as Lindsay."

Tess reached to cradle the fabric to her chest and stiffened. Her head drooped, and dark hair curtained around her face.

Marcy's heart rammed against her chest as she flew to her side. Driven by curiosity, she sucked in a deep breath and flattened a hand against her friend's back.

\*\*\*\*

*Uncomfortable in the fussy, heavy pink dress, Ellen Sanders slouched in the back theater pew and fumed. Onstage, her castmates leapt up to dance to the latest Monkees' tune blaring from a transistor radio. Her feet tapped along, but with annoyance rather than pleasure.*

*Nan and Rod were late to rehearsal, holding them all up. Her lucky best friend had the day off from Woolworths, and she'd probably spent hours with her new boyfriend. He was known to cut his college classes. Why sit through a boring lecture when some adoring girl would give you her notes—and her number.*

*Ellen's lips puckered with distaste. Nan had lost her marbles; she'd barely rallied from her depression after being dumped by the last jerk. Technically, her "fiancé," before he knocked up another girl. And this one was primed to hurt her, too. She slumped lower on the hard pew, pondering how to tell her best friend what she'd overheard the night before. The revelation would rip her heart in two again, and she might not withstand another blow.*

*Pounding footsteps and laughter interrupted her thoughts. The lovebirds burst into the room and jogged up the aisle holding hands. "Sorry we're late," he hollered. "The Shake Shack was hopping." They didn't look sorry, all gleaming smiles and bubbling laughter.*

*Ellen frowned and tugged up the flowing long skirt to head toward the stage. She sidled next to her starry-eyed pal and hissed under her breath, "What's the deal?"*

*"Nothing to worry about." Nan tossed her mane of long, black hair over her shoulder. Her eyes followed Rod across the room as he joked with a pal.*

*"How was last night?" She tried not to sound bitchy, but it took effort.*

*"Magical." She practically glowed, leaning in close to whisper "Fill you in later. Not here. Too many big ears."*

*Nausea rose in Ellen's throat. He was using her. She'd definitely have to share the juicy tidbit she'd overheard. But what if Nan got furious—at her?*

*Bette, the director, clapped her hands to corral the cast. "All right everyone. Let's begin with Rod's entry into the garden."*

*Ellen's mouth fell open. Of all the scenes, she'd have to play opposite him and ooze immediate attraction. She stood stone-faced as he approached, wafting the faint scent of fried food.*

*Ebony hair curled over his forehead, nearly swooping into the dark-lashed eyes as he read from the script. "Cecily, ever since I first looked upon your wonderful and incomparable beauty, I have dared to love you wildly, passionately, devotedly, hopelessly."*

*"Yeah, right."*

*His head flew up at her sarcastic, improvised words.*

*The rest of the cast tittered, and the director cleared her throat. "Do you need the line?"*

*Ellen shaded her eyes and peered out into the darkened room, feeling a blush of embarrassment sweep* her cheeks. "Um, no. Sorry. The dialogue's super cheesy."

"We call it satire, my dear." The woman left her seat to stand below them. "The scene's pivotal. We need to believe in an immediate, swoony connection."

"Fat chance," she muttered, unable to control her tongue.

Bette crossed her arms over her chest and narrowed her eyes. "I won't delay everyone who's come here ready to work. I'd strongly suggest the two of you meet early tomorrow and work on your stage chemistry. You both know how to project affection. Start the scene again." She retreated to her seat. Silence lay thick over the room.

Tears pricked behind Ellen's lids. When she finally composed herself to look up, he scowled. Jerk. She doubly shared the sentiment. She gritted her teeth and willed herself into a semi-convincing delivery as the action flowed on.

At the break, she avoided everyone and ran off toward the green room. She had to pull it together, fast. A couple of gossips already had teased about her sour attitude toward the guy. She shoved the door open but, instead of finding refuge, thumped blindly into another body. They knocked heads, with arms and legs entangled. "Oooww." Dazed, she clutched her aching temple.

Without a word, the person pushed her away. Arms flailing, Ellen slammed against the door shoulder-first, hard enough to bruise.

Lorna, the stage helper, glared in front of her. "Clumsy ass." Her thick brown braids swung below a beaded headband. Cleavage erupted out of a gauzy peasant top.

*Fueled by pain and frustration, Ellen levered up to stand nose to nose, smelling a mix of patchouli and pot. "What are you cooking up with Rod? I heard you two last night when I was on the stairs."*

*The girl held her ground and smirked. "You're such a square. If you really heard anything, you'd know. I'm warning you, stay out of other people's business." Her face hardened, and she poked a finger into Ellen's painful shoulder before pivoting to stalk away.*

*"We're not done," she shouted after her, rubbing the sore spot.*

*The bitch shot a middle-finger salute.*

Chapter Six

Marcy's head swam, and her limbs trembled as the vivid images flared, then faded. She breathed deeply to recenter herself and registered a hand rubbing small, soothing circles on her back. Her eyes fluttered open, and she looked down into Tess' concerned face.

"Did you join in the vision?" her friend questioned. "Are you okay?"

"Ye-ess. To both." She squinted toward the corner. The light had blinked out.

"What exactly did you see?" Tess still clutched the pink dress to her chest, the long hem sweeping the floor. Her aura floated a gentle purple to reflect her sincerity, imagination, and intelligence.

Still a bit unbalanced, Marcy focused to recall as much detail as possible. "A young blonde wore the gown at a rehearsal for Earnest, to play Cecily. I got an impression of her name. Ellen. Plus, her friend Nan, and Rod and Lorna." She began to steady, and her voice strengthened as additional highlights tumbled out. "Definite drama surrounded the four of them."

"You're echoing my perceptions." Tess tucked the garment onto the rack. "We don't yet know the name of the girl who died here, but Chase did say she played the role you've been reading."

"I'd rather forget that part."

Below them onstage, a phone jangled a classic rock

ringtone. They both jolted as Mike's voice answered. After the hellos he paused to listen, and so did they, aware he must be standing beneath the half wall. They'd spoken in low tones but definitely didn't want to be overheard. Marcy raised her eyebrows at Tess, hoping the call wouldn't take long so they could resume their conversation.

"Damn it, Nicki." His voice pitched higher, and louder. "You could've told me you were auditioning for both shows to weigh in my decision to cast you…"

In the loft above, they exchanged dismayed expressions.

"Okay, that's exactly why you didn't tell me. I get it. But let me give you a little advice. Directors tend to get pissed when they're jerked around, and the rep'll follow you."

Marcy edged toward the opening, imagining his stormy face. She didn't want to see him yet couldn't help the eavesdropping.

"I know. You're sorry. So am I." His tone softened. "But we're kind of up a creek here. Hey, hey, don't whimper… No, I promise I won't be mad at you forever. Gotta go. Goodbye."

"Damn it!" His repeated curse rocked the quiet.

Yikes. He'll be a real bear tonight. Marcy considered a quick exit out the back door to avoid his claws. Though he also might need her to read again. The tromp of feet held her rooted as the cast began to herd across the wooden stage. Tess tiptoed to join her and peeked over the half wall as he began to address the group.

"Nicki also auditioned last week for *My Fair Lady* because she always wanted to play Eliza." His flat voice floated up. "Through some airhead thinking, she decided not to come to rehearsal here—or tell us—till she knew the result. They chose her, and we need a new Cecily."

Cast members murmured. He talked over them. "We didn't have another age-appropriate person audition who could handle the role. Do we know anyone who has the ability and isn't tied up in another show?"

A few names were tossed out and rejected onstage. One girl had moved. Another was getting married on a show weekend. With the drama playing out below, their ghost hunt would have to wait, along with the costumes. "We should go," Marcy mouthed to Tess.

"What about Marcy?" Will's voice stopped her dead in the intended retreat. Her heart thumped wildly, and she spun toward the wall again as he continued, "She had a great feel for the character when she read. Accent and everything."

"Marcy?" The director responded with an obvious note of dismissal. "She's never done anything. The show's dialogue and comic timing are challenging even with experience."

Her teeth clenched at his smug tone.

"She nailed both." Chase had joined the argument. "Come on, man. What've you got to lose?"

*Aww, such a sweetie.*

She couldn't resist popping her head over the open ledge. "I have acted before," she blurted, scanning the surprised, upraised faces.

Mike's chin wrenched up. His jaw worked above his tight crossed arms. She skimmed her gaze right past him. "Guys, thanks for the vote of confidence. I've had a blast reading with you."

Chase gave her a thumbs-up. "You'd be awesome."

*Yes, she could be...*

Her eyes flickered to Mike. He stared up at her for a few charged moments, giving the wacky impression of playing a reluctant Romeo to her Juliet. Wait, she *wanted* the role. "I'd really—"

"I usually—" He spoke at the same time. She deferred to him to finish, her nerves dancing double-time.

He held up his palms in mock surrender. "Sorry to come off as a tight ass. We don't have a lot of time here. If you want to try the role, let's give 'er a shot." He focused on her with unnerving intensity, as if the two of them were sharing an intimate, private joke. His lip lifted in a half-smile. "I suppose I should ask first if you're willing."

Her heart tripped into her throat, leaving her speechless.

Beside her, Tess' head bobbed in support. Marcy noted similar gestures of approval from the actors below. "Absolutely," she confirmed, confident in the answer.

The others erupted in cheers, and she thought she detected a hint of relief flitting across Mike's face. He clapped his hands and broke the spell. "Come on down to rehearse, Cecily. I can either open early or stay late some nights, so you can work on the costumes."

"Right, boss." No option to slack off, despite the new responsibility, but she didn't mind. She'd do her best to shine at both activities. Acting might even help satisfy her ever-present, unresolved artistic longings. She stepped away from the wall. "I'm in the show," she tried out the phrase. "I'm. In. The. Show."

Tess grasped her arm, bestowing a wide, twinkling smile. "I'm so proud of you. No doubt you'll kick some creative booty onstage and off." She dropped her voice to a whisper. "I'll try to return in a few days to see if we can gather more impressions from the clothing. Someone definitely has a message to relay. Hopefully between us we can uncover it."

"Thanks so much for sharing your gift to help me." Marcy matched the low tone. "If we're lucky, when Justine returns, she might be able to see the…whatever." A shiver fingered along her spine at the thought, though she truly desired to achieve the outcome. Dealing with benign auras seemed much safer than encountering ghostly embodiments.

They headed downstairs to join the others, and Tess said her goodbyes. When the cast leaped into action, Marcy tamped her tingle of nerves with a quick internal pep talk. *You've already been reading the part. Heck, you've got some of it memorized.* She might not be the most experienced, but she'd make up for it with enthusiasm, focus, and dedication. Feeling calmer, she eased into the interaction and discovered she also remembered most of the blocking.

At the end of the evening, Mike approached. "Red, thanks for jumping into the fray with us. You did good tonight. I'll give you more pointers tomorrow, and we can hang around Wednesday after rehearsal if you want some extra time upstairs."

On a positive adrenaline high, she ignored the nickname, bounced on her toes, and returned his blocking script. "I promise to work really hard. You won't regret giving me a chance."

"I know you will." He glanced at her dancing feet. "Now go home and get some sleep. Don't drink any caffeine. You're already pumped to the ceiling. Got to get used to the acting high."

\*\*\*\*

With the theater empty, Mike walked down the side aisle toward the lobby. He reached for the velvet curtain separating the spaces and caught a faint clunking sound behind him. He spun to listen. Probably the ancient heating system, which could clang and wheeze, channeling a cantankerous old man. When the silence hovered, he walked through the doorway and outside to complete the lock up.

Feeling ancient and bruised himself, he rubbed the back of his stiff neck and crossed the street toward his vehicle. Of course, he'd known some sort of issue had come up with Nicki. Yet he'd preferred to bury his head and cross his fingers it would resolve. On the job, people were paid well to perform to his standards and plans. In theater they were all good-hearted volunteers. Her action had been thoughtless, but not unforgiveable. At least they were early in the process. He'd heard horror stories of leads dropping out of shows within a week or two of opening.

He stepped up into his black pickup, berating himself for dissing Will's suggestion to consider Marcy. Especially within her hearing. Weird thing was, he couldn't say *why* he'd done it. Her fill-in reads actually had impressed him. The sharp British accent had outshone some of the others. She'd nailed the comic delivery.

No, there was something else about her he couldn't pinpoint. Not the crazy fashion sense. Or her attitude. She radiated kindness, sunshine, and positivity. He started the engine, recalling how she'd turned to jelly in his arms at the swish of a flying mammal.

Maybe that was the problem. When she smacked into his chest and clung, his engine had roared, as well. "Frickin' testosterone," he muttered, hitting the gas a little too hard as he swung into the street.

He wasn't a player, and he'd been with Tara for— what, eight months?—after a fixup by mutual friends. Her relationship had ended, while he'd never seriously connected with anyone since moving to the area. His initial take on her: hot, but showy, and probably demanding. Yet she also could be fun and engaging, and they'd surprised themselves by sticking together.

He peered through the windshield into the starless night, admitting he and Tara had cooled a bit during the summer. She loved to dress up and party. He preferred jeans or sweats and hanging with a few close friends. With her new job, managing an upscale health club, she'd started to develop an edgier attitude. At adult night with the cast, he'd noticed her snide remark to Marcy but hadn't wanted to make an issue, in case she'd picked up on some subconscious vibe from him.

All the more reason to lay down his internal ground rules around the new girl. They'd stay professional. Director to actor. No attraction allowed.

Chapter Seven

The next night, eager to hit the stage, the whole cast assembled. With directorial reminders on blocking and character, the show rolled into action. Marcy noted the actors added mannerisms as they found their comfort zones. She'd have to catch some quiet moments to ponder and finesse her own character. Between working two jobs, helping her mom, and costuming, the packed schedule left zero room for her artwork. She had no goals to achieve anyway. Her chin drooped. She missed creating watercolors and whimsical scenes. Maybe she should volunteer to help paint the set.

"Red?" Mike's voice pierced through her musings. "Got a question?"

It took her a moment to realize she'd missed a cue. Then the burn set in. "Um, no. And my name is Marcy. In case you've forgotten."

OMG. The snark had popped out. Growing up, boys had taunted her because of her hair color, and she'd resorted to thumping their heads with her knuckles. Until one tattled to the principal which earned her a detention.

Lindsay tittered across their imaginary tea table.

The director stared at them, his face studiously blank. "Right. Marcy." He chopped out the name and turned to the others. "How about we take ten."

She'd probably pissed him off. Throat parched, she skirted around him to head for her purse which she'd stashed in the first row of seats. With a water bottle halfway to her lips, she saw him approach. Her nerves zinged a warning, and she grabbed a quick gulp. Would he give her grief for challenging him? She didn't want to come off as a diva. Like Tara.

Her spirits tanked as he stopped in front of her, exuding cool masculinity and a hint of spicy aftershave. "You're doing a pretty good job of interpreting Cecily." *But…*

She gripped the bottle and waited. A splash of water gushed onto her sandal, and she ignored the wetness creeping between her toes.

"For everyone here, the most important thing is to play the role straight." He searched her eyes for comprehension. "No matter how outrageous the comment, the characters are totally committed."

She nodded, compelled by his total concentration, on how his face lit in discussing the work. "In your interaction with Chase, the audience has to be reeled in to believe these two meet and are immediately smitten, to the point they're engaged within minutes." He hesitated, thick, dark brows drawing together. "Generate strong chemistry, but don't let him pull you too far."

*What exactly did he mean?*

Her confusion increased as he extended his hand and leaned forward to encroach on her space, closing the distance between them. Aftershave tickled her nose, and her heartbeat rocketed in her chest as his face loomed above. He was…he was…reaching past to nab the script on her chair. She exhaled a shaky breath as he stepped back to thumb through the pages, and hoped her cheeks weren't as red as they felt.

His index finger jabbed a passage. "To revisit the

actual words, 'Cecily, ever since I first looked upon your wonderful and incomparable beauty, I have dared to love you wildly, passionately, devotedly, hopelessly.' " The British accent was strong, the tone flip, yet sensual. He met her eyes and held them.

Her pulse fluttered in her throat. *Wildly. Passionately.* The way she'd want to be loved if the right man ever came along. Heat skimmed down her body, and she struggled to recall his initial point.

The corner of his lip curved before he seemed to catch himself. His face blanked again, and he dropped his eyes to the page. "Yeah. You respond, 'I don't think that you should tell me that you love me wildly, passionately, devotedly, hopelessly. Hopelessly doesn't seem to make much sense, does it?' "

He slapped the script shut, and she jumped at the sharp movement, spilling more water on the carpet. "She's not off guard or overwhelmed by the sudden, passionate declaration of love. You see? She expects it as her due."

She did see.

He tapped the book again with a blunt fingertip. "You have to make us believe in the attraction. The spark. I want to work with you two on building the scene."

Marcy offered a tentative comment. "You want a controlled sizzle." If only they could wrangle what had swirled between them in the loft the night before. Her mind raced, excited by the idea of expanding her character knowledge. "Does it help if we touch?" To illustrate, she placed hers on his muscled forearm, finding the skin warm and taut.

He stepped back, and her hand fell away. She tucked

it under her arm and tried not to let the mortification show on her face. He sure was a moody one.

"Try the movement onstage, and I'll decide." He turned and strode in the opposite direction.

Shaking her head, she lowered into the closest seat to wipe off her damp toes with a tissue. "Lacking in social skills," she muttered. Those muscled, he-man types were far removed from the poetic, hippie rebels she usually ran with and dated. Too often ones with shaggy hair and scraggly goatees, without visible means of support and an uncanny ability to sponge off her own limited resources.

Coming out of the reverie, she wadded up the tissue and caught a whiff of a semi-familiar perfume. One she'd smelled recently. She sniffed, trying to place the scent, and looked up into sharp brown eyes heavily rimmed with mascara. She gulped and tried not to jolt with surprise. "Oh, hi."

Why in the world would Tara be standing over her, face creased like she'd chewed on a lemon? "I hear you're onstage now, too. I suppose congratulations are in order." The low voice carried a hint of mockery.

When had she arrived? In time to witness the little discussion with her boyfriend? Marcy straightened in the seat, swallowing an internal sigh. The woman stood too close for her to gracefully stand and meet her eye to eye. "I'm glad to help out. The role is fun and challenging." She kept her voice light and non-confrontational.

"They're taking a risk with you. Mike should know better after losing his last big bet."

*Bet? Was he a gambler?* That didn't mesh with his control freak tendencies. Yet the idea meshed with Will's mention of "bluffing" at the bar. She held her tongue and wished she could drop through the floor and escape.

To compound the painful encounter, the director had caught sight of them and was taking long strides down the aisle. His girlfriend's face rearranged into a pleasant welcome. He stopped and kissed Tara on the cheek, wrapping an arm around her shoulders. "Babe, I didn't know you were coming by tonight."

"Spur of the moment." She tilted her head at him. "I wanted to support your progress with the big change."

His brow wrinkled.

Marcy held up a hand. "I think she means me. How sweet." *Oh yes, she could act.* "If you'll excuse me."

She slid out the opposite side of the row and looked for someone—anyone—to interact with. The others were gathered, oblivious and chattering, near the stage. Before she could slink over and immerse herself in another conversation, Mike came forward to recall the cast. Tara trailed behind and dropped into the second seat at his director's table. Great, she was staying to watch. Her stomach churning, Marcy focused her gaze above the woman's head. Yet after a few minutes, she'd immersed and forgotten everything but the immediate onstage action. They spent nearly an hour running through the remaining pages before he stopped to issue notes. She dared to peer out into the theater space and discovered Tara had vacated. Must've gotten bored. Or maybe she'd already achieved her goals in sniping at her.

"Marcy." The director said her name, and she guiltily tuned in. "I asked if you and Chase can hang around a couple minutes? The rest of you can leave, but I want to try a few things with your introduction scene."

Of course, he hadn't forgotten their earlier

conversation. Maybe his girlfriend had given him a few "helpful" suggestions.

"Chase, you're not seducing her." Mike mounted the stage and jumped right in, focusing his attention on her partner. "You're wooing. There's a difference."

His target lifted an eyebrow. "Do tell."

He ignored the sarcasm. "Lighten the tone. Algernon should be attentive but self-absorbed. Run the lines again. Please." He moved off to watch them and interjected after a few moments. "Marcy, you asked whether to touch him. Go ahead." Since Chase closed the distance between them, she repeated the previous line and laid her hand on his arm as she had with Mike. To her, the gesture came off flat. Uninspired.

"No." The director seemed to agree. "Doesn't add anything. The scene revolves around tension *without* touching."

After their sizzling eye contact at the break, she could grasp the concept. She attempted to portray a heightened attraction with the next effort, ignoring the distraction of the man watching them. He let them run before interrupting. "Better. Pursue the same direction tomorrow. Make us believe you two are really into each other. But, Chase, behave yourself." He waggled his finger at him and left the stage.

The younger man snickered. "He's no fun." He reached for her hand and wrapped his fingers around the palm. His handsome face dipped toward her. "I'm all for method acting, but you're doing fine."

At least somebody here respected her efforts, and she didn't detect any creepiness behind the joking comment. Despite the swagger, he appeared to be a good guy. Otherwise, she'd have caught a negative vibe from how the other cast members reacted to him.

"Break it up, you two," a chiding voice sliced between them. "Time to lock up."

Chase released her fingers. "Tomorrow. Same bat time." He sauntered off backstage.

She couldn't help but smile, as the reference reminded her of the costuming. She peered into the darkened theater, trying to fix on Mike. "Can I come in early tomorrow to work upstairs?" Tess might not be available to join her again, but she could finally pull some pieces.

He appeared below her. "I can do six." He crossed his arms over his chest. "Hey. Sorry I called you Red earlier."

She waved the apology away and descended the steps to his level. "I didn't mean to make a deal out of it. It doesn't really bother me though I got my share of teasing when I was little."

"Were you ever little?" His eyes swept over her in an obvious, humorous fashion.

"For a couple years, before I towered above all the boys. They retaliated by calling me a matchstick."

He snorted out a laugh. "Sorry, that was a hot one." He snickered again. "Can't help it. I'm into bad puns."

She groaned, pleased he'd finally loosened up. "Thanks for the warning. I'm out of here." She retrieved her purse and trotted toward the door. She'd have to find her rhythm with their gruff leader, but apparently, he had a softer, corny side in addition to the rigid one. She def preferred cornball.

Tomorrow, she'd tackle the costume area again. She exited through the heavy wooden doors and wondered if the ghostly glow would greet her again.

## Chapter Eight

Mike opened the theater early Wednesday and settled to consult his script while he waited for Marcy. He stood when he heard footsteps, and his gaze swept the long line of leg, emphasized by stilettos under a slip of a dress. Damn. She looked hot. He disguised the thought with a scowl. "You're planning to carry costumes in those stilts?"

She looked down. "Sure, I wear heels a lot. I'll be careful. Or take them off." She removed the shoes, baring hot pink toenails.

His breath lodged in his throat. Annoyed, he cleared it. "I'll help. Don't want to have to replace you, too, due to hauling injuries." He turned sharply to head toward the stairway through the stage left door, determined to bound up the stairs ahead of the miniscule skirt. If she raised her arms to drag down a costume, he'd keep his eyes averted.

At the doorway, she hesitated. "Could you check for the bat, please?"

In his agitation he'd forgotten the damn bat. He took a deep breath and forced himself to stride to the racks and ruffle his hands over them. No swooping wings emerged, thank goodness. "All clear. Do you have anything for me to take down?" Best that they make a quick escape in case the intruder lurked nearby.

Her brow furrowed, and she circled the room. "The

mannequin was bald last night." They both stared at the curling black wig perched on her head.

"Somebody's got a sense of humor." He shrugged, impatient to leave. "A couple of board members have keys. Maybe somebody came in to clean up." He jerked a thumb toward a pile of men's suit coats waiting to be rehung. "The place could use an overhaul. Go ahead and load me up with stuff to carry down."

Faint voices started to filter to them as cast members arrived, and he glanced toward the half wall. To his right, he noticed a small side door standing ajar. He'd never seen it before. Must be additional attic storage. In case the bat hovered inside, he shut it. The thought made him antsy, and he checked his watch. Ten minutes till start time.

Marcy turned from the racks hugging a half dozen garments. "These might work for the women. I'll catch people at intermission to try them on."

She transferred them to his outstretched arms, but the slippery weight of the fabrics pulled two of the dresses to the floor. When she knelt to gather them, her own tight dress slid up the smooth, tanned thighs.

His pulse quickened. Shiny curls bounced around her face, emitting a scent of coconut as she rose and stood—too close for comfort. Not intentionally, but to hand off the items. He slapped a hand on the pile to secure them and took two giant steps back. "Come down as quick as you can so we can get rolling." He didn't wait for her answer as he balanced the pile and strode to the stairs, still smelling the sweet hint of coconut.

****

She watched him exit, brusque as usual. The man really needed to chill. As she began to select pieces for the men, a bright light winked in the corner and disappeared. *Interesting.* Preoccupied with his presence, and the bat possibility, she hadn't thought about or witnessed the glow earlier.

Yet the wigged mannequin raised new concerns. Did the ghost—yikes, she didn't want to think in those terms—have the ability to *move* items? The hair rose on her arms, and she drew a shaky breath to ponder a new realization. Justine had been in the loft many times in the past, but she'd never once said anything about encountering a spirit.

Was *she* the catalyst? And if so, why?

A burst of laughter from below grabbed her attention. They'd be starting soon, and she needed to finish. She hauled the additional garments down, stepping carefully on the steep stairs. If these pieces worked, she'd be able to refine her needs for Friday's planned trip to the South Bend costume shop.

With no sign of Mike in the theater, she decided to flag down one of the support characters for a fitting. Bryant, an easygoing man in his forties, played the butler. He gamely tried on a formal coat with tails, which sculpted his broad shoulders.

He agreed to provide black pants; she'd add a cummerbund and cravat. "Milady." He bowed to her and slipped away to try on the white dress shirt with fine tucks. Next, the older gentleman playing the Reverend Chasuble slipped a black choir robe over his girth. With the addition of a white collar and his own slacks, she christened him costumed. She'd also discovered a simple, wide-sleeved gray blouse and dark skirt for the governess, plus a muted decorative shawl.

Maria wrapped the fabric around her shoulders and

tugged back her black hair threaded with gray. "Will I pass for a feisty spinster?"

"The Rev won't be able to resist you."

Marcy searched the room for Lindsay and found herself tensing when the director headed toward them. She willed herself to relax, reminding her that his proverbial bark was worse than his bite. Or so she hoped. An image leaped to mind of him leaning close to nibble—ooh, danger. She did not poach on other women's boyfriends, and especially this one. Darn her parents for encouraging her overactive imagination. She usually appreciated being able to translate words into visualization.

Mike stood before her with his dog-eared script. "We need to jump into Act I. Are you finding some clothing matches with the cast?"

She indulged a spark of pride at the progress. "I am. Plus, I'm making a list for my treasure hunt in South Bend."

He contemplated the governess' shawl, and she poised for a snide comment or suggestion. Instead, he shared a costume budget figure that she hoped would cover their needs. The website hadn't included prices.

They all shifted gears into rehearsal and finally broke for the night after three intense hours. As the actors tossed off cheerful goodbyes, Chase sauntered toward Marcy and grabbed her around the waist. "Don't forget adult night tomorrow."

After their frequent stage interactions, she didn't mind the close contact. "I wouldn't miss it."

"Excellent." He disengaged before strutting back down the aisle.

She made additional notes on her pad, humming a

little tune. When she flipped the notebook closed, she found herself alone with Mike. She wished their rapport was as easy as with the rest of the cast. "Sorry if I've kept you. I didn't want to forget anything."

He shrugged into a leather jacket. "You're fine. If you're ready, I'll lock up."

She ignored the preference to grab her things and run ahead. Just because he unnerved her, there was no need to be rude. She had to get used to his moods. They walked out of the theater together, not talking, into the dark, cool night. She crossed the street, shivering in the sleeveless dress, and wished she'd brought a sweater. A hint of fall had crept into the evenings, chilling the air and sprinkling gold and rust-colored leaves among the abundant maple trees in the town. Fitting for LaPorte which had been dubbed the Maple City. She waved an airy goodbye to the director and settled in her car, anticipating a boost of heat.

The Bug's engine whined and sputtered. She tried again, and the scary noise died away to silence. Shocked, she twisted the key to repeat the motion, with zero response.

Mike approached with a question on his face. "Problem?"

To her distress, tears pricked her eyes. "I've had a teeny bit of engine trouble lately."

"Let me try."

She clambered out carefully in the tight, short dress and exchanged places, chewing the inside of her jaw. He maneuvered his large frame into the car and tried the key with the same silent response. "Could be the starter." He looked up at her. "Sorry. Not much I can do in the dark at ten at night."

"I guess I'll call…"

With Tara's sharp comments echoing inside her head, she flushed and hesitated, not wanting to utter the juvenile words "my mom." Who likely would have taken a sleeping pill in an attempt to get a few hours away from her pain.

His lips twisted. She held up a finger and pivoted away to dig out her cell.

"I'll give you a ride home." His offer whipped her around in the middle of the quiet street. He finagled out of the tiny vehicle, holding the keys. He started to hand them to her, then halted. His eyes widened. "I rode my bike."

A bicycle? She followed his gaze to take in a cherry-red…motorcycle.

Chapter Nine

The sunny day had been too inviting to ignore, and
Mike wanted to ride as much as possible before the
weather turned. He stood next to the whimsical little car,
and his mind tumbled through other transportation
options. He wouldn't leave her here alone, waiting for a
ride. The community was safe, but still. And he wouldn't
drag her mom out late at night. Unless she preferred to
wait here for her. He'd open up the theater and stay. Her
pale face registered a trace of panic in the dim light of
the streetlamp.

"If you're scared to ride, I'll wait with you."

"No." She hugged her arms to her chest as her gaze
darted to the hulking machine. "My mother often takes a
sleeping pill and goes to bed early. I'd rather avoid
waking her."

He restrained a groan. She'd be straddling him.
*Good God Almighty*. He didn't think the words as a
curse, but as an appeal for his fraying sanity. Over the
summer, he'd cajoled Tara to ride with him more than
once, anticipating a sexy trip. She'd refused, worried her
hair would tangle. Now another woman, in a crazy short
skirt, would be plastered behind him. *Keep your cool*, he
thought, and noticed she was shaking from the cold.

He was being a dick. "Here." He pulled off his
leather jacket.

She hesitated but wisely accepted the warmth.

Muttering under his breath, he walked across the street to retrieve his helmet where he'd strapped it onto the back. She didn't move, and he carried it back to her. "You wear it. I'll be careful."

She flipped her mass of curls out of the way to slip on the heavy headgear and buckle it under her chin. Her head dipped, and she made a snuffling noise.

*No, don't let her cry. Ah, geez.*

A giggle erupted, and she raised her face, contorted with mirth. "Good thing you wear a large to fit all my hair." She swiped a hand across her lips but couldn't erase the merriment. "Sorry. I'm not trying to be difficult or ridiculous. I need to get home. You've got a ride. We're adults. We're friends. And I'm babbling." She laughed again, ending in a little snort.

"You're right on all counts." Thank goodness she had a sense of humor. Maybe someday he'd look back and chuckle, but tonight the logistics were unnerving. "Can you climb on, or do you need help?"

She avoided his eyes. "In usual circumstances I'd be fine, but—" Marcy ended on a yelp as he also averted his eyes and took the initiative to lift her. With no other choice, she swung a leg over the wide back seat and immediately clasped her knees together.

The maneuver made him snicker, as well. "You know that won't work."

She grinned back. "Yeah. Close your eyes and…sit."

*Mount. Straddle. Get on.* The unsaid words hung between them. Bracing the bike, he was close enough to note a hint of pink spreading across her cheeks. She angled away and fiddled with the zipper on his jacket.

"Hang on and hold your balance," he gritted out,

grabbing the handlebars and avoiding those bare thighs clenched on the seat. Eyes forward, he swung his leg over the seat, catching a peripheral glance as she opened her legs. He landed, hoping they wouldn't be arrested for public indecency as the skirt had undoubtedly peeled backward. She tried to tug it down, jostling her legs against him.

He gritted his teeth, gunned the engine, and sped down the quiet, darkened street filled with older residential houses. Within a couple of minutes, he buzzed through the downtown area toward the industrial zone. In the awkwardness of the situation, he realized he had no idea where they were going.

At a red light he asked, "Where do you live? Around Rolling Prairie?" He'd heard her tell the others where she'd attended high school.

The light changed, and he accelerated, revving the engine. She leaned closer to speak toward his ear and began to share directions. He tried to concentrate; he really did. But his body was too aware of her soft female form pressed against his. Of the hands cupping his waist. His teeth ground together, and he gathered the barest basics of what she'd said. The ride would take a good fifteen minutes. Fifteen minutes of torture. With Tara, he'd enjoy the sensations, stroke the silky leg, revel in the closeness.

He didn't dare enjoy tonight's ride. He sped up as they hit the edge of LaPorte and followed the winding four-lane highway. The wind would've been brisk, but invigorating, wearing his jacket and helmet. Yet he welcomed the cold, to keep from fixating on the warmth enveloping his butt and back. The motion of the machine had eased her body even closer.

He hit a bump, and her arms twisted tighter around his waist. When she didn't readjust, he told himself she'd taken advantage of the wind-block, plus he'd boosted their speed to shorten the ride.

Agonizing minutes later, he came to a crossroads, and she tugged his left arm. "Turn here," she shouted.

He leaned the bike onto the black-topped rural road, and her body hung with his. They had to be close now. He gripped the handlebars and forced himself to envision Tara. They hadn't gotten together since adult night. She'd offered the excuse of a busy weekend, and he'd agreed. Four nights of rehearsals meant he hadn't done laundry, or cleaned much, or shopped for groceries. Thankfully, his current work project at the condos proceeded with relatively smooth precision.

"Next right," Marcy instructed.

He let off the gas to turn into a driveway framed by towering dark pines. They approached a small house constructed of logs, with a lone light on inside.

Now for the dismount. He pulled in a deep breath and braked before leaping off the bike as quickly as he could without toppling. With his eyes toward the half-moon, he lifted her body over the seat.

****

Marcy wobbled when he jumped off—moving as if the engine was on fire. She didn't have time to clamp her legs together before he grasped her around the waist to lift her off the bike. Her arms flailed, and she drew her calves and feet up to clear the seat. Riding a motorcycle in stilettos definitely wasn't recommended. He released her onto the gravel drive, and she tilted in the heels with a high, wordless exclamation. Blindly, she braced her hands against his chest to gain balance. "Sorry." Her voice came out breathless as she met the intent gaze.

Her body tingled—everywhere—from the intimate ride. For a moment, under the twinkling, starry sky, every thought flew out of her head, leaving her tuned to the flush of feeling. As if there was no one and nowhere else, except for the two of them cocooned in a heightened moment.

The familiar bang of the screen door barely registered, but her mother's voice drove straight through her consciousness. "Marcy, are you all right? Where's your car?"

Chapter Ten

Mike's head flew up to witness a woman standing in a halo of light in front of the house. The mother. Damn. He'd hoped to drop her off and speed away, to submerge his body's churning. Instead, he was standing in what might appear to be an embrace. He disengaged, and Marcy's hands fell from his chest. She tugged out of the helmet and handed it to him before she whirled and picked her way over the gravel in those wobbling heels.

"Mom, nothing's wrong," she reassured. "Well, the car conked, which is a huge hassle. Thankfully, Mike gave me a ride home."

"Nice to meet you, and thanks for the rescue," the woman called. "I'm Marcy's mother, Pat."

He considered jumping on the bike to ride away into the night. *Nope.* His mom had raised him better. He left the helmet on the seat and walked toward the house, slow and on-edge.

Pat peered up at her daughter, as she stood a few inches shorter. "You could've called and spared him the drive. I couldn't sleep, so I've been puttering around. Let's offer the reward of one of your brownies." She opened the screen door, and he noted a similar facial structure, though the eyes were darker blue, and the shorter, reddish curls tinged with gray.

"Glad I could help." He extended his hand. "Nice to meet you."

"I'm sorry. I'm not able to shake hands." She said the words easily and lifted her palms.

He took in the gnarled, curved fingers. Before he could think of anything to say, she relaxed her hands to her sides. "I made decaf. You're lucky I didn't binge eat the rest of the brownies."

He wondered at the cause of her malady as he gestured to indicate they should go first. Pat entered, and her daughter tossed him a questioning glance, as if she'd intuited his preference to leave. He kept a straight face and followed them into a living room decorated in a colorful, eclectic vibe with a mix of newer and antique furnishings. The walls were painted a bright, sunflower yellow and covered with artwork. The dozen framed pieces ranged from a detailed pencil sketch of a golden retriever to a vivid impressionist garden worthy of Monet.

The older woman watched him closely. "Marcy is a first-class artist. These are all hers. If you've been to Northside Deli, she painted the wall mural." She nodded fondly toward her offspring, who rolled her eyes.

They were hers? The hidden talent surprised him. "They're really good." Intrigued, he took a moment to inspect each piece in the low light.

The artist joined him. "Thanks. These wouldn't fit on the refrigerator. We had to find another spot."

He couldn't help but frown at her self-deprecating words. "Don't downplay talent. Your artwork's impressive, and your acting debut will be, too."

She appeared pleased but didn't comment, while her mom beckoned him to follow her. An enticing coffee aroma filled the air as they entered the kitchen, where the appliances dated back decades. The cabinets were distressed, stripped down, as if they'd been rescued from a much older home but never refinished. On purpose. The décor worked in the rustic space.

"Have a seat." Marcy stretched into an overhead cabinet to gather mugs. As her short skirt rose, he forced his gaze toward her mother, who'd retrieved matching glazed pottery plates. He reached to take them then wondered if she'd be offended, but she didn't react and sat to join him at the table.

A steaming hot mug landed in front of him, welcome after the cool ride.

"Black, I presume?" Marcy's lip curved in amusement.

He nodded. "Yes, thanks." No frou-frou coffee. But those brownies. A tray of them rested in the middle of the basic pine table. The fast-food burger he'd gulped for dinner had worn off long ago. He practically salivated, smelling the dark chocolate studded with nuts and a ribbon of caramel.

She settled two more mugs on the table, both lightened with cream, and sat across from him. "Those are from the deli. I do some baking between the breakfast and lunch crowds."

"Another commendable talent." His fingers twitched, and he stopped himself from reaching out to grab and gobble the treat. She nudged the plate closer. With that permission, he indulged, biting into the wedge of gooey goodness. A moan of pleasure escaped as he swallowed.

Pat lifted one onto her plate. "Sinful, aren't they? The girl has so many talents. If she'd give in and choose one, she'd go places."

Her daughter looked down and broke a brownie into

small, precise pieces. "I'm not looking to go anyplace soon. My so-called talents will wait." Her voice had lowered with intensity. "Besides, I'm dabbling in a new one with the theater. Who knows where the muse will lead?"

"To your art. Always. You have to start prioritizing yourself over me."

A charged undercurrent swam beneath their words. He didn't have time to decipher the comments before Pat swiveled to regard him. "I have rheumatoid arthritis. Challenging to do some things, but I get by. I don't drive anymore, so we only have one car. She's a sweetie to live here with me, but she'll tell you I keep trying to prod her out of the nest. Because someday she'll move out, and I will survive. Just fine." She emphasized the last two words.

"I'm happy living here," her subject interjected with a pointed look. "Until I land a *real job*, I'm thankful for the chance to save money."

He wiped his sticky fingers on a napkin, trying to keep up with the rapid-fire conversation but aware a mini drama had just played out. "What kind of job are you considering?"

She didn't meet his eye. "My dream would be illustration. Children's books. But I need specific training and connections."

He sensed she preferred to change the subject, but he stayed the course. "I'm no expert, but from your artwork, I'd say go for it."

She finally turned the liquid-blue gaze on him. A slight smile played over her lips. "My skills are genetic. Mom's an excellent potter. She threw everything we're eating on." Her finger traced the edge of the mug, colored in a haze of copper tones. "Dad's a painter out west, specializing in landscapes." Her hand tightened and stopped, covering the top of the cooling coffee.

"I could use artwork for my house. I'll have to check him out."

Hopefully they'd all parted on civil terms, and the ladies wouldn't take offense at his casual comment. Anyway, he'd caught the underlying explanation. Her mother couldn't handle the craft any longer. Her father lived states away. How many years ago had divorce ripped into their family? Fortunately, his parents stayed married, and they'd grown happier over the years as he and his two rambunctious brothers matured, and they all moved on. He hadn't returned home after college—but his parents didn't depend on him. Anymore, he amended. They'd done so plenty in his teen years.

The cozy warmth of the kitchen had seeped into his bones, and he stifled a yawn. Not that the company had been boring, but he should leave before he nodded off, filled with decaf, chocolate, and family revelations. "I'm grateful for the snack, but I'd better roll. Those brownies are killer." He stood, and they did the same.

"Take the rest," Pat urged.

No way would he refuse. "I appreciate it. They're too darn good to turn down."

He stretched his arms back, loosening for the ride, as Marcy gathered foil and wrapped up the treats. She returned, and her mouth flew open when she handed the packet to him. "Oh, I'm wearing your jacket."

With her height, the sleeves were only slightly long, but the size swamped her. He grasped the arms to help remove it and immediately slid into the waist-length leather. Body heat and a cinnamon scent wrapped around him. A heady combination. He flashed on the image of her body pressed against his on the back of the bike. The ride home wouldn't be nearly as interesting.

He diverted his unwelcome horniness with another hot concern. "Will you have a vehicle tomorrow night?"

She wrinkled her nose. "I suppose the Bug will have to be towed tomorrow. Tess probably could pick me up for work and drop me home. After that, I'm not sure."

He squeezed the package in his hand, crinkling the foil. "I…we need you there. If they can't fix the car tomorrow, call my cell and I'll pick you up. In my truck. Cell number's on the cast list." Or he could give it to her now for her phone. But he didn't. Exchanging numbers could swing as an invitation to call him.

Pat came to stand beside them. "Thank you again for the generosity. Rudely, we were so caught up in chocolate and art I didn't ask what you do for work."

He appreciated the interest, proud of his job combining skill and precision. "I'm a project engineer, mainly with housing complexes. My art funnels into CAD—Computer-Aided Design—and theater sets. I'm overseeing construction of the new apartment complex on Clear Lake in LaPorte." He found himself wanting to elaborate. "The luxury units will offer new housing options, but more affordable housing is a pressing need in the county. The company's considering a cost benefit analysis I compiled for a lower-income project. I hope they'll be open to pursue that when this one wraps."

"How commendable." Pat beamed her approval. "And I'm sure you're very competent at whatever you take on."

"Competent, efficient, and wearing down. Thanks again, ladies. You don't have to see me out."

Marcy stepped away. "Drive safe. I appreciated the ride." A hint of color flushed her cheeks before she ducked her head and began to collect their dishes.

Her mother started to help. Which couldn't have been easy as her fingers angled away from the wrist and the hands were topped with knobby ridges. What a nasty condition for an artist. He left them and headed through the doorway into the living room, again glancing at the pictures gracing the walls. Yeah, her daughter was super talented. And more than a little sexy in the short dress, whether in stilettos or bare feet. He ground his teeth and jogged out the door and into the night toward his ride.

Chapter Eleven

After an early Thursday call, Tess agreed to provide transport to and from Divine Vintage. In the afternoon, Marcy heard from her mom, who'd arranged for the car to be towed to the mechanic's shop. The news sucked: a kaput alternator.

"What's the price tag?" She stared out the shop's bay window and envisioned money flying out of her lean wallet.

"Don't worry," her mother soothed. "We'll split the damage. You run the errands and take me around, so we share the repairs." She paused. "Actually, I should handle the total cost."

"Mom—"

"You're busy. We'll talk later. Don't forget to call Mike about the ride to the theater," she said quickly and clicked off.

The "ride" conjured images of a cherry-red motorcycle. Fast, fun, and yes, arousing. Legs spread wide, her silky thong had provided zippo barrier between her vibrating, sensitive parts and his jeans-clad butt. The firm back and abs also reminded her she hadn't attempted a relationship after she and Trey Dunmore's cousin, Jake, admitted they were better as friends. That was more than a year ago.

She also hadn't been on a motorcycle for years since riding behind her dad before his big "finding myself" move to New Mexico. Last night had been world's different, of course. Sensual, despite her firm intentions to remain detached. How could she detach when the rough road pressed her against his back—which also provided a haven from the whipping night breeze. Thank goodness for the helmet or the wind would've whipped her hair to resemble Medusa.

Tess walked out of the back room where she'd been tackling the financials. She appeared happy, which meant the numbers had balanced. Over the past three years, between online and in-store sales, she'd made a go of the niche business. "Good news on the car?" she asked.

"No such luck." Marcy plopped onto the stool behind the counter and filled her in. "I'd better call for a rental, but I don't think our insurance covers one."

"Don't. The work shouldn't take long, and I'm happy to chauffeur you to and from work." She tipped an imaginary cap.

"Aww, thanks. I'll bake a double batch of brownies for you and Trey."

"Who says I'll share?"

"You will."

Tess' smile might be devilish, but after two years, she and her hubby were lovey-dovey to the point of sweetness overload. Both managed to toss in worthy zingers, yet their sex appeal flamed off the charts. The kind of relationship she'd want to find someday.

In the meantime, harmless, sexy banter with Chase was a safe option. Much safer than rubbing up against the director on a cool fall evening. She scowled, reluctant to reach out to him, but she also didn't want to burden her boss. "I'd better call Mike for a ride to the theater, as he offered." She grabbed her phone, having taken the number from the cast list and added it to her contacts.

Tess leaned her elbows on the counter and waggled her dark brows. "I'm sure he won't mind."

"Don't get any ideas."

"Me? I never have ideas. Used to be a romance skeptic myself. Now look." She patted her rounded stomach. "I'm not suggesting a baby, though. Better to build the relationship first."

Marcy rolled her eyes and stalked away from the counter, and the teasing. "He has a relationship with a perfectly gorgeous woman. Well, not perfect. But she is gorgeous." She nearly collided with a mannequin and pointed toward the door. "I'll call him from outside."

Laughter followed her, chiming with the doorbell as she escaped into the sunshine. Vehicles rolled down the one-way street, and she tugged on one of her curls and sat on a bench beside a planter of still-vibrant flowers. She jabbed at his number. The call went direct to voicemail, bringing a mix of relief and disappointment. She left a short message as a woman walked past with a waddling Corgi, who stopped to greet her by sniffing around her feet.

****

Marcy thanked Mike later when he picked her up from home in the gleaming black pickup. "I'm fortunate you and Tess are so accommodating."

He smirked, eyes masked by dark sunglasses. "We're motivated. She wants you at work. I want you onstage."

"Cynic. She's a genuinely nice person." She let the joking comparison hang a moment. "She offered to let me keep a day off tomorrow, but without a car I won't be able to make the appointment in South Bend."

"You had to set up an appointment?" He'd reached the end of the blacktop road she lived on and turned onto the four-lane highway.

"They recommended it since they're open limited hours on Fridays and Saturdays due to a reorganization. Unfortunately, I usually work those days. I'll have to figure out a date later in the month." She angled toward the window to appreciate the delicate pastel sunset floating above the fields and pastures. The lovely view reminded her of her first blurry attempt at watercolors.

"If they don't stock everything we need, you'll have to find it somewhere else." He stated the obvious and yet she detected a note of strain. Of course, he prized sticking to an efficient timeline.

"I'll have to research other options." She fingered her seatbelt as they entered the city limits.

"I'll drive you."

The words snapped her head around. He didn't appear particularly pleased with the offer. "You'd be willing to hang in a costume shop on a Friday afternoon?" She left out the two most important words—"with me."

"I don't want to risk putting us behind, especially if we'd have to search out or sew a new piece. I worked a few hours the last couple Saturdays, so my boss won't have an issue. Call me crazy, but let's not scramble or compromise, or I'll never hear the end of it."

"From the board?"

"The members I play poker with." He pulled up in front of the theater and shoved the gearshift into Park. "We can discuss logistics later."

"O-kay." Her curiosity grew over the betting

connection, but she unbuckled and hopped out of the high cab. After he unlocked the massive theater doors, he held one for her to slip inside. She hurried toward the stage; he followed more slowly. They'd spend a few more hours together tomorrow between the drive and the costume selection. She hoped the day wouldn't be awkward, as most of their interactions leaned.

Thankfully, other cast members began to arrive, with everyone in high spirits in anticipation of adult night. In the brouhaha over the Bug, she'd forgotten the weekly outing. Tonight, she'd be at Mike's mercy as the chauffeur.

She talked and joked with the others until he called them to begin, reminding, "Folks, the goal's to be off book a week from tonight."

Off book. Memorized. She'd begun to feel at ease in her character and spent much of her downtime silently running the lines. As the action progressed onstage, she tried to avoid using her script as much as possible. She flitted and flirted, growing in sync with the witty Cecily. The friendship with Chase enlivened the rapport between them and added believability to the accelerated courtship, or so she hoped.

After they wrapped for notes, the other cast members headed to a nearby Mexican restaurant with a bar that stayed open late. She approached Mike, asking, "Do you have a couple minutes for me to run up and check for hats?"

"Sure. I'll go with in case you need help hauling stuff."

He tossed his notepad on the table, and she led out of the room following the now-familiar path. They were halfway up the back staircase when the lights flashed off, immersing them in inky darkness and thick silence. She stopped dead and gasped. His hands braced on her back as he tried to halt his own forward momentum. She swayed with the impact and groped for the railing, holding tight for security.

"Mike?" Her voice quavered. If the white glow appeared, she might climb over him and run for the door.

"I don't know what's going on." She heard annoyance in his tone, but no alarm. "Hey," he called, "did one of you guys shut off the lights? Stop kidding around." He sighed. "I'll try the switch again."

Before he could retreat in the dark, an unidentifiable noise seared the air—loud, grating, metallic. She fell back against him as the clanking sharpness, reminiscent of a dragging chain, neared. A horrible groan erupted above them.

A shriek tore from her mouth and drowned out the clatter. He gripped her arms, and she rammed back against him, fear quivering through her body.

"Stay steady," he commanded, but she could tell his alarm level also had amped. "Someone's joking around. Turn slowly and hold onto my shoulders."

"Move!" She pivoted and shoved him forward. Her limbs quaked, and she half-expected an icy hand to pull her backward as they scrambled toward safety.

****

Bracing both hands against the walls, Mike inched his way down. Though the hideous noise had ended, Marcy's anxiety matched his which was translated by the tight, almost painful squeezing hands on his shoulders. He didn't complain; the sensation helped ground him. He'd nearly screamed himself when the startling noise clanked above them. Finally reaching the hallway, he ignored his frantic, thumping pulse and groped for the light switch. The lone bulb popped on. Marcy moved in front of him, face ashen, eyes dilated. She opened her mouth, but no words came out.

"Let's go." He nudged her, none-too-gently, down the dim path to enter the green room. He slammed the door behind them, and she dropped to huddle on a bench, arms wrapped tightly around her midsection, eyes darting wildly around the room.

He sprinted over to the door to make sure it remained locked. When he rejoined her, she jumped to her feet. "Do you think this was a joke? Or is the place haunted?" Her voice shook, but she'd regained color.

"Will tried to wind you up the other night. He was kidding." His own stress-level began to ease. "Probably just the old boiler heating system trying to kick in for the first time in months. I'll recommend a service call." He wouldn't admit aloud that the eerie groan had sounded human. And why would the lights have zonked? If somebody had pulled a prank on them, they were going to regret it. Messing with him was fine, but she could've been hurt. He gauged her wellbeing. Still shaken but calming. "Do you want me to take you home?"

She shook her head, curls swaying, and rubbed her bare arms. "No. I really need a drink now."

So did he. Attempting to look cool, all the while listening and watching intently, he followed her quick steps toward the front and flipped off lights as they exited. He locked the door and, as they got in the truck, strained to see if any telltale lights bounced in the windows. The hulking brick structure remained quiet and dark.

Her trembling had returned in the cooling night air.

Of course, she'd be traumatized by the shock. "Come 'ere." He reacted on instinct and scooted her under his arm, where her head burrowed on his shoulder. He leaned his chin on the soft cloud of hair and closed his eyes, inhaling the soothing coconut scent. They sat for a few long moments to unwind.

The tension had eased from their bodies. He straightened and rubbed her chilled left arm with his palm. "Nothing in the building's going to hurt us. Sorry you were spooked."

"Sorry for being such a baby," she mumbled into his leather jacket.

"If it makes you feel any better, I was scared shitless, too."

Vibrations rumbled against his chest as she giggled. "This calls for tequila therapy."

Better than the trembling, but the warming of his body indicated they'd best head to the restaurant. He fired up the engine, and she took the cue and returned to the passenger side. He drove away from the theater, realizing he hadn't even talked or texted with Tara since she'd shown up unexpectedly on Tuesday night.

He felt a little guilty for hoping she wouldn't join them for adult night. Having to explain that he was giving rides to Marcy might not go over well.

She definitely wouldn't hear about the motorcycle ride. No need to ruffle her up unnecessarily.

Chapter Twelve

At the Mexican restaurant, Mike entered with Marcy and analyzed the cast's reactions. Everyone was acting naturally—or as natural as they ever were. No one snickered or cut a joke about the scary gag they'd played on them.

Despite the earlier fear, his stomach rumbled in reaction to the scent of sizzling meat. At the same time, his rattled mind recoiled at the noise level. Conversations bounced around the crowded room, and Latin music provided a lively, thumping beat.

Maria, who tended to be perceptive, frowned as they approached the table. "You two look frazzled."

He gathered himself and raised his voice above the din. "We were heading up the back stairs when the light flipped off. Not a big deal, but then we heard some crazy, strange noises."

Marcy grabbed the back of an empty chair, fingers clenched tight. "The sound reminded me of a huge, clanking chain, followed by a loud moaning noise."

Chase winked at her. "And now you're pulling our chain. You should've waited closer to Halloween."

The others looked confused, not guilty. Mike crossed his arms over his chest. "Unfortunately, we're not kidding. We were hoping one of you pulled a prank."

Denials circled around the table. Will shook his head, hard enough to dislodge his glasses. He nudged his frames into place with the tip of his finger. "No way. We all left together and got here at the same time."

They weren't lying.

Mike shrugged, then sat. "Must be a kink in the boiler or the pipe systems that run around the theater. The old relic's been limping along for ages."

His companion for the incident shuddered dramatically and took the other open seat, next to him. "I was super freaked and almost wet my pants."

Maria reached across the table for her hand. "Sweetie, I'm so sorry. Have a drink and relax. I'm glad you weren't alone up there."

"Me, too." Marcy peeked over at Mike. "You helped keep me semi-sane. I felt trapped though, with your bulk blocking the doorway."

"That must be why your fingernails dug gouges in my shoulders." He was glad she'd relaxed enough to tease him. The table began to break into smaller conversations, and he perused the menu as the waitress arrived.

Chase closed the distance between him and Marcy. "Is Tara coming out tonight?"

"Not that I know of." He made a show of pulling out his phone to check. "I think she had plans with friends." He shifted topics. "Are some of you planning to get out of bed Saturday for the set build? Remember, in community theater, we're all needed to pitch in to build and decorate."

Marcy's hand shot up. "I'll be happy to help with painting scenery, but I'm scheduled to work this weekend."

"We won't need you until the canvas flats are prepped." They'd make good use of her artistic talents.

He paused to order, then decided to shoot a quick text to the board president suggesting boiler maintenance. The message downplayed the graphic details of the scare. No need to be alarmist about a situation he couldn't quantify. Though if it happened again... No, they'd check the boiler and correct any issues.

He put the incident behind him, surrounded by the easygoing, joking camaraderie—a main reason he directed shows. Theater people were creative, fun, and supportive. When he craved order and analysis, he hung out with his engineer buddies.

With the first drink round finished, the older cast members began to bid farewell. Chase gestured to the waitress. "A round of tequila shots, on my tab."

Mike declined. "Not me, I'm driving."

The others accepted, including Marcy. "Sounds fabulous to take the edge off," she said. Her adrenaline still appeared to be revving as she fidgeted in the chair and folded, then refolded her napkin into a tiny triangle.

Across the table, Lindsay intertwined long fingers under her chin. "I bet you were crazy scared. I can't imagine. At least you didn't run into a ghost."

Will poked her in the shoulder. "Doesn't mean one wasn't there."

"Shh." She swatted back at him. "She won't want to go up to the costume room again."

Marcy laughed. "I wouldn't go that far. Yet." Her face sobered, and she unfolded the napkin again. "On a semi-related topic, I googled the accident from 1966 but didn't discover any details."

Mike heaped a tortilla chip with salsa and observed, "You're awfully interested in an old story."

She avoided his eyes and toyed with the saltshaker.

"After being warned about a curse, of course I'm curious."

The curse theory again. Darn Will for his fun-loving antics. "The truth's been forgotten through the years, so the story's embellished. Theater folks love drama." His voice gentled to defuse her concerns.

She swiveled toward him. "Could you also ask the board about the plaque? Just for kicks, so we can see it?"

"Sure." He puzzled over her perseverance, but he'd indulge the request. "I imagine the piece went into storage when they painted and redecorated."

The tequila arrived, and he sat back to watch the familiar ritual. Down the liquor. Lick salt off damp thumbs. Suck lime slices. A citrus burst filled the air, and a quartet of shot glasses clattered onto the table, accompanied by exclamations. He also enjoyed the occasional shot but preferred to remain in taut control after the stairway incident.

The conversation changed course again, and near midnight, tabs were settled, and hugs shared as they all walked to the parking lot. Mike strode into the chilly night, lit by a shimmering crescent moon, and remembered he had to drop Marcy home. Her eyes had begun to droop with fatigue. He shared her reaction and hoped he wouldn't nod off during the longer drive.

Inside the truck, she leaned back into the seat and covered a yawn. "What a fun night. A most welcome antidote to the scare."

"We needed one. Hopefully now we can sleep tight." *Why in hell had he referenced "we" in the same sentence as sleep and beds?* Annoyed with the slip, he adjusted the heater. "Anyway, don't let the situation spook you."

"Between tonight and the bat, the loft isn't my favorite place right now. But I'm no scaredy cat." She yawned again, curled her legs on the seat, and closed her eyes.

Content with the silence, he rolled out of town to the rhythm of her deep breathing and took his own advice not to fixate. His snoozing companion stirred but didn't wake as he slowed to turn into her driveway in the pitch dark. He parked near the house and shook her shoulder. "Hey. You're home."

She opened one blue eye and closed it to stretch her arms over her head. "Wow. Must've nodded off." Her voice slurred with sleep and tequila. "Thanks again for the ride, plus being such a hero at the theater. We should have the Bug back tomorrow." She leaned forward to close the distance between them.

He froze as soft lips landed on his cheek.

"G'night."

She clambered out to walk in a fairly straight line to the house. He watched her safely inside, with a jumble of emotions. The kiss had been innocent. An unconscious action she might not remember. Yet if he'd twisted his head, their lips would have connected, maybe tasting of a lime / salt tang. His chest tightened, and he jerked the truck into gear and roared out of the drive, fumbling for his cell. No message from Tara. In reality, he had no idea what she'd done all evening. He tossed the phone into the seat and barreled along the empty highway, cranking the radio to reroute his mind, opening the window to cool his jets.

Chapter Thirteen

The next morning, Marcy woke up huddled under the floral quilt, sluggish, but with no lasting effects from the tequila. She sat up, swung her legs out of the bed, and froze with them dangling over the Hello Kitty rug. *OMG, she'd kissed Mike.* On the cheek, but she had *kissed* him. When she'd awakened in the truck, blurry from the short nap, the action had been perfectly natural. A thank you for his support during the tense scare. An acknowledgment of sharing a strange and momentous encounter.

Today, mortification ruled. She groaned and clutched her now churning stomach. He might believe she'd tried to start something. She absolutely had not. Loyalty and trust were values she both maintained and admired. Hopefully he'd attributed the peck to a tequila buzz, and from now on she'd stay ultra-professional. Friendly but aloof.

Dwelling on the lapse would drive her crazy. In search of caffeine, she leaped out of bed and found her mom in the kitchen working on a bowl of raw eggs. As Marcy poured a cup of coffee for herself, she noted the slow turns of the whisk in her mother's hand and gave her the respect not to commandeer the task.

Pat pointed toward the table. "Sit for some brunch and tell me how rehearsal went. You came in pretty late."

She obeyed and took a first blessed sip. "Adult

night. We had margaritas and a couple of tequila shots."

Her mom snickered. "I thought tequila made your clothes fall off."

"Not mine." She recalled the kiss and felt her face flush. "Last night, I'd have been too spooked from what happened at the theater."

Pat swung around. "Did someone give you a hard time?"

"No. Well, nothing human anyway." She hadn't shared about the aura, not wanting to alarm her mother until she had more info. Now she longed for advice.

"You'd better elaborate, and quickly." The eggs were forgotten. Her mom came to join her at the table, face scrunched with concern.

"Stay chill, and I'll tell you the story. But the details will take a while." Marcy retied her robe and stood to head for the stove. "I'm going to finish the eggs while I talk, because I'll need the energy boost."

She started the tale with seeing the aura and joining the vision with Tess. With the scrambled eggs bubbling, she popped bagels in the toaster and shared about the noises from the night before. A brief, sanitized version, as her mother would be appalled at the true level of her terror.

In the dark, claustrophobic stairwell, her blood had literally chilled. Until Mike's voice centered her, and his strong hands propped her up. "I can't help but wonder if the sound generated from the white glow," she concluded. "If so, the…manifestation…must be strong to present through sound. But Tess and I didn't sense any malevolence."

She buttered the bagels while her mom rose to dish up the eggs. "Are you sure the place is safe? Please be careful. The boiler may be to blame for the noises, but the aura is an unknown quantity."

"I know. I'm glad Tess has agreed to help me."

At the stove, her mom stifled a gasp and cradled her hands to her chest. Marcy darted to her side as she gritted, "Spasm."

"Sit. Please."

They locked eyes. Her mom caved and followed the order, slumping in the nearest chair and breathing in slowly, eyes closed. The twisted hands rested on her thighs, fingers trembling.

Marcy tried to calculate the pain level. "Can I get you anything?"

"No. Keep talking. The muscles are relaxing, and diversion helps."

"Well, actually, here's another important factor. The cast says there's a supposed curse on the play related to a death fifty years ago."

Pat's closed eyelids flew open. "And you've been sitting on all this?" She sighed. "I know. You don't want to worry good old Mom." She straightened in the chair, pondering. "This curse, you think they're tied together? Since I didn't grow up here, I've never heard of one. But my friend, Bonnie, is fifteen years older. She did a few shows in her twenties and might recall details."

"Worth a try." After Marcy plated the food, she delivered it to the table. "Could you maybe call her? Say I'm doing the show and wondered about the curse? Hold back on the ghostly details."

"That goes without saying. I'll try her when we're done. What time is Mike coming by?" The spasm apparently had subsided or become more bearable.

"Eek. I'd better dash. Sorry."

In her room, she munched through the eggs as she pulled out skinny jeans, a short sweater, plus a matching purple thong and bra. After a brief shower she finished the last bites, tamed her hair, added simple makeup, and dressed at max speed.

Nearing his arrival time, she trotted back to the kitchen. Before she could ask the question, her mom answered. "Bonnie remembered vague details of a girl who died during rehearsals for the play. She thinks they ruled an accident, though there were suspicions at the time. I didn't prompt her on the name, and she tossed out Evelyn or Ellen."

"We're onto something for sure." Marcy hugged her purse to her chest.

"If there is a spirit up there, you, Tess, and Justine should be able to figure out what's needed." She rose to carry her empty plate to the sink and paused. "Have faith in your abilities. All of them."

She appreciated the pep talk. "I hope you're right. I don't need the distraction with lines to learn and costumes to handle, but the mystery is intriguing." Marcy heard the crunch of gravel as a vehicle pulled up. "My ride must be here, so I'll see you later."

She zoomed toward the front door, wondering if she'd dumped too much information. Her mom had enough issues without worrying about spooky, possibly threatening, entities.

****

Mike didn't have a chance to exit the vehicle before Marcy bounded out the door, red hair flying. He couldn't help noticing her legs in the tight jeans and heeled sandals as she maneuvered into the low leather seat of his sports car. The close-fitting sweater didn't escape his notice, either, but he turned away to focus on his driving.

"Morning." She buckled in and tossed him an amused glance. "How many vehicles do you own anyway?"

"Two, plus the cycle." He patted the burgundy leather dashboard with pride as he followed the driveway to swing back out to the tree-lined road. "This baby's vintage, and I restored it with my dad and brothers. I only drive her in fair weather. I figured we needed some trunk area today. Granted, there's not much."

She bounced on the seat, oozing enthusiasm. "I'll rein in the temptation to try on loads of stuff."

He wished he could be so upbeat. The idea of spending hours surrounded by costumes drained him. But with her attitude, he grudgingly admitted the day could be almost fun. The powerful car hugged the rural highway, opening views of flat farmlands punctuated with clumps of trees. A symphony of fall leaves swayed in swirls of gold, red, rust, and orange. The scenery mellowed him, and he cranked the stereo as a favorite alternative rock song played. Marcy sang along on the chorus in a fluid alto. When she stopped, he interjected, "Next, you'll have to try a musical."

She shuddered. "Ooh. I'm barely winging my way through a straight play." She wrapped her hands around her crossed knee. "Do you sing?"

"Baritone." As she joined the chorus again, he added harmony through the end of the song, enjoying the blend of their voices. The music shifted to a slower ballad.

"Nice voice." She swayed in time with the beat. "Do you direct musicals, too?"

He stared at the taillights of the semi rumbling ahead of them. "No, not my genre. Earnest is a stretch for me.

Kinda fluffy."

She frowned. "Only on the surface. As you've pointed out, Oscar Wilde wrote a biting commentary on polite society—which convicted him of 'perversion' and tossed him in prison. I can't imagine the intolerance." Her lips twisted. "Sadly, yeah, I can. Such a shame. He died young and broken."

"A loss of creative genius, for sure," he agreed, signaling to pass the truck. He preferred a clear view of the oncoming highway.

"If you're not into the genre, why are you directing?"

He'd prefer not to relive the sorry details, but she'd probably hear an embellished version from someone else. He might as well provide the true, unadulterated tale. "I lost a bet," he finally admitted.

She threw him a quizzical glance and waited.

"A bunch of us were playing poker. Drinking and beating our manly breasts about our many talents. No, not all sexual." He grinned at her wrinkled-nose disgust. The girl didn't have a poker face; every emotion telegraphed across her features. "I've earned a rep for directing darker, edgy stuff. I was running low on chips, and they let me wager a virtual bet. Lose the hand, I'd have to direct a show of their choosing."

He'd been sitting pretty cocky, with three kings. His pal had stunned him and slapped down a full house. "Thankfully, they took pity and chose a classic with social commentary, instead of a basic romantic comedy. Which is why I'm determined to present a good show."

She regarded him for several seconds and burst into laughter, nearly doubled over as she wheezed out, "You're directing the show to protect your machismo?"

He gripped the wheel and gunned the engine to press her back in the seat. "With that spin, it sounds pretty lame," he agreed over the revving noise as the car roared down the road. "I'm protecting my reputation as a decent director. One who isn't afraid to cross boundaries." He'd raised the speedometer to ninety and lightened his foot on the pedal. He'd look a further fool if he got a ticket.

Her laughter contained, she released the tightened hold on the armrest to give him a knowing look. "I think you're a great director. For my virgin initiation into the theater, I'm glad you were the one guiding the action."

He couldn't help snorting at her word choice. But when he spun and took in her wide eyes and open mouth, he realized she was embarrassed at the reference. Sweet and unexpected. "Thanks," he answered simply, not wanting to fluster her further. He blew into the South Bend city limits and lowered the speed again. "We're only a few minutes out."

Following his phone GPS, he maneuvered the purring car through the outskirts of South Bend, lined with nondescript businesses and houses. He obeyed the spoken direction to turn right and drew up to park in front of a sprawling two-story brick building. *Meyer's Costumes,* the signage declared.

They left the bright sunshine outside to wade into an ocean of clothing: dresses, suits, hats, shoes, accessories. He stopped inside the doorway to swallow his apprehension.

She skipped down the aisle in delight. "Sooo cool."

A kid in a candy store. He'd have to keep them on target. "Chill."

With a light hand on her shoulder, he maneuvered toward a long, battered wooden counter. Surrounded by the scent of a popular odor eliminator, he tapped on the old-fashioned metal bell as his companion whipped her head around. Energy vibrated in her bouncy reactions.

An older woman with long white hair entered from an open doorway, adjusting her bifocals.

"Hi. I'm Marcy Alexander, and this is Mike Figueroa. I'm the one who emailed from Little Theatre. He's the one we have to impress, as he's directing *The Importance of Being Earnest*." A wide grin spread over her face. "Unsupervised, I'd go cray-cray in here."

The woman plucked a piece of paper off the counter. "You have full permission to indulge your whims, but I did pull some pieces." She stared toward Mike. "I love Earnest, both for the costumes and the whip-smart dialogue. Hope you do it justice."

He hid his amusement. "We plan to, ma'am. Our cast has the ability to allow Wilde's brilliance to shine." His companion's eyes fluttered wide, and her lips curved again. He lifted a brow in acknowledgment.

Their helper stepped around to join them. "First, you can check out my selections." She led them through the maze of rows, appearing to be in costume herself from the '60s rack. A long skirt swirled a kaleidoscope of colors as she headed toward a back corner.

He kept his partner-in-crime in front of him, to avoid her being distracted. Still, she stopped more than once to exclaim and handle garments. He nudged her as she halted in front of a pearl-covered top in a shiny fabric, saying, "I imagine you'll want to spend more time here when you return the stuff."

The woman waited in an open area in front of three curtained dressing rooms. She flipped a beringed hand toward the nearby hanging rack. "I hope these work for you. Feel free to try them on then browse around or come find me."

"Thanks. We will." Marcy dug in her bag to produce a list and a tape measure. She began comparing items as the woman sauntered away.

Already losing interest, he scratched his head and looked around the warehouse space. Who'd kept all these old clothes, and how had they made their way here? The concept interested him more than the actual garments, but by the look in her eyes, Marcy seemed thrilled enough for both of them.

She swung a checked suit off the rack for his inspection. "In my research of the late 1890s gilded age, I discovered men often wore frock coats or single-breasted three-piece suits. Algernon is flamboyant, and this pattern would be charming on Chase. He could switch to a darker, elegant coat for act two, along with a new cravat."

*Charming.* Good ol' Chase. Mike had been pleased to witness the growth of the pair's onstage chemistry, but not the offstage flirtation. The boy had earned his rep as a ladies' man. If they got involved and the relationship tanked before the show, how would they play off each other? They weren't hot and heavy, thank goodness, but he discerned the interest. They were both young and attractive, and shows often fostered quick, intense relationships and friendships. But he was responsible for putting on a first-rate run and didn't want that success jeopardized.

He also didn't want to see her hurt, or the peppy innocence erased. *For the character*, he told himself. His concern centered on the stage. Nothing personal. She stared at him, holding the suit aloft for his approval.

"Fine," he agreed, to hurry her on.

She returned her attention to the clothing. Yep, they'd be here a while. Two plush armchairs upholstered with huge cabbage roses rested against another wall. Ugly, but serviceable. He sank down on the soft cushion. At least he had a comfortable seat, but she'd already approached again, holding a bright yellow getup. His brows rose at the huge, puffed sleeves the size of dinner plates.

She tilted her head. "The yellow silk will set off Lindsay's complexion and dark hair. The black serge dress is severe enough to suit Lady Bracknell, plus, the burgundy taffeta skirt and waist." Marcy tapped a finger on her chin. "That fabric will swish when she walks. Do you think it'll be too distracting?"

"Adds to the character," he deadpanned as she retreated again. He dug in his jeans for his phone. Whenever he took time off, he checked messages, in case an emergency arose on the jobsite. His head jerked up at her squeal.

"I love this for Cecily. You think?" She danced a few delighted steps.

Who got so worked up by old clothes? Give him an engine or a CAD drawing to work through, and he'd get lost for hours. He squinted at the dress, picking out a daisy pattern, rounded neckline, and similar gigantic sleeves. A great choice for the garden scene, and a stroll among pots of flowers. He envisioned the mass of red hair pinned atop her head and a curl or two escaping. *Charming* echoed in his head.

"I have to try it on." She left the pad and tape on the matching floral-explosion armchair, and with a swish of the curtain, disappeared from view.

He shoved away the image of the zipper sliding down those skintight jeans and the waist-length sweater rolling over her head. He jumped to his feet and roamed to a safe corner, away from the thin curtain.

"Mike?" Her voice floated out, sounding distressed.

He halted on a sigh. *Really?*

"Can you give me a hand? I can't reach these little buttons to tell if they'll close or not."

*Crap.* He wasn't a frickin' saint. Despite having a desirable girlfriend, his hormones weren't cooperating in a gentlemanly fashion. He scrubbed his palm across his chin and waited, fighting a touch of anxiety.

"Sorry." She peeked out and opened the curtain. "If the dress doesn't fit, I'll have to find another option. The theater doesn't have one in my size." She stepped into the room to peer in the full-length mirror, turning her back toward him. Her fully exposed back. A rush of heat overwhelmed his body, pooling behind his own zipper. His throat dried as he dragged his feet to stand behind her, willing his hands to remain glued to his sides. "Those buttons are too tiny." Damn it. His voice came out hoarse. He cleared his throat and retreated.

Her frown was reflected in the mirror. "Can you do up three or four? I need to see if I can lift my arms. "

She didn't seem aware of how wide the dress gaped, exposing creamy pale skin, the purple lines of her bra...and no...not a thong. He almost groaned and debated calling the clerk to help, but he didn't want to call attention to his conflicted thoughts. Earlier he'd advised her to chill. Now, he had to.

He pulled a deep breath and inched his hand forward to tug the material closed, to hide the soft skin from his view. Better. Of course, he could assist, he wasn't ruled by his crotch. He bunched the fabric together and trailed up to grasp the top button, fumbling for several seconds while cursing internally. How had Victorian ladies managed? Hmph, the rich ones had maids. He managed to slide the tiny loop around the cloth-covered button and experienced the thrill of victory. Down an inch, he repeated the motion, trying to drown his discomfort in concentration.

He attempted to call up a picture of Tara in his bed but felt kind of creepy and disloyal, and his keyed-up mind refused to be distracted. The dress' snug fit, molding every curve, teased his imagination and body. Even nerve endings had become hyper-sensitive, in his fingers…and elsewhere. "Why don't they have music in here?"

Lack of background noise added to the awkward tension as he stood close enough to hear her shallow breaths. She didn't respond, having gone rigid as he shifted lower, mastering each challenge, toward her waist. Probably urging him to *finish the damn job*. His nose twitched—hell, everything twitched—at the spicy smell of cinnamon rising from her skin, beckoning him to taste. Just a little nibble of the exposed shoulder.

*Jesus deliver me.* The prayer burst out of silent desperation. Delivery from sin? Temptation? Despite years of trying, his mom hadn't been able to mold him into a good practicing Catholic. He re-blocked the image of the sexy undergarments and approached the final button, resting on the curve of her butt. A shapely butt. Downright enticing if he was in the market.

He wasn't. And the damn button resisted his awkward efforts. He'd have to balance his hands on her to manage the task. He cursed under his breath, and she jolted at the sudden noise but didn't respond. The fabric parted again, revealing the strip of sassy purple elastic. So easy to glide a finger under. His manhood throbbed as he mustered the resolve to finish. When the slippery loop latched, he practically leaped away from her.

"Done." He caught her eyes in the mirror. Wide. Cheeks as flushed as his own. His gaze lowered to the form-fitting neckline enhancing her cleavage.

She couldn't wear the dress on stage.

The damn thing was perfect for the scene.

He stalked several feet away and grimaced. "Can you breathe?"

She lifted her arms and filled her lungs in an exaggerated test, which thrust her breasts forward. He held in a groan and stared above her head.

"Uh-huh. A little snug, but doable. If you approve?" She waited. "Or should we keep searching?"

Did he approve? Good Lord. Chase would salivate, but the style wasn't too revealing and would come off as demure and lovely. "This'll suffice." He'd somehow managed a flat, disinterested tone.

"O-kay." She didn't move. Her forehead creased. She rubbed a hand over her arm in a jerky motion and peered past him. "You'll need to unbutton me."

He swallowed hard, willing Tara to call. For the fire alarm to blare. Anything to break the sensual allure of the moment. Her eyes fluttered closed, and she turned to present her back.

He counted to ten to center himself. Reversing should be easier. He didn't have to look. He focused beyond her left shoulder as his fingers tripped over the top buttons. At the middle, the material parted to reveal the titillating purple lines. He reached for the lower closures, nestling on the indentation of her spine. His hands shook, and he gritted his teeth to unhook the last tiny button.

In his relief, he gave in to an overwhelming urge to briefly…touch.

**\*\*\*\***

Marcy stood at rigid attention, regretting giving in to her excitement over the dress. She should've waited to try it on when Lindsay could help with the buttons. His hands trailed along her back, undoing those he'd struggled to engage, pulling the fabric across her breasts. She clasped her hands tight as his palms drifted to her hips to grapple again with the lowest loop. He'd be appalled if he knew how his actions, the soft brush of his hands, stirred her imagination. He wouldn't see the situation as sexy. Rather, a necessary nuisance. Maybe she should go out on a date, and soon.

In the mirror in front of them, his taut face reflected concentration and irritation. She stood mesmerized as the heightened emotions flowed around him in a crimson stream. She'd never caught an aura in a mirror before. In her momentary distraction, the final button released. His fingers trailed across her exposed skin before the warmth snatched away.

Surely, she'd imagined the lingering touch. She whirled, breathless, and tingly. The color hadn't dimmed. "Thanks. I won't be a sec." She backed into the dressing room, running into the curtain, jerked it aside, and hid from view. For several seconds she breathed deeply to stabilize her emotions. *Don't make a huge fool of yourself.*

She jumped at hearing his floating voice beyond the thin barrier. "I'm going to check out some wigs."

Thank goodness. The weirdness had to pass, never to be spoken of. She cupped her flushed cheeks for another few moments of centering meditation, dressed in her own clothes, and exited the cubicle. With the dress clutched in her arms, she gazed around the cavernous room. Mike stood with his back to her, at the opposite side of the building. She didn't hurry to his side. A little space would be smart.

After transporting the costumes to the front counter, she wandered the aisles packed with eye-popping, magical costumes. Their needs for the show had been fulfilled, so she could indulge her imagination. A majestic gold and plum Medieval gown called forth the Lady Guinevere holding court in *Camelot*. Two rows over, *Mame* could've belted a showstopper in one of the glittery sequined formals.

In the Edwardian section, *My Fair Lady's* Eliza Doolittle would have charmed horse racing fans in a dramatic, black and white satin confection. *Thanks, Nicki, for giving up Cecily to play that role.*

To be thorough, Marcy checked the Victorian-era rack, but she didn't find any better substitutes. She ambled nearer to the director, in a platter-sized lavender hat with feather plumes and hydrangea blossoms. "Not on our list, but how divine." She tilted her head with exaggerated coyness and achieved the intended reaction. He chuckled.

"Indeed, mademoiselle. But back to biz. Maria's hair is short. We'll need a wig, and I think this will work." He twirled a dark one with an oversized bun on his index finger.

"I agree. You've found a close color match." Their earlier camaraderie had returned, and she breathed easier. "We're almost done, but don't forget the shoes and hats."

He groaned, and she gave an imperious wave for him to follow. They joked through selecting high-button boots, fancy shoes, and slippers for the women. Basic oxfords would suit the men. Hats were next, and she took off the oversized one and gathered the matches she'd selected for the gowns. "You've mentioned the top hats are in the loft. Not that I plan to go anywhere near there again." The claim was semi-serious. She'd prefer to have a nightly bodyguard to protect her from the bat and otherworldly influences.

He plopped a Roman warrior mask of lightweight metal over his face. "Dig deep for your she-warrior," he growled. "You won't shirk the task." Mike brandished the accompanying fake sword and executed a Zorro slicing motion.

She narrowed her eyes as the air stirred past her. "Darn. You've pegged me. I'm a reliable do-gooder. I wonder if they have a toga in your size?"

The sword clattered to the floor, fortunately, away from their feet. He bent for it, whipped off the mask, and flipped them onto the shelf. "Have you got everything on your list? We should head out."

Oops, she'd overdone the flirty talk. But she'd only been teasing. She pretended to consult her notes as they returned to the checkout counter. Pleased with the success, they paid, stashed the load in the trunk of the car, and retraced the streets toward home.

Chapter Fourteen

Mike pulled up to a stoplight after leaving the shop and quickly checked his phone. Tara had texted. —*Out w/ grls 2nite*—

He shoved the cell back in his jacket. He'd have to pin her down tomorrow with their schedules. Otherwise, time would keep ticking by. *Neither of you are particularly worried, or reacting*, a shitty little internal voice taunted.

The light changed, and he accelerated and dialed up the radio to drown out the snark. "When did your mom and dad divorce?" The question popped out. A strange icebreaker.

She didn't act put off by the nosiness, but more contemplative and sad. "They didn't. He moved away. They needed to live in a different space. Their marriage stands, in limbo."

Stoic words. He didn't want to pry further, so he stayed quiet and drove back through the city streets toward the highway.

She rubbed her neck and stared out the window. "New Mexico is a great place to visit, and I love the artistic vibe. My dad wants me to consider moving there eventually, but…"

"You don't want to leave her."

"Mom can take care of her basic needs now, but everything's much harder, and the pain's getting progressively worse." Marcy thrust out a heavy breath. "She's been so supportive of me through the years, when I struggled with confidence in my art. Even when she was reeling after he left. Now she can't throw pottery and has no steady income until she can land disability payments. My dreams can wait."

"Admirable dedication. Though she's got to be torn at your sacrifice." He noted her wince at the word, but she didn't rebut him. Time to shift to a more pleasant topic. "You said you want to illustrate children's books which is the opposite end of the spectrum from my precise design work."

"Yin and yang." She regarded him steadily. "No, you're not at all whimsical. Today I've seen a different side, though. You should do chill more often."

"Do I come off that uptight?" He didn't take offense but gripped the wheel, invested in hearing her take on his personality.

"Sometimes." She rubbed a finger over a worn spot on her jeans. "Experts tell us a person's backstory helped mold them. Plus, their astrological sign, for those who believe. Myself, I'm pretty open and free-flowing, mostly due to my parents' creative lifestyle. You're much more...structured."

"A PC description for a tight ass."

"Not what I said." She slid him a side eye. "Anyway, I know you didn't grow up here."

"What gave me away? My accent?" He chuckled. "I'm a Midwesterner, too. Raised in Ohio by two hard-working parents who sacrificed for us. I probably appreciated it more than my two laid-back younger brothers, when I got over resenting the responsibility I shouldered in making sure they stayed out of trouble."

*Where had that come from?* Emotional confessions had never been easy for him. Next, he'd be spewing about how he'd sweated through intervening with a teacher, to keep the bros from being expelled after a dumb prank.

He leaped again for safer conversational ground. "My job brought me here seven years ago. I bought a house on Fish Lake for the water view and the fishing. Couldn't afford the Lake Michigan shore."

"Most people can't anymore. I wish my parents had bought a little beach shack years ago, but they were rustic and went with a log cabin they built themselves. Though really, the style suits us unpretentious artists." She gestured to the window. "Do you mind? The weather's gorgeous." They were traveling along the four-lane road again, lulled by mellow sunshine and the rows of crops drying to papery, pre-harvest readiness.

"Go ahead. If you don't mind the wind whipping your hair."

"Hardly. I've channeled Medusa before, to great effect." She hit the button, and the wild auburn curls swayed in the breeze as she resettled in the seat. "I've been wondering if you've ever acted yourself?"

He snorted. "Once, in high school. You're right. I do prefer 'structure' and being in charge as a director. When I landed here, I was looking for a way to meet people, and a co-worker brought me along to work on a set. I was asked to assistant direct a couple of shows."

"You have the vision and proved yourself," she said.

The words pleased him. Cast members usually thanked him at the end of a run, but along the way, they were too caught up in their own on and offstage dramas to shoot him a compliment. "Thanks. One of my favorite things is finding sweet spots to make a production shine. Plus, nurturing actors to develop their full potential and flesh out the characters fully. No doubt Earnest will excel in that department."

Her demeanor brightened. "After working past the basic nerves, I love playing Cecily, and exploring her nuances and characteristics."

"I'm sorry for being grudging about offering you the opportunity." He'd been dead set at the idea and regretted the knee-jerk reaction. "Don't get me wrong, Nicki's talented. Your innocence is a better fit for Cecily."

She slapped her hands on her knees and snickered. "You think I'm innocent? That's sweet, I guess. Depends on your context." Her voice had dropped to a throaty purr.

"Strictly theatrical." She was kidding. He knew it, but best to avoid dangerous territory. They were nearing her home, and he used the location to change topics. "I'll drop you and take these to the theater, so we don't have to haul them around between vehicles."

She didn't appear fazed by the quick sidestep. "They're heavy. I won't complain if you carry them up to the dreaded dark loft."

He signaled to turn into her drive. "I'll exorcise the bat and any ghosts while I'm there." Hopefully, he wouldn't encounter either.

"Make sure you do." She punched him lightly on the arm. "Thanks again. I'm certain you had a blast spending your day with the costumes." The car rolled to a stop, and she unbuckled and leapt out with a quick wave.

He watched her walk inside. In full light, he didn't have to be concerned for her safe entry but enjoyed the sway of tight butt and long legs. Great, now he'd gone and introduced the image he'd managed to block of her nearly naked back. Pale, curving, soft. The dimple above the thong line. He fought back a surge of desire, purely hormonal and surely unwanted, and forced himself to drive away.

Back on the highway, he set his cruise to maintain a speed five miles above the limit. Otherwise, he might push the car much faster as he tried to submerge mental snapshots from the day. After dropping off the costumes, he anticipated much-needed relaxation on his deck facing the lake. She'd nailed the assumption: he was too uptight and hadn't found a way to balance the need for a controlled environment in his life versus downtime to unwind. Maybe that's why he wasn't bothered at spending time without Tara. Sometimes, her expectations added to his stress level.

Chapter Fifteen

The weekend passed, including a busy Saturday at Divine Vintage, where between customers, Marcy regaled Tess with stories from the foray to the costume shop. She left out some of the more intimate points—specifically the button-unbuttoning episode. Her own imagination needed to be checked, not boosted by a friend's teasing take. Wandering down that path would only lead to further embarrassment.

When she returned to the theater on Monday, she discovered the construction crew had made strong headway. Two-sided canvas flats which would revolve between acts to reflect the garden or indoor scenes ringed the edge of the stage. Blank canvases beckoned and inspired her to envision the lovely possibilities. One side would feature an abundance of blooms, blue sky, and grasses. The flip would boast elaborate wallpaper and wainscoting. She'd already cleared an upcoming Saturday morning to paint them. A hint of nerves danced through her system. Was she really up for the challenge? She pivoted and paced to the opposite side of the stage. For more than two years she'd tamped her creative urges, and this was a big-scale undertaking.

*Start small*, she told herself. A single flower would blossom into a clump, then an entire meadow would spring from her fingers. Sketching the costume ideas proved she hadn't lost her ability.

*Costumes.* Her more pressing project tonight revolved around dealing with the new selections. Which were stored in the loft.

When Chase entered from the side door, she breathed a sigh of relief. "Would you come upstairs and help me carry down some costumes?"

"Anything for my Cecily." He ignored the steps and vaulted onto the stage next to her. His blond head gleamed under the lights. He always appeared confident and put together, and in a transition between summer and fall, wore cargo shorts and a long-sleeved fleece. "What did you find for me, Miss Marcy?" The aristocratic British accent was spot-on.

She curtseyed low. "A most fitting suit, my lord." When he leaned close and grasped her hand to help her up, his palm felt warm and smooth. A gentleman, and a flirt. Why not, they were both single. And available. He'd be a fun companion...and a welcome distraction. Pondering the thought, she led the way through the backstage maze. When they reached the familiar staircase, her heart rate kicked at remembering the last attempted visit. She stepped aside. "You go first."

He didn't razz her and bounded ahead. She took her time, shivering at the memory of the horrific noises. The others could tease, but she'd rather not come up here alone again for a while. Chase popped his head back through the doorway. "All clear and quiet. No bats. No chains."

"Ha ha." She joined him, pleased to see Mike had hung the new acquisitions on the rack. The pleasure dimmed when from the far corner, the aura flashed a welcome. Determined to ignore it, she gritted her teeth and riffled through the garments. "We found this fab plaid suit for a dandy like you."

"You mean like Algernon," he clarified. "I'm many things, but not a dandy." Chase took the jacket from her and plunged his arms inside, but his bulky fleece pullover bunched at his middle. "Hold on."

Before she could comment, he'd pulled the shirt over his head, tousling his hair in the process, then tossed it over the rack. She opened her lips but couldn't dig up a snappy comment.

A nice chest. Very nice, actually. Smooth, with a light tan. Not a six-pack but toned. She felt the heat rise to her cheeks. He closed the distance between them and plucked the jacket from her arms, holding her eyes with his dark brown ones. "Should fit better. Right?"

She nodded and noted a little sizzle low in her body. He didn't move back and took his time to shrug into the jacket, drifting a faint, agreeable scent of aftershave. She could almost feel the heat radiating off him. Yet, she didn't note an aura from him. He could be an orange risk-taker, or another mellow yellow with his fun, friendly side.

He closed the last button, and she examined the fit. "Couldn't be better."

He smiled, thickening the charm. "I have an idea. To advance our character study, we should go out." His hand lifted to trail warmth across her cheek.

"Alone?" Her voice quavered. Despite her earlier considerations, she hadn't actually anticipated moving beyond flirtation.

He chuckled. "A friend's band is playing in Michigan City Saturday night. Say you'll go with me."

He'd expect her to agree. Women didn't turn him down. And why should she? Hadn't she been thinking she should get out and date? He was the most attractive man she'd connected with in a long time besides… The director flashed into her mind, standing close behind her as he undid each tiny button.

"I'd love to." Her response veered a tad too enthusiastic. Hopefully not desperate. She grabbed control of the situation and sent him a pointed look. "Of course, we'll *behave*, because we want to enhance our stage interaction and not mess anything up."

"Absolutely. Maybe I'll wear the snazzy suit." He finally added space between them, spinning in a circle to show off the jacket. "Better check if the pants fit, too." He stopped and reached for them.

She clutched the slacks tighter, to derail any possibility of him dropping his shorts in her presence. "I'll take some of these pieces down. You can try those on and bring them with the rest, if you would."

He breezed past her reaction. "At your service. We'll talk date details later in the week."

*Date details.* She grabbed an armload of items, handed him the slacks, and darted out of the room. Saying yes might not have been wise, but they could keep the relationship easy and friendly. She maneuvered down the stairs, musing that while they apparently found each other attractive, his emotions hadn't presented an aura. An unfair advantage perhaps, but a handy "tell."

In her limited experience, the flush of color from an aura could generate from positive, or negative, energy. She wasn't skilled enough at reading people to determine the difference on face-value and had to rely on actions, expressions, and words to clarify. Such as with Mike at the costume shop. Irritation with working the tiny buttons undoubtedly had sparked his crimson aura.

\*\*\*\*

Moving around the stage to consider set options, Mike caught floating snippets of conversation from the loft. He tried to tune them out, especially when he heard Chase make his move on Marcy. His chest tensed, and he strode to the far side and out of hearing range. Damn, worse yet, his imagination filled in the blanks. He rubbed a palm across his chest and attributed the concern to worry about the show. If the two of them clashed and fought, the onstage camaraderie would suffer. Yet if they connected personally, a new layer of depth could be played on.

Couldn't the dog have waited until after they closed the play?

He gave up on the set considerations and stalked off the stage. To be brutally honest, he wouldn't have waited either with such a fun, interesting, open-hearted woman. A flash of silky, lean, *naked* back flashed through his mind. He banished the image immediately, and loudly, calling, "All right, guys. Time to hit the stage."

Interesting that he didn't notice a heightened heat level between the two as Marcy arrived, followed seconds later by Chase. Which was a good sign—for the show. He relaxed and settled into the rehearsal rhythm, pleased with the overall performance level. Folks were nailing their blocking, developing the characters, and attempting to wean away from their scripts. When he wrapped for the night, their spirits were high, and so was his. He offered a minimum of constructive notes.

During the break, Marcy flitted between the cast, sharing new costume pieces. As the others left for the evening, she gathered some of the items to hang in the green room.

He grabbed the additional garments and joined her. "Are these all working out?"

Her eyes sparkled as she straightened the shoulders of the yellow gown. "Not everyone's tried theirs on yet, but Chase's plaid suit rocks."

"I bet." Had he stripped down up there in the loft? He really didn't want to know. "Try to get the rest of them fitted tomorrow, so you can fill in any holes."

"That's the plan." She proceeded him out the door to enter the theater and stopped dead. He looked around to catch pin dots of light dancing across the walls and ceilings and nearly ran her over.

"Mi-ike," she stammered as she backed into him. "Do you see…"

"Lights. What the—" He ran past her to investigate, increasing speed to leap up the steps onto the stage. The shower of lights disappeared. He spun in a slow circle. Could the rumor be real? Nah, of course not. He had to control his imagination.

Anxiety pinched her face as she ventured to the edge of the stage. "Is the place really haunted?"

"No." He barked the word louder than necessary. "There must be a sane reason. Maybe headlights from cars are filtering in, and we aren't aware of them when the place is lit."

She peered around her. "I've seen a light in the loft, too, without any obvious, traceable source." Her voice sounded tentative.

His blood iced. He struggled to stay manly. "I'll talk to the lighting crew and try to get answers. The place is more than a century old. The wiring's been updated, but older, hidden stuff might malfunction. Including the boiler."

She rubbed her arms and frowned. "I'm all for coincidences, but they're stretching my gullibility."

He strove to keep her calm. "Nothing will hurt us here. Don't get yourself and the rest of the cast spooked. We don't need anyone bailing on the show."

"I won't. Promise." Yet she appeared ready to bolt and run.

He walked down the steps and indicated she should proceed him down the aisle. "I promise we'll get answers. Come on." He kept his pace measured and steady but couldn't help twisting for another look around the place before he ventured through the curtained doorway.

She hovered while he locked up, pacing on the sidewalk. "Sorry for freaking. I'm sure you're right regarding logical answers."

Unfortunately, he didn't have any. He pocketed the keyring as the night air swirled around them, kicking up leaves. "I'm clueless as to what the heck is going on," he admitted, "but I'm going to take a look around soon."

She stopped and stared at him. "Don't do it alone."

"I'll call for reinforcements." He bracketed his hands on her shoulders and faced her straight on. "Don't psych yourself out. I would never let anything happen to you." Their eyes held, and she finally nodded. "Go home. Have a glass of wine. Get some sleep."

He removed his hands, and she drew a deep bolstering breath and trotted to her car. He watched until she got in and started the engine, which now puttered gamely. She tossed a wave, and he returned it, wishing he could convince himself the strange happenings were benign.

Chapter Sixteen

Tess agreed to return to the theater on Tuesday to summon additional visions. In the lobby, Chase sauntered up to join them. "Ladies. Lovely as usual." He stood close to cup Marcy's elbow with his hand. "The band starts around nine on Saturday. If I pick you up at eight, we can catch a table and talk before they blast into action." His fingers caressed her skin with a feather touch, raising a tiny shiver of awareness.

"I'm always up for fun and good music." Marcy kept her voice upbeat yet neutral and shared her address, aware of her friend's interest.

He tapped the contact into his phone and glanced up, the intimate look reinforcing the previous tingle. The guy knew how to build tension—though was it a reflection of actual interest, or a practiced approach? "You're locked into my calendar. Meet you onstage." He whistled a show tune as he headed through the curtains.

"My, my." Tess pursed her lips as she watched him leave. "You've been holding out on me."

"Nooo. He asked last night, and you and I didn't work together today to catch up on our personal lives." She smiled, enjoying the surprise.

"Quite the hottie. Little bit of a rep, from what I heard when I helped Justine costume last year." Her friend turned serious. "Probably hype."

Marcy lifted a nonchalant shoulder, but her mood

deflated. "Don't worry, I'm aware. We're casual." Brave words, yet true. She wouldn't become an easy conquest for him. "I think he's more playful than a player. Not ready to settle down, but neither am I. We'll have fun with no strings." She didn't want to analyze the possibilities, which would only create unnecessary anxiety. "Anyway, I'm more concerned about what we *can't* see in this place."

They made their way through the building toward the loft and shared greetings with the cast. Mike wasn't among them, which was fine. She'd taken a risk last night in mentioning the light in the costume area. While he hadn't been able to offer an explanation, at least he intended to investigate. The evidence seemed irrefutable that the aura tied to Ellen, but did it also link to the noises and other occurrences?

When they reached the back staircase, Marcy hesitated at the bottom step. She should've asked one of the guys to check for the bat, or worse.

Tess intuited the reason for their pause and walked around her. "I grew up on a farm surrounded by woods. Bats don't faze me."

They ascended together. Thankfully, no noises filtered down. Her protector reached the top, slipped inside, and seconds later hollered, "Clear."

Marcy entered and stopped dead in the doorway. The white glow still pulsed from the corner but appeared much stronger than before—as if the entity approved of their purpose. Apprehension crawled through her veins when the source brightened and expanded. She gasped and pointed, tempted to approach, to check for actual heat, but chickened out.

Tess followed her finger and shook her head. "Nope.

Auras are your power. I have to touch a catalyst." She stepped to the blush-colored Victorian gown that had triggered the first vision. "Last time, this beauty showed us young lovers, a jealous friend, and a stage manager with an attitude. Let's see if she holds more secrets." She reached for the hanger. "Are you joining in?"

"Absolutely." Marcy moved forward and anchored a hand on her shoulder, resting the other on the slick fabric. A wave of disorientation took her under, muting sound and color until the vision flooded her senses.

****

*"Truce." Ellen stood at the foot of the stage and cradled a plate of chocolate chip cookies, offering them to Rod. "Look, I've been a bitch. And I am sorry." She forced her lips into what she hoped would read as a self-deprecating smile. "You've gotta understand, Nan and I have been friends forever and I've lived through her heartaches. I couldn't bear her being hurt again."*

*Scents of butter and chocolate wafted from the plate. She lifted the plastic wrap with a finger, trying to interpret the emotions flitting over his face. He didn't trust her, but damn, he wanted the treat. She'd banked on the strategy to lull him into a false sense of security. Then she'd pounce to wrest out the truth about him and Lorna when his guard dropped. "Oh, come on. You want one." She eased a gooey cookie off the plate, lifted it to her mouth to chew.*

*"Later. We should focus on our scenes before the others arrive." His face remained wooden.*

*The cookie caught in her throat, and she swallowed hard to dislodge it. His reserve had resettled.*

*He crossed his arms over his chest, flexing the tanned biceps. "Before we start, let me make one thing*

118

*clear. I don't intend to hurt her. Ever." He raised his voice to reinforce the message. Or to issue a warning?*

*"Cool. Got ya." Her hopes dashed. He wouldn't be easily trapped. She plunked the plate on the edge of the stage and mounted the steps. At least he'd agreed to come early and work with her. Only because they still hadn't developed the intimacy the director sought.*

*Bette had finally exploded two nights before. "For goodness' sake, we at least have to believe you like each other. I specifically asked you to come early and work these scenes together."*

*The rest of the cast had snickered, and Ellen had wished for the scuffed wooden floor to open and drop her into the void. Everyone in the theater stuck their noses in other's business, but she seemed to be the only one who'd learned the truth about Lorna and Rod. The rest of them ate up his charm, no questions asked, whether male or female.*

*She didn't believe his lame declaration about not hurting Nan, but they'd better work the scenes or risk getting chewed out again. "Once more with feeling," she deadpanned, settling to lounge on the garden chaise.*

*He surprised her by snorting out a chuckle. Apparently, he'd recognized the source of the comment from The King and I.*

*Hmm, he'd loosened up, if only for a moment. "Did you catch the play or the movie?" she asked, to prolong the interaction.*

*"Movie."*

*"Me, too. Yul Brynner's so manly. Brave enough to go shirtless. Those were spiffy costumes."*

*He twirled a finger around his ear in a symbol for craziness. "I can't imagine working with all those kids."*

*"Deborah Kerr could've swept them all under her humongous hoop skirts." She giggled.* Wait, were they having a civil conversation?

*"Hello young lovers." He named one of her favorite songs from the musical. "And with that, we'd better knuckle down."*

*A tad more relaxed, they ran through the dialogue and movement in their introduction. Both were able to project additional openness and connection. The interaction began to gel.*

*He seemed to agree and didn't offer suggestions. "Another time through?" His lip curled in an engaging grin. One she'd turned her nose up at before, when the other girls swooned.*

*She wanted to do a second run-through, to explore where the new improvements would take them. They glided into the action with heightened energy, at least sharing the goal to offer a good show. As they lowered their guards, she could almost understand what drew Nan in. She didn't mind when he inched in closer to deliver the flirtatious lines.*

*He stood within an arm's length to tip a finger under her chin. "What a perfect angel you are, Cecily." His eyes lit with mock-adoration.*

*She quaked a bit at his nearness.* No, her character reacted to him. She certainly wouldn't. *"You dear romantic boy." She followed the director's suggestion to touch his hair. Caught in the moment, she twirled an ink-dark curl around her finger. "I hope your hair curls naturally, does it?" Her hand brushed his cheek.*

*He stopped and stared at her. She'd never noticed how dark and full his lashes were. Or how the indigo blue intensity of his eyes could make you feel...special.*

*Her heart fluttered, and she felt a blush stain her cheeks.*

*"Hello, babe." Nan's voice boomed across the quiet space.*

*They jerked apart. Blood rushed to Ellen's head as she swung toward her friend standing below them, arms akimbo.*

*Rod shifted back, to put the length of the tea table between them. "Hey. Did you finish early?"*

*"We were slow today, and I wanted to check out your progress." She emphasized the last word and glanced between them, rolling her lips in a familiar attempt to curb anxiety.*

*Did she believe they were too cozy? Was she jealous? Excellent. If her friend learned he was two-timing with Lorna, the image of flirting with her, too, would cement a final wedge between them. Ellen rounded the table and grabbed the abandoned plate of cookies. "We've accomplished sooo much. Here, have one while we finish the scene and show you how enamored Cecily and Algernon are with each other."*

\*\*\*\*

Marcy blinked three slow times as her friend's somber face came back into focus. "You emerge out of these visions much more centered than I do," she whispered, grasping the clothing rack while waiting for the dizziness to recede.

"I've had more practice." As her aura faded to lavender, Tess replaced the gown on the rack. "Let me recap while you recover. I saw Ellen and Rod onstage; something new perked between them, then Nan interrupted. Are we looking at a possible love triangle?"

"Maybe." Marcy pondered the suggestion. "But I caught the vibe she's still worried about her best pal and acting to protect her."

"Sure wouldn't be the first time someone tried to steal a pal's boyfriend."

"Breaking the friend code is unacceptable." She grimaced. "Well, poaching lovers in general is pretty heinous." Marcy paced away, her mind still whirling with snippets of the vision. "Too bad we don't have the true backstory on these folks. I'm swamped through the weekend, but I'll make time next week to visit the newspaper. The old archives will provide a few basic facts, at the very least." The light in the corner intensified. She sighed. "The glow agrees."

"No surprise," Tess said. "If everything lines up the way we're thinking, Ellen has a strong message to share. We have to help her, as we did with Phoebe at Carver House."

Marcy wrinkled her nose and turned away from the corner, unable to control the shiver that rolled through her. "Yes, but don't forget, Phoebe was murdered."

Chapter Seventeen

Throughout the week, the vision from the loft hung in Marcy's mind, taunting her with questions. On Saturday morning, hoping to achieve some answers, she drove by the newspaper and cursed when she found the building locked tight. She'd taken time off from both her jobs to drop in there before painting backdrops.

Frustrated at having to wait for answers, she drove on to the theater. Onstage, she set up her supplies and sang along to the songs playing from someone's cell phone. Within minutes, she'd immersed herself in creating a floral explosion for the manor garden scenes. Surrounded by music and the staccato pounding of nails, she shaded blues and purples onto impressionist, vining morning glories. When she dipped her brush into the jar of water to clean it, her nose also picked up the welcome scents of coffee and sugar.

She scooted around on her butt to spy a box of donuts on the nearby table and a six-pack of coffee cups in a holder. "Ah, I could use a—" The words caught in her throat as her eyes traveled to the woman perched on the edge of the couch.

Her makeup was impeccable; the short skirt barely covered toned, tanned thighs. Nope, definitely not dressed to work. Marcy felt a flush rise to her face, noting the paint on her baggy T-shirt and both hands. "Hello, Tara."

The brown eyes narrowed, as if she couldn't fathom squatting on the floor, clothes and skin covered in stains. "Yellow. On your cheek."

Marcy's hand rose, and she barely stopped herself from adding a blue smudge to the mix. "Oh, right. Thanks. And for bringing snacks."

"Sorry I don't have enough coffees. Didn't know you'd be here."

*Why else would you come decked out like a wet dream?* Marcy waved a paint splattered hand to blow off the intended slight. "I've had plenty of caffeine for one morning."

"Well, I haven't." Mike entered through the stage doorway. "Thanks, babe. Didn't expect to see you, but you're always a welcome sight." Dressed in comfortable sweats, he went to her side, and she lifted her mouth for his kiss.

Marcy concentrated on standing, to flee having to witness their love fest. Princess Tara must have some hidden qualities, because she couldn't imagine why Mike stayed with her.

His voice stopped her. "Better grab a donut before they disappear."

Did he have no idea his girlfriend was shooting daggers at her behind his back? Marcy drew herself to full height, shoulders back. "No. I've got a date tonight. Think I'll save the calories for the alcohol and munchies." Let them guess who she'd be joining later. Tara should just be happy to know she was dating someone.

She couldn't read Mike's face as he bent to grab an apple fritter and a coffee. Before he'd straightened, she'd escaped through the door.

\*\*\*\*

At home that evening, her system jittered as she prepped for Chase's arrival. She hadn't dated enough to be truly casual about going out with someone—especially a good-looking smooth-talker. In high school she'd hung with a mixed crowd of friends, mainly for group events. Her college arts focus thrust her into a circle of creatives. She enjoyed their company, but most of them seemed to be trying on a bohemian presence and moodiness.

She stood in her closet, remembering how she'd developed her own avant-garde fashion sense early, drawn to her grandmother's hippie leftovers: fringed vests, patched wide-bell jeans, and swirling skirts to hide her long legs. Eventually, she'd come to love her height and favored minis. Tonight, she'd dress casually in skinny jeans and a lightweight teal sweater, with a swish of makeup: mascara, pale eyeshadow, and rust-colored lip gloss.

A swing of reflected lights through the window revealed a car had pulled in, and she trotted toward the living room, breathing deep to center herself. Her mother stood guard at the door as Chase ambled up, also in jeans and a V-neck pullover.

"Very cute," Pat murmured.

Still drawing calming breaths through her mouth, Marcy stood back as he rapped on the door. Her mother opened it.

His smile was intended to charm. "Hi, I'm Chase."

"Pat Alexander. Nice to meet you." She motioned him in.

He took note of the gnarled fingers yet pretended not to. "You, too. I see where your daughter gets her looks."

"An old line but effective every time." Her head dipped in a near-coquettish movement. *Mom wasn't immune to the woo, either.*

Marcy interjected, "Welcome to our humble, artsy home."

"Hey. You look great." He kissed her cheek and dropped his hand to the small of her back.

When she turned, her mother beamed. *Fantastic. Telegraph to him how desperate you've been for me to date.*

"You kids have fun." Her mom gestured to the overstuffed couch littered with throw pillows in clashing patterns. "I'll lay around here and relive my glory days."

Chase chuckled. "I'm sure we'll have a tame night compared to your memories. The next time we meet, you can share the best ones."

He grasped Marcy's hand, and she waved as he led through the door, toward a siren red convertible illuminated by the outside light. The car gleamed as if freshly washed and buffed. He reached to open the door for her.

She whistled her approval. "Do all you guys drive hot cars?" She folded her legs inside and skimmed her palm over the leather dash, looking up to catch his raised brows. "Mike drove me to the costume shop in South Bend in his speedster. Must be a testosterone thing because I'm fine driving my vintage Bug."

He frowned and jabbed the button to start the engine. "Why'd Mike take you? Never knew him to be enamored of costumes." His tone edged on curt, surprising her. Had she missed an issue between the two men?

"I told you, my car tanked." She watched his face

loosen. "I had an appointment, and he's committed to keep us on schedule."

"Makes sense. He lost the bet, and he doesn't want to give them any more bragging rights." He drove down the drive slowly, probably to avoid kicking up gravel onto the car.

"He discussed the infamous man-bet. Were you there?"

"Nah. I prefer playing for higher stakes at the casino. What fun is it if the risks aren't high?" He reached the blacktop and punched the car up to fifty. When they reached the highway, he accelerated further, showing off the fast engine.

She snuck a look at the speed. Seventy and climbing. She should have run in to grab a hat or a headband, and a jacket. The wind would tease her hair into a bouffant, but she reveled in the freedom of the open car. If necessary, she'd tame her curls with water in the bathroom. Or maybe she'd embrace the wildness. Her mom shouldn't be the only one with youthful memories.

He draped his hand over her shoulder. "Let me know if you're cold."

A curl whipped across her eyes, and she shoved it behind her ear. "The temperature is kinda brisk, but I love the fresh air."

"There's a blanket in the trunk if you need it." He didn't remove his hand, and the warmth seeped through her sweater.

A blanket. She wasn't sure she wanted to know the previous use. A quickie at the beach? She missed some of the details he'd shared on the band they'd be hearing. One of the members was his friend from high school. She corralled her thoughts to listen more intently.

"I've played bass guitar with them occasionally," he said, as they rolled into the outskirts of Michigan City.

"You must be good. I've never played an instrument. Too caught up in my art. I wish I'd learned the piano. They did value my talents earlier at the theater."

The breeze had mussed his hair into a sexy, careless tousle. "Ah, you were recruited, as predicted."

"I volunteered. Happily."

She waited, but he didn't ask questions, leading her to notice her mom hadn't pointed out the artwork on their walls, as she had to Mike. Chase also hadn't commented, despite knowing she was an art major. Not that the oversight wounded her ego. If tonight went well, they'd likely date again. Yet she'd prefer him to express some level of enthusiasm toward her interests. She'd find out more of his and do the same.

When she asked what activities he enjoyed, he worked through hiking, boating, and soccer in the minutes until they reached the popular Zorn Brewery. After parking, he hopped out to grab the door again, and they entered the restored 1890s building. "I'm glad when people repurpose cool old places instead of tearing them down," she said, admiring the distressed brick which flowed inside, rising up past the exposed timber beams.

He wound through the expansive open room and introduced her table by table, inviting people to attend their soon-to-open show. His evident popularity broadened her insights into his personality, with everyone hanging on his words and offering best wishes. The room had begun to fill, and they halted the grand tour to snag a two-top near the middle. A waitress took their drink orders, and a tall man with stud earrings and dreads pulled into a tail sauntered up to joined them. She'd noticed him setting up the band equipment.

Chase offered a high five. "Hey, bud. Have a seat. This is Marcy. Reg sings lead and plays a mean guitar riff."

The man folded himself into the extra chair. A colorful tattoo slithered from the shoulder of his shirt, up to his earlobe on the left side. In the dim light, she made out the scales and fiery breath of a dragon against his brown skin. "Good to meet you. Nice tat. Local ink?"

He snickered. "Uh-huh. Meg does good work. The rest of mine are covered."

Chase leaned close. "Do you have one?"

"Maybe." She tried to project an air of mystery.

He reached for her hand on the table and skimmed a finger over the palm. "Come on, give it up."

"I might have a Celtic Unity Knot," she shared. The design symbolized her maternal Irish heritage.

"But where?" he persisted, and both men grinned.

Oh, she hadn't flirted in too long. She stretched in her seat and glanced around, as if insuring she wouldn't be overheard. "Lower back, right side," she whispered. "Visible in a bikini."

Or a thong. She jolted. If Mike had noticed, surely he'd have commented at the shop. She didn't welcome his introduction into her consciousness.

Reg smirked. "With that enticing image, I'd better go get ready. Thanks for coming out tonight." He rambled away toward the makeshift stage area.

Chase brought her hand to his lips. "Definitely something I'd like to see."

*Whoa, ease down the flirtation.*

"You should be so lucky." She extracted her hand

and tossed a smile to take any sting from the words. She preferred the connection and commitment of a relationship to feel comfortable with sexual involvement. No one had intrigued her enough to do so since college. She and Jake had dated several times and enjoyed themselves. Yet a spark didn't ignite to lure them beyond the friend zone into bed.

Would Chase be the one to break the drought? Or was he too much of a player to settle down? Well, not settle down. Eewww. But if they clicked and were exclusive… The blonde waitress returned with drinks, all attention focused on him. Marcy diverted herself by licking salt from the rim of the margarita glass. Way too early to consider such thoughts. The date might turn into a dud.

She caught him watching her and almost flicked her tongue out, but she didn't want to project mixed signals. The band began warming up, loud enough to prevent conversation. He brought his chair around next to hers. Not only to get a better full-on view of the stage, but to position his arm around her chair back. The music swelled around them as he murmured comments in her ear. She swayed in her seat, enjoying the mix of original alternative and cover tunes. Reg and his mates performed mostly upbeat songs, but as the lead, he also sang a few ballads.

At the break, conversation swelled around the room. Chase swigged the last of his whiskey and cola. "What do you think?"

"They're tight. The originals are pretty awesome with his rasp."

"Thought you'd approve. The sound level doesn't encourage talking. Let's grab dinner next week before rehearsal?"

He'd already decided on a second date, and she was having fun, too. "There's a plan." She finished the margarita and entertained a mellow buzz. Other band members wandered by their table to say hello as they spread out to grab their own drinks and greet friends.

In the second set, he pulled her up to dance to a popular, high-energy tune. She twirled around him, laughing, curls swinging. With work and helping at home, she hadn't been out in way too long. Partly because her closest friends were married or seriously coupled, she missed hanging out with a group of confidantes. Hopefully, she'd stay tight with Lindsay, Will—and Chase—after they closed. The music slowed, and he tugged her into his arms. Her cheek grazed his chin.

She registered a hint of pale stubble and cologne as she rested her arms on his chest. His encircled her back, and they swayed together comfortably. He wasn't as muscled as Mike, but his body swayed, toned and firm against hers. She realized she'd compared him to the director's fit physique. Since when had he become the male standard?

He pulled back, startling her. "What say we ditch this place."

"Sure," she stuttered, wondering at the quick decision. Yet the cool air would clear her head of the tequila fog, which had lured her thoughts into a danger zone.

Outside, he retrieved the blanket from the trunk and draped it over her before driving up the quiet streets toward the Uptown Arts District. The dashboard clock read 11:10. The air had grown colder, and she huddled into the blanket, thrusting out her hand to point. "There's Divine Vintage. I dressed the window yesterday." The mannequins posed in 1940s formal gowns, surrounded by paper flowers the size of basketballs she'd crafted in rust, red, gold, and orange tones.

He barely noted her handiwork. "Uh-huh. Nice."

She frowned in the dark. He might've shown some polite pretend-interest. When he didn't ask questions, she didn't elaborate. He drove through a couple more blocks, the streetlights casting shadows on empty sidewalks. She tried again, with a gesture toward their right. "Northside Deli's close enough to walk between my two gigs when I want a little exercise."

"Must help. You're in pretty rad shape." He took her hand. "Sorry to leave early, but we don't have many nice nights left. Thought we might walk on the beach."

"I haven't strolled the beach at night in forever." Moonlight, sand, and surf sounded enticing.

"Girl, loosen up and have some fun." He squeezed her palm as he wound the car through the entrance of Washington Park toward Lake Michigan. She heard and smelled the Great Lake as they approached. A gentle splash and roll tinged with a tang of fish. They parked in the paved lot, along with a handful of other cars, and he folded the blanket to carry. "The sand'll be chilly if we decide to sit."

Reaching the beach, she pulled off her strappy sandals and dangled them from two fingers. A three-quarter moon shimmered in the inky darkness. They headed east, holding hands for several quiet minutes before sitting. Her eyes had adjusted enough to make out gentle waves cresting with white tips. She burrowed next to him in the cool breeze, and he pulled the remainder of the blanket over their legs. "I love the water," she said.

He held her eyes for a long moment, cupped her chin, and kissed her. The lips were firm, and *nice*. His hands caressed her arms as the kisses deepened. She leaned into him and parted her lips. His tongue caressed. She floated in the sensations, in the lovely feel of his mouth, his chest.

He whispered against her lips, but she couldn't decipher the words. He pulled away, resting his forehead against hers, his voice low and sexy. "Show me your tattoo."

The spark sputtered. She anchored her hands on his chest to provide distance. She could give him grief or toss the comment off as a joke and chose a mix of the two. "You are a very bad boy."

He looked surprised. "Sorry. I'm not trying anything. You left us with a sexy image tonight." His voice trailed. "I got carried away."

"No harm. Really. But we'd better go. I'm tired after working and rehearsing all week." She scrambled to her feet. They remained silent again during the walk and revived the small talk on the drive back, after agreeing to put up the convertible top. Thankfully, he hadn't taken offense. If he had, she'd have kicked him to the curb.

At the house, he walked her to the door. She held her distance and pecked his cheek, drawing away immediately. "Thanks for a great time tonight."

"You know it. Catch you soon." He threw a mock salute, and she unlocked the door, sweeping inside to make her way through the dark house by feel. The band had been terrific; he'd been fun. A bit pushy on the beach, but he backed off when she called him on it. All in all, a successful first date.

She tossed off her clothes and prepared for bed, determined to advance one slow step at a time. No need to rush, especially with the show opening soon. At least she'd replaced unwanted thoughts of the director with someone else's desirable image.

Chapter Eighteen

After they'd settled on the mutually open date, Mike swung by to pick up Tara for dinner on Saturday night. Since the temperatures hovered in the comfortable high '70s, he decided to ride the cycle. He hoped she'd agree to at least hop on for five minutes to reach the restaurant facing LaPorte's Pine Lake. Maybe he could tempt her into a longer ride tomorrow and exorcise the image of a redhead hanging on behind him.

He used his key to enter the newish condo when she didn't respond after two blasts of the doorbell. The foyer led into the living room, decorated in the cool, earthy tones she favored. The place always smelled good, too, with candles scattered around. No wonder she preferred him to sleep-over here, surrounded by tasteful decorations and artwork, instead of staying the night at his stark bachelor pad.

She rarely made the trek out to his small-town cottage on Fish Lake, despite the water view. In fact, the differences between them seemed to widen with time. Early on, the attraction had been hot enough that her preference for sophistication hadn't clashed with his simpler, homey leanings. He buried the traitorous thought by calling, "Hello. I let myself in."

He stifled a groan when she popped out of the bedroom door in a robe, her hair still in a towel. "Sorry. Running late after my workout." She gestured toward the kitchen in the open-concept room. "Grab something to drink and feel free to watch TV."

He sat on the stiff-backed couch and clicked on the replay of a NASCAR race. After a few laps, his mind wandered to the previous afternoon, when he'd left his worksite early to pull together some of the male theater crew for an impromptu search party. With flashlights and lanterns, they'd combed the building to search for signs of trouble like hinky wiring related to the weird lighting-related incidents or possible changes in the boiler. They hadn't been able to get a repairman in yet for a non-emergency call.

The whir of Tara's hairdryer mingled with the roar of motors as he relived his relief at not finding any issues, or winged mammals, in the loft. Feeling brave, he'd even crawled through the half-sized door at the back of the largest costume room. Despite fighting claustrophobia and sneezing from the dust, he'd gathered a pop can and a snack wrapper, tossed in with old fabric, drapes, and a blanket. No big revelations there, or anywhere else in the building.

Tara emerged with a sleek hairstyle, wearing some sort of jumpsuit. Perfect. He hadn't thought to mention appropriate attire for the motorcycle. "You look beautiful, as usual," he said. "Glad you're wearing pants. I thought we could hop on the bike for the short distance."

Her hand flew to her hair, and her forehead creased. "Are you kidding me? I just spent all that time straightening it."

"Why don't you let it go natural? The wave is nice."

The frown deepened. "Curls are too frizzy. Like with the new girl."

"Marcy." He tried not to show any emotion, but he didn't get the dig. Her hair always looked fine, in his opinion. Wild and bouncy.

She moved past him to turn off the TV. The room deadened from revving engines to silence. "Speaking of her, putting a total novice onstage is a big risk for the show. I'm surprised you stuck your neck out when you're so concerned with the big bet."

One had to pick their battles in a relationship. This skirmish was worth the effort—a challenge to his directorial decisions from someone who'd never participated in the theater in any way, despite his invitations. "She's been onstage before." He controlled the burn attempting to rise in his tone. "When she stood in for Nicki a couple times, the accent and the read were spot-on, and the cast suggested her. Options for other actresses weren't overflowing."

"Let's hope she pans out and doesn't develop stage fright or something." Tara plucked her purse off a hook. "We'll take my car and eat inside. I'm in the mood for seafood."

Annoyed, he tossed out the name of a local fast-food chain, knowing how she'd respond, but unable to resist the setup.

"Yuk. You know I don't do greasy fish." She flounced out the door.

His lip lifted. *Yeah, something's fishy.* What the heck did she have against Marcy? His mirth diminished. If he'd been throwing any signals of interest, he'd better bury them, quick.

Chapter Nineteen

On Monday night, Chase and Will entered the theater together. Sitting at the table jotting notes, Mike picked up on the not-so-hushed conversation. "We had a great time. The band rocked, but we left early to walk on the beach." A laugh snorted out. "Dude, I've gotta tell ya'—she's got a hidden tattoo."

Will hooted. "Where?"

"Lower back, right about…"

Mike turned to watch Chase's hand glide to a point on his left upper butt cheek. Unexpectedly, his temper sizzled. Were he and Marcy sleeping together already? Of all the stupid, asinine ways to screw up the show. He shoved back the chair and ground his teeth as he strode toward the makeup room. No destination in mind, but he needed to clear Chase out of his line of sight. He halted inside the green room, rubbing his fingers against tired eyes, as if erasing a mental image.

A new thought taunted. He hadn't seen a tattoo at the costume shop. The ink must be farther down. Annoyed that he gave a damn, he stalked toward the back stairs. They hadn't yet collected the top hats; he could use the search as a way to chill. *They're big boys and girls*, he told himself as he reached the smaller room and dug into a plastic tub. He found three other styles, but no top hats. The other half dozen containers offered the same results.

He gave up. The costumer could do her job and seek them out later. He descended the stairs, indulging his foul mood, and picked up the chatter of the cast on stage. Joining them, he discovered Marcy giggling with Will and Chase. She must've enjoyed the date, too.

He couldn't avoid frowning at her. "Hey. I searched for the top hats, but damned if I could find them." His voice came out harsher than intended.

Her head jerked up. "Sorry. I haven't had time to get to those yet."

She didn't appear very sorry. Chase regarded him warily. "Is everything cool, Mike? Tara's not yanking your chain, is she?"

"Nope. All good."

Shit. Regulars at the theater knew every time he did a show, his girlfriend would get jealous of the time commitment. Saturday night had fallen strangely flat, with neither of them able to muster much enthusiasm. After her reaction to the motorcycle suggestion, he'd assumed she'd have no interest in a Sunday ride. They hadn't even made future plans at the end of the shortened evening. With both feigning tiredness and busy schedules, he'd ridden home in the dark.

Waving hello to everyone, Lindsay joined the group. With the cast assembled, he instructed them to start at the top of Act I and sat down at his table, telling himself to get his own act together. Tonight, they were laying all scripts aside, which could lead to flubs and calls for lines. He'd be prepared to toss them a few words if needed.

Yet to his satisfaction, the requests were few as the action progressed. The actors were growing in confidence, and characterizations flourished without the crutch of scripts in-hand. At the end of the first act,

Marcy took her place in the garden scene, and his jaw worked as the attraction blossomed between Cecily and Algernon.

"What a perfect angel you are, Cecily."

"You dear romantic boy." Tonight, the scene seemed to carry an extra spark of realism. She twined her fingers, as instructed, through Chase's blond waves. "I hope your hair curls naturally, does it?"

"Yes, darling, with a little help from others. You'll never break off our engagement again, Cecily?"

Mike jumped to his feet to pace, eyes tracking the actors onstage.

"I don't think I could break it off now that I have actually met you. Besides of course, there is the question of your name."

As their initial meeting drew to a close, Chase leaned in for a kiss. The action read as sexy and enamored.

"Wait, where'd the lip-lock come from?" Mike glared up at them. "No." His hand sliced the air. "A kiss doesn't work. The introduction scene already stretches reality. Don't knock us over the edge."

Chase's eyes narrowed. "Okay. You said to overplay the characters. Thought I'd experiment."

"Overplay within a fine line. Subtlety's underrated." He rubbed his tense jawline to relieve the pressure. "Try kissing her hand."

They repeated the last two lines and substituted that action. "Better. Somewhat." He paced away again. "Move on."

At the break, he walked outside before anyone could waylay him. He stood in the bracing air to call Tara, anticipating she might blow him off. Then he'd really be honked off. After four rings, she surprised him by picking up. "Hello, stranger." Her detached voice floated over the speaker.

"Hi, sweets. Catch you at a bad time?" He faked a pleasant tone. Muffled voices hummed in the background behind her. The noise dimmed as she moved away from the television, or other people in the room.

"No." But her voice pitched low and guarded.

He didn't have time for a long explanation. They'd make nice when they got together again. "You free for the weekend?" He waited through a long pause, wondering if she was checking her calendar.

"I'm working extra hours. Have to cover for vacations. You're caught up in the play, as usual. Maybe we can touch base next week."

*Maybe.* She must be upset for some reason, but he wouldn't force the issue. "Babe, I'm sorry time's been getting away from us. Shoot me a text when your schedule opens up."

"Absolutely."

Did she sound relieved? "Okay, I have to—"

"Get back to rehearsal," she finished.

"Yep. The play's coming together pretty well tonight. Mostly off-book already."

"Mmm, good. Bye now."

The conversation carried less intimacy than a prostate exam. He shook his head and shoved the phone into his pocket to return to the building. Buying a piece of apology jewelry probably should be on his agenda. Yet her schedule was the problem this weekend.

The action progressed onstage again, and his final notes were brief. Afterward, as the cast filtered away, he overheard Chase say to Marcy, "See you at five fifteen tomorrow."

Pre-rehearsal dinner? None of his business. He wadded up a scribbled note and ignored the little voice that reminded him of the happy early days of his and Tara's relationship. They could and would recapture the good times. They'd done so before.

Even though each effort drained him.

\*\*\*\*

Lindsay grabbed Marcy in the green room after rehearsal. "I wanted to catch you alone for the real dirt."

"We enjoyed ourselves. The band's rad." She'd intended to head upstairs to search for the top hats. Mike had been in a pissy mood after announcing he couldn't find them.

"The band is awesome. I went to school with Reg, too. Most important, though, did Chase hit on you?"

The question rocked her. "I'm not a pushover."

"Of course you're not." Lindsay flapped a hand in the air. "I'm only asking because I'd kick his butt if he got out of line. He's a great guy, but women fall all over him, and he might make assumptions." She dug into her purse and found a tube of lip gloss. "The boy could benefit from a challenge." She bent toward the mirror and applied a pale pink coat.

"I'll provide one. Definitely not interested in anything heavy. We're meeting for a quick dinner tomorrow before rehearsal, though."

She tossed the tube into her purse. "You must've had fun together."

Minutes had ticked by. Marcy decided they could continue the conversation on the move. "Hey, would you mind running upstairs with me to look for hats? You know I'm a tad spooked in the loft."

"I'll protect you." The girl smiled and propelled her forward with a hand to her back. "I've been running around here for years, and nothing's dared to present. Will shouldn't have shared those old haunting rumors."

"I value your bodyguard abilities," she teased as they reached the stairs. "Hopefully we'll find the formal hats stashed in the main room."

As they turned the corner to enter, she stifled a groan. The light glowed from the corner, beckoning her in. She whirled to her companion who had moved to the back corner to explore, oblivious to the otherworldly presence. They opened a variety of boxes and containers, with Marcy staying on the opposite side of the room. She worked through them all and turned to join her friend, swallowing a gasp.

Lindsay stood dead center in the pulsing glow before she bent and disappeared from view. Her voice floated up through the racks. "Oh my gosh. There're boxes of old scripts here. I wonder how far back they go." The light quivered around her, resembling a wavy desert mirage.

Marcy's skin prickled, and she stood on tiptoe to try to see, without edging closer. "Ahhh, we should probably go. I'm sure Mike's ready to lock up."

Her companion stayed out of sight. Rustling sounds filled the air. "Cool. All the show dates are on the covers. Maybe we could find a place to display these in the lobby."

The temperature had risen, blanketing them in a muggy haze. Perspiration bloomed under Marcy's arms. She fanned her face with a hand. "Is it getting hot in here?"

"They checked the boiler earlier. Heat rises, you

know. Hey, look at this." Popping up with a triumphant wave of her hand, Lindsay brandished a script. "Here's a copy of Earnest marked September 1966."

The room had begun to resemble a sauna, sweltering and damp—the first time she'd experienced an impact beyond color. Marcy shaded her eyes against the glow. The realization made her dizzy, as her curiosity peaked. "Let me see."

The script flew toward her in an arced toss. She caught the book in both hands and nearly fumbled it as the cover singed her fingers. *Illusion*, she told herself as her heart thrummed a rapid staccato. She ignored the sensation and flipped it over to view faded handwriting.

*Ellen Sanders.*

Her equilibrium spun, and the world went black.

Chapter Twenty

She moaned and squeezed her eyes tighter as a large, warm hand dropped onto her forehead. "No fever." An anxious voice entered her consciousness. "Marcy. Hey." The tone sharpened. "Do we need to call 911?"

*Mike's voice.*

"I'm fine," she muttered.

Or thought she did. She braced her hands on the hard surface beneath her and attempted to sit. Her head swam, and he caught her shoulders from behind. He must be kneeling on the floor. Boneless, she propped against his torso. And started to slide.

"Whoa," he commanded. "Don't move too fast."

Ragged edges of memory flooded. The heat. The script. *The name.* Marcy scrabbled her hand along the floor to search for the book but didn't find it. Her eyes finally focused upward. The glow pulsed, yet the intense heat had receded. *Umm, yes, she got the message.*

Lindsay moved into her line of vision, hands cupped to her mouth, emanating a magenta haze. "Who is Ellen Sanders?" She spoke between her fingers, then bent for the discarded script and opened the cover.

"I think she's the one who died in the theater," Marcy croaked. The white flash intensified in the corner—a game show buzzer signaling a correct answer. She squinted and closed her eyes again.

Mike's grip on her shoulders tightened. "Did you get

145

a chance to research the details of the accident?"

"Not yet. I'm following a hunch."

No way she'd reveal the insider info from her visions with Tess. Yet she needed to pull herself together. Despite the appreciation of his solid presence behind her, she sat straighter to disengage. "As for fainting, or whatever, I think the heat took me down. I didn't drink much water today." Not ready to stand, she scooted away and wrapped her arms around her knees to steady them.

Lindsay joined her on the floor, cheeks flushed. Her aura had faded, the magenta reflecting a bright, entertaining, but determined personality. "You scared the bejesus out of me. I shrieked so loud Mike came pounding up here, probably convinced the bat had attacked again."

His concern still hovered as a red outline around his body. Marcy attempted a smile to reassure them both, but her lips trembled. "Sorry. I promise to drink plenty of water every day. Tomorrow I'll go to the newspaper to uncover details on Ellen. To see if she's our...actress." No, she couldn't say victim.

"We might be able to confirm the name here." Lindsay's tone carried confidence. "Right after I lobbed the script, I saw a wooden plaque in the box. You fainted before I could dig it out."

"Quick, bring it here." Forgetting her condition, Marcy scrambled to her knees. She fought back the dizziness as the light glimmered with approval.

Seconds later, they had the proof she'd been seeking.

Chapter Twenty-One

The newspaper office in LaPorte nestled in a historic building off the downtown square. Marcy drove past the Victorian-era red sandstone courthouse before she finally reached it. She parked out front and entered the door marked Herald-Argus.

Inside, the newsroom carried a stale air of disuse, with a jumble of empty, mismatched desks slotted between faded cubicle dividers. She'd heard the local newspapers had downsized over the years and wondered if they were still staffed locally. She rang a bell on a front desk and waited. A head popped around the corner, topped by short, graying hair. The woman approached, smoothing her cardigan. "Can I help you, hon?"

"Yes, thanks." She considered how to phrase the request. "Could I access newspapers here from the year 1966?"

The woman adjusted her glasses. "Can we narrow down the dates more specifically?"

Duh, she didn't have the actual date of the production. Though if the theater had offered a traditional schedule, shows would've run January through May, breaking for the summer months then resuming in September. She shifted from foot to foot with indecision. "Let's start with September. I'm in Little Theatre's production of *The Importance of Being Earnest,* which we're told hasn't been performed in fifty years. We're interested in digging up some history for our promotional efforts."

"You want the scoop on the accident." Her voice flattened.

"Yes." The insightful guess startled her. "Partly." Not wanting to come off as ghoulish, she added, "I'm surprised you remember."

The woman's lip lifted, emphasizing tiny lines around her mouth. "I've worked here forty-five years, and for a decade I wrote obits. The incident happened earlier, of course, when I was in middle school." She regarded Marcy intently, as if sizing up her real interest. "The event impacted me. All of us, really. LaPorte's a small town, and we're interconnected. My older sister had classes with Ellen and the others."

The name drove a shiver of awareness through Marcy though she'd engaged in the visions and seen confirmation on the polished wood plaque. That commemoration included spare details: name, role in the play, date of passing, and "Beloved Friend and Actress." She clutched her hands together and attempted to appear unaffected. "Would you be willing to tell me what you recall?"

"Well, I only remember a few highlights. We can sit for a couple minutes if you'd like." She indicated a forlorn row of plastic chairs against the entry wall. "I'm Glenda, by the way."

"Marcy. Thanks for your time." She followed and perched on one of the ungiving seats. "You said the girl's name was…"

"Ellen Sanders. You hold onto a name when tragedy's attached. She was pretty enough, with light brown hair, I think." She squinted in recollection. "The show hadn't opened when the accident happened."

Anxious to keep Glenda going, Marcy teetered on the edge of her chair. "The accident?"

"At first, they had to investigate, you know. Rumors started flying of possible foul play. Especially around the young man playing opposite her. Rod was quite the hunk—and such a dreamboat for all us girls with that James Dean level of cool." She sighed and sagged back. "They couldn't prove anything and closed the case. So sad for everyone involved."

If this woman was a reporter, she had a frustrating way of meandering through a story. "What happened to Ellen?"

"Spotlight. Fell right on her head."

Marcy gasped, then shuddered. Her fingers tightened around the chair seat as she imagined the glow in the loft flashing in distress. "How did they think that might've been caused by someone?"

Glenda regarded her without flinching or overdramatizing. "I guess they wondered if the spot had been pulled down on her."

Wow. She hadn't anticipated such a serious possibility. "Thank you for sharing what you recall. You also indicated I could access the archives?" She jumped to her feet, determined to read the factual details.

****

Flush with new information, Marcy trotted into Divine Vintage at noon. Two customers were browsing, so she caught Tess' eye, held up the bag of food she'd brought, and headed toward the office.

As usual the shop looked impeccable. She wove through the industrial racks displaying garments from the late 1800s to the 1990s. A red lace dress from the

'50s poked into the aisle, and she paused to align it with the others. Above the clothing, hand-painted boughs of draping flowers adorned lavender-colored walls. She'd painted them early in her employment when she'd been actively planning to pursue the certificate program—before her mom's health issues intensified.

She shifted her gaze away and entered the back room, debating whether she had time to set up the steamer and work on the stack of Victorian camisoles. Before she'd decided, the front doorbell tinkled. Tess burst in. "Ooh, I hope you brought me a loaded chef salad with extra bleu cheese."

"Of course. Special delivery for your cravings, along with some straight scoop. I visited the newspaper this morning."

"Scoop, eh? Then shoot, ace reporter."

"Maybe I should start with last night, when I passed out at the theater."

Her friend's face morphed to concern. "Are you okay? Come sit down." She abandoned the food to pull up a chair for her.

"I'm fine." Marcy waved her away. "You eat and I'll talk."

"I don't want to get distracted by food. Though I'm hungry as usual." She pointed to the chair. "So please sit. And talk fast."

She did, describing how the glow had intensified during the script and plaque discoveries. "I caught the script, saw Ellen Sanders' name, and toppled. Woke up with Lindsay and Mike hovering over me. Totally embarrassing."

"I can relate. You recall I fainted in experiencing my first lengthy vision." Tess opened a take-out container and popped a cherry tomato in her mouth. "Did you tell them about the light?"

"They'd think I'm nuts. I mean, first the bat and the crazy noises. Now I see *auras*." She waggled her fingers in the air and noticed she'd chipped the blue polish on her thumbnail. "I did mention the light to Mike, in a very offhand way, hoping they might discover a physical reason."

Tess sat and plumped the skirt of her vintage gold eyelet dress. "Our visions cement the linkage to Ellen, I'd say. But believe me, I understand your hesitation. Now, please get to the newspaper stuff, or I'm going to rip into the salad."

"They haven't had staff to upload articles to microfiche over the years, which is why I couldn't find anything on the Net. The staffer, Glenda, found the actual clippings from September 1966, and these articles thankfully were grouped together." At the discovery, the woman had left her alone to speed-read the basic details. She'd handled the fragile pages gingerly to protect them for future generations.

The facts were burned in her memory. "Long story short. A couple weeks from opening, Ellen was backstage and somehow a spotlight fell on her."

Tess shuddered and clasped her hands together. "Oh, how horrible. I'd tried not to imagine the actual cause but thought maybe she'd slipped and hit her head. One time I ran smack into a beam backstage during a rehearsal."

"Ouch. The cast and crew were traumatized, of course. They questioned them all, but with no evidence, they didn't file charges." Marcy's mouth had gone dry, and she wet her upper lip with her tongue. "Glenda said they'd especially talked to a guy named Rod, who played opposite Ellen. And get this, a later piece said they'd delayed the show but opened with a girl who'd been in the crew taking on the role. Any ideas who that might've been?" A shiver had trembled through her at just reading the name.

"Lorna?"

"The same."

They exchanged searching looks. "I'm not so hungry anymore." Tess nudged the food away. "After reading the articles, do you think Ellen's trying to send you a specific message?"

"Yes, I do. But why me?" The responsibility of being chosen as a conduit still unnerved her. Yet, apparently, she had no choice. Marcy stood and peered out the window to center herself, watching a pickup rumble down the alley. "Justine's costumed several shows. Why hasn't she discovered the spirit?"

"Because you have some special connection Ellen's been seeking."

A gentle hand landed on her arm. Marcy hadn't heard her friend approach. Her stomach fluttered with apprehension. Sunlight glinted across Tess' dark hair. "Phoebe waited a century to share her visions through me. Ellen needs something from you."

Needs something.

The outside shop door burst open; the bell pierced the somber atmosphere. Three chatting young women entered. With one last empathetic glance, Tess left to join them.

Marcy opened the alley door to draw in deep breaths of fresh autumn air. "Come on, you're not a wimp," she admonished aloud, mulling over her boss' final words.

In fact, the two of them shared a running joke of being Warrior Chicks.

*Courage.* She envisioned the word, meditating it into a mantra. Her lips curved as the cowardly lion from *The Wizard of Oz* roared into her consciousness. If he'd transformed into a brave, adventurous soul, so could she.

Chapter Twenty-Two

Mike observed Chase and Marcy entering the theater together that night. Pain, akin to indigestion, stabbed his chest when he saw Chase's arm around her waist. Stress of the show and his job, he told himself as he rubbed the area with the heel of his hand. Maybe he shouldn't have eaten a second bowl of his homemade chili.

Instead of wandering past him, the couple halted at his table. Chase spoke first, his face animated. "Marce made it to the newspaper today, and has she got a tale. You might want to call the cast to listen before we start."

Preferring to stay on schedule, Mike frowned. "Must be noteworthy for you to make such a dramatic announcement." He stared past him to Marcy. "Speaking of dramatic, are you all right today?"

Her lips quirked. "Sure. But thanks for asking."

At least she looked normal, rather than white-faced and frail. Last night in the loft she'd nearly sent him into a panic. His chest twinged a second time, and he ignored it to holler for the rest of the actors and crew. "Hey, guys. Grab a seat before we start." When they'd all assembled, he perched on the edge of his table.

Marcy stood before them, hands tucked into the pockets of a funky leopard-patterned jumpsuit. "I went to the newspaper office today, and we figured you'd be interested."

As she layered the facts, he hung on her words with the others. When she reached the cause of the accident, gasps, exclamations, and questions flew. She held up a hand and continued with the initial police suspicions toward the actor who'd played Algernon. "They cleared him, though, and the articles didn't even state his name. So that's the sad truth of what happened to Ellen Sanders."

Now she looked a little peaked, Mike thought. He stood to join her, and his eyes swept the group's serious expressions. "With these considerations, I'd recommend the board downplay any celebration aspect to our opening. Not that they planned to make light of the history, but now we know more, it might seem crass or exploitative."

Maria nodded from the first row. "I agree. Though a brief memorial mention would be appropriate?"

"Possibly. Maybe I'll note the anniversary and have a moment of silence each night in the director's welcome." He shook his head. "If my poker buds had known, I imagine they'd have chosen a different show for me to eat crow with."

Will stretched up from his seat. "I'd have voted for *Steel Magnolias*."

"How about *The Women*?" Lindsay suggested. "I'd pay money to watch you wrangle more than two dozen females."

"Right. Thanks for the comic relief." Mike took advantage of the segue to shepherd the actors onto the stage. Throughout the rehearsal, he found himself keeping a watchful eye on Marcy. Thankfully, she stayed upright and didn't faint. If she had, Chase made a habit of standing so close he'd catch her. He frowned and scribbled an instruction to add space between them, for the sake of Victorian standards.

After they'd wrapped, everyone said their goodbyes and shuffled out. He followed, reminded of the previous night's mad dash up the stairs after hearing Lindsay squeal. His heart had nearly stopped at finding her bent over Marcy, who lay sprawled on the loft floor.

How devastating for the 1966 cast to discover Ellen decades ago. The scene would've been gruesome. He craned his neck toward the stage where the metal-encased spotlights attached fourteen feet above, each weighing around twenty-five pounds. When was the last time someone had climbed up to ensure their safety? Another recommendation he'd share with the board.

He grabbed his notebook and headed down the aisle. Sliding through the velvet curtains to the reception area, he nearly mowed into two people. *Ah damn.* Chase and Marcy stood even closer than they had onstage. They separated to get out of his way, and he muttered, "Sorry," and barreled past. He couldn't lock up till they left, but he'd wait outside and hope they'd hurry…whatever they were doing. He grimaced and reached for the door.

To his surprise, they followed. Outside, the couple moved away to murmur together. He twisted the key and headed toward the truck. Her voice stopped him midway. She joined him on the sidewalk at the corner of the building, while Chase got into his car. "I meant to go up for the top hats tonight, but I got distracted. I promise I'll search tomorrow."

He swung to face her, jingling the keys in his fingers. "Did you look everywhere up there?"

"Not on the far end. Lindsay was making her way around when she discovered the script."

He scratched his chin, hearing the purr of the engine as Chase drove away. "If you can't find them, we've got to order asap. I'll run back in." He returned the key to the lock and grasped the door handle.

"I'll go with to learn the hiding places." She lugged her oversized purse over her shoulder. "In case I'm ever in a weak mood and give in to the huge demand to ply my costuming skills again."

Before he could reply, his eyes were drawn up by a sudden arc of light dancing through the windows. "Stay here," he commanded, flinging open the door to break into a run.

**** 

Disobeying the order, Marcy trotted behind him. They ran across the lobby and into the theater, lit only by the emergency exit signs. The rhythm of footsteps pounded across the darkened stage in front of them. The breath seized in her chest when she spied a moving form.

"Stop!"

She jumped at Mike's bellowed command. He jogged up the aisle while she followed more slowly and groped for the light switch to illuminate the seating area. Her gaze scanned the cavernous room. Where had he— *and it*—gone? She edged toward the green room, hyperventilating. With concern. And growing fear.

Loud, sharp voices rang out behind the closed door. With a burst of courage, she flung herself into the still-dark room. Two figures jostled nearby.

An angry oath echoed in the murky room. "Lemme go, asshole."

"I will when you stop fighting me." Mike's voice. Stressed, yet in control.

She again grappled to find the lights, afraid of what

she'd see. Her fingers located the switch, and her mouth dropped open. Mike stood nearby, legs braced, gripping a skinny kid by the forearms. The boy twisted to release himself and kicked out with a scuffed athletic shoe.

The director flinched at the assault to his shin but held tight. A heated red glow wavered around them. "Cut the crap. Promise you'll sit and talk to us, and I'll play nice."

At first, she assumed the color had drifted from Mike. But no, both reflected the angry flame.

"I don't have to talk to you, dipshit." The boy—young teens maybe?—attempted another futile twist.

"You're trespassing. I guess the cops can deal. Call them." Mike directed the terse order to her.

She hurried to dig for the phone in her bag. A kid. Was he also responsible for the lights they'd seen the week before?

"Don't call," the young voice pleaded. "I'll spill."

Her hand paused in the cell search.

Mike's face reflected thunderclouds as he loosened his grip. "Sit down and tell us why in the hell you're in the theater. The truth. No bull."

The boy stood for another defiant moment before he slumped onto the bench fronting the countertop.

Pulse racing, she joined the director to form a human barrier in front of the intruder. Though the boy tried to project bravado, she read panic in the darting eyes. His jeans were baggy and frayed over a wiry frame, and the black sweatshirt showed smudges of dirt. Intuition told her he hadn't broken in as a lark.

"What's your name?" She kept her voice soft and unthreatening.

He hung his head, and a slash of dark hair tumbled

onto his forehead. "David," he mumbled.

She resisted the urge to smooth the locks back, to offer comfort. "Sorry to go all commando, but you scared us silly. Well, me at least. This guy's pretty macho."

The boy wouldn't meet her eye.

Mike leaned in, his jaw clenching. "Have you been staying here in the theater? I found a blanket and some trash in the small side room upstairs."

"Maybe. Sometimes." David scrubbed a hand over his cheek. "When I don't have another place to crash."

"You're homeless?" she asked.

He squinted as if weighing whether to trust her. "Technically, I've got a home." Sarcasm laced the words. "Just tired of being my stepfather's punching bag."

What a horrible way to live. If he was telling the truth—and she believed he was. "Your family's here in LaPorte?"

"My mom. She puts up with him." He dragged the toe of a worn sneaker on the floor. "A month ago, I got fed up and left. I didn't have money, and my friend's dad started getting suspicious of me being there, so I had to find another place to sleep some nights. We don't have any relatives I could call."

Mike crossed his arms over his chest, though the tension in his face and body had relaxed. "How and when did you get in here?"

The boy flung a defiant smirk in Mike's direction. "You left the door open."

"You little—" He bit off the words, eyes lasered into him. "You're lying. Call the cops."

Marcy flung up a hand. "Not yet." If he was bad-copping, she'd gladly play good. "We don't want to get you in trouble, but you need help. Otherwise, you'll waste your life running and hiding." She lowered to sit next to him. "We will call the authorities, but first, we're looking for straight answers. I suspect you might be behind some other weird stuff around here."

One lip curved, and he snorted out a chuckle. "You mean the bat and the noises? You didn't wanna spend much time up there afterward."

Mike's lips thinned. A definite bad-cop. "You can laugh, but how would you feel if this nice lady had fallen down the stairs and broken her leg or arm? You scared her bad."

She arched her brows at him. As if he'd been cool and unaffected. "Wait." Her attention zeroed back to the intruder. "How are you responsible for a bat?"

The boy now appeared sheepish. "The thing's not real. Probably a prop from a Halloween show or something. I found it when I explored early on. Had to rig a fishing line to trigger from inside the closet room." He held up his fingers as if zinging a bat into the air.

"For Pete's sake." Mike rubbed his temple. "I assume you also made the clanking noises. So, I'll repeat, how'd you get in?"

The boy delayed, picking at a frayed spot on his jeans. She couldn't help wondering if he attended school regularly. Probably, or they'd have called the mom. Though maybe they had. If the woman lived with the threat of violence, she might have supported him getting away. Or been too weary to go after him. She couldn't imagine being a poor young kid, alone, with nowhere to sleep. While her parents had separated, she'd always been assured of a secure, clean bed.

David lifted his dark blue eyes. "The first night I had to leave my buddy's house a couple blocks over, I wandered around trying to decide what to do. The lights were on in here, and I remembered coming in on a tour with our grade school class. I walked up and sat on the back steps. The door was cracked open." He hesitated and rocked a little on the bench.

"Go on," Marcy urged, recalling nights when the door had been opened for air flow.

"I remembered the bathrooms were right behind me. I decided to slip in and out quick and didn't turn on the light. Then I heard footsteps, and the door slammed shut out there." He bowed his head and resumed working the thread on his jeans. When they didn't comment, he added, "I didn't know what to do. Honest. I waited a while, and the voices stopped. I came out here by the light of the emergency exit. Everything was dark."

Mike pulled up a plastic chair and sat in front of him. "You stayed and came back. Trespassing."

The kid's head shot up.

"But I would've done the same. Look, we're on your side here. Finish your story."

The young voice sped up, relaying details of sleeping on the chairs the first night, and figuring out he could leave and sneak back in. His friend had passed him a flashlight to avoid turning on the lights.

Mike nodded and seemed to accept his explanations. "Thanks for coming clean, bud. But you know we can't leave you here. The police have to be notified."

The boy's eyes darted to the door.

She stood, blocking the path. "How about we call Bryant first for advice since he works at the juvenile center. He can tell us what we should do."

The director twisted his lips and considered. "Makes sense." He pulled out his phone and made the call, stepping away to fill in basic info.

Marcy dipped into her purse for her emergency stash of an apple and a granola bar. The boy took them with tight-lipped thanks. His foot tapped an audible rhythm, and he glanced toward the outside door. Without warning, he leapt to his feet to sprint around her.

"Don't go." She sprang after him, the bulky purse banging against her thigh as he reached the outer door. He struggled to flip the deadlock, allowing her to catch up and grab the back of his sweatshirt. "Where do you think you're going?" she panted. "They'll help—"

Mike pounded up beside her and latched onto the boy's arm. "Really, dude? How do you think you'll survive when winter dumps a foot of snow around here?"

His heaving breath swished across her cheek. Neither of them released their holds.

After a few seconds of squirming in their grasp, the teen raised his hands. "Back off." He faced them like a wary, penned animal.

They retreated a few steps. Mike exchanged a glance with her. "Bryant's coming. He advised me to call the police, and I did. Go take a seat." He slung a thumb toward the green room, and they all returned to wait, with the director pacing while keeping his eye on the visitor.

Marcy stood beside the boy and squeezed his hand. "Hang in there. You're strong and a survivor. Bryant's great, and he'll ensure the system works for you."

"Never has before." His head drooped, yet he remained standing, as if willing himself to face down all adversaries. *Poor guy. How could she preach about systems she'd never encountered?*

Tears threatened, and she busied herself organizing the clutter on the counter behind them to keep from dissolving into an emotional heap.

Within minutes both Bryant and the police had arrived, and questions and explanations blurred into a whirl of voices. She eased out of the room and found herself wandering toward the costume loft. Yet she couldn't make herself enter. The white glow would pulse at her to help, to do something. She'd provided enough SOS assistance for one night. She sagged onto the top step and checked her phone for the time. Only an hour had passed since rehearsal ended, but the minutes had been intense. Adrenaline ebbed from her body, and she attempted to ease herself into a meditative state.

She'd been so consumed lately, with the play, helping at home versus leaving for school, Ellen, and Chase that she hadn't allowed time to decompress. Her eyes floated closed, but David's story commanded her consciousness. A tear rolled down her cheek, and she stifled a sob.

"Here," a soft voice from below offered.

She opened her eyes to a bleary outline of Mike at the bottom of the stairwell. He climbed toward her holding a navy bandanna. "Thanks." She plucked it from his hand and wiped her eyes, hoping to catch the smearing mascara.

He squeezed in to sit next to her. "I know it feels sucky, but we did the right thing."

His gentle tone cracked her composure. She sniffed into the bandanna as more tears trickled over her cheeks. His arms came around her, and she didn't think, merely collapsed into the clean scent of his shirt, pressing her forehead into the warm skin at the base of his neck. His hand rubbed comforting circles on her back, loosening the tension.

"S'sad," she whimpered.

"Shh. I know."

Oh, how tempting to curl into him and anchor in the shared understanding. To submerge her raw emotions and float in wordless oblivion.

Compelling, but a very bad idea.

He had a girlfriend, and she was with Chase. She shifted and found him looking at her with an expression that was difficult to decipher. Compassion? Or perhaps something…more? His deep brown eyes were intense. Probing. Her chest tightened. She couldn't look away.

He lifted his hand to cup her cheek, and she stilled, knowing the kiss was inevitable. Oh-so-wrong, but unavoidable. Her body flooded with sweet anticipation as his lips lowered.

"Mike?" Bryant hollered from somewhere below. "We're ready for you to lock up."

The yearning inches between them dissolved into a foot divide. He pulled back and stood in the tight confines, without a word or glance. Faint crimson waves radiated as he trotted down the stairs, stuffing the damp bandanna in a back pocket. She frowned as his tight butt disappeared around the corner.

Good Lord, surely she'd misread his intentions. Otherwise, they'd nearly crossed an epic line. And she'd been a too-willing participant. She wrapped her arms around her knees, lips tingling. The absolute, way-smartest option was to keep her distance. She was dating Chase, and definitely not interested in Mike.

*Was she?*

*Was he?*

No, of course not. Their hormones had run amuck after tonight's craziness. Or she'd confused comfort with lust. He'd probably been about to whisper another comment about David in her ear.

## Chapter Twenty-Three

Midnight ticked past but lulled by a croaking frog chorus and the familiar fish-tinged scent, Mike didn't budge from the back deck of his cottage. Moonlight reflected in the rippling water as he settled an empty beer bottle on the table, right next to the first two.

After tonight's usual efficient rehearsal, he'd anticipated ditching his clothes before diving straight into his king-sized bed. His body generated considerable heat, and he never wore pajamas, even in the most frigid temps. After a demanding day at the work site, he'd hoped to sleep soundly.

The kid, David something, sure dashed those plans. He hadn't sprinted that fast since playing high school football, and his body revved with taut energy. He'd probably pay with strained leg muscles tomorrow. But at least they'd determined the cause of the weird lights and noises. And the damn bat. Though rumors had persisted over decades, he'd never believed the building was haunted.

As for the kid, he sincerely hoped the system would work for him. Bryant would advocate to ensure he wasn't shuffled off and forgotten—or worse—sent back to that hellhole of a home. The responding police officer said he was aware of the situation, having responded to a couple of what he termed "domestic calls" in the past. Yet, he said he hadn't known a minor child was involved.

Not a child, he corrected himself. A resilient young man. His age had been revealed as fourteen.

Drained by the consuming interaction, Mike eventually had disengaged and wandered out of the green room. He'd itched to lock up and leave and assumed Marcy had done so earlier. But then he heard her muffled sob from the back stairs. The sound walloped him, and he almost convinced himself to let her handle the emotions in her own way, alone. Yet he'd trudged in to witness tears pouring down her reddened cheeks. He wasn't cold-hearted enough to slink away.

The affecting shared experience led him to drop beside her on the stairs, to naturally fold her into his arms. He'd have done the same for any of the cast members.

*You wouldn't have tried to kiss them.* The thought tumbled into his brain with taunting clarity.

*Fool.* He ducked his head against a gust of breeze and stuffed cold hands in his jacket pockets.

*Asshole.* He'd never been one to cheat, and they were both in relationships. What the hell had possessed him?

He shoved to his feet to gather the bottles, and they clinked against each other in his fast retreat to the house. Flinging them hard and fast across the water would provide a physical outlet, but protecting his home lake overrode. He didn't stop as he tossed the glass into the recycling bin and headed off to bed.

Chapter Twenty-Four

Marcy wiped down tables after the deli's Wednesday morning rush, glad the activity rerouted her mind from the crazy night before. She'd hardly slept in thinking about David's situation…then the confusing, shivery interaction with Mike in the upper stairwell. At least she didn't add contact with "the glow" to the equation.

Behind her at the baked goods case, Theo wiped perspiration from his balding head. "They near cleaned us out." The owner nodded toward the glass-fronted display, round cheeks still reddened from standing over the stove. "You want to bake brownies and cookies? I've already got some dough rising for the rolls."

The small corner restaurant had earned a dedicated following over three decades, partly due to mouth-watering, cinnamon-stuffed rolls the size of a salad plate. Some featured thick swaths of maple or vanilla icing. Others were covered in caramelized pecans. He'd only allowed her to attempt them a handful of times in the five years she'd worked here, because he enjoyed reliving the process he'd learned from his grandmother.

No matter what she baked, Marcy appreciated the opportunity to indulge her culinary artistry. Serving the regulars and newcomers raised her spirits, but experimenting with ingredients took her to a special Zen place. She especially anticipated the relaxation today.

Yep, a definite double-chocolate day.

She cleaned the final, red-topped table and pointed out her kitchen destination to Sherri, the other waitress on-shift. The wiry blonde chatted with two old-timer customers.

While lathering her hands at the kitchen sink, Marcy heard the front doorbell. Theo peeked past her. "Appears Sheldon's back home safe and sound," he muttered. "I wondered if he'd stay out there with his son now that Pauline's gone." With a pleased expression, he squeezed by to greet another of their loyal patrons.

The white-haired gentleman was one of her own favorites, and she missed his lovely wife, too. The memory struck her of how they'd all reeled when a heart attack took Pauline in July. They had pulled together to pamper Sheldon with caring and comfort food in the weeks preceding his extended trip to his son's home near Seattle.

She dried her hands and headed to the dining area. Theo opened his stance to include her, his face creased with humor. "You'll have to get your menu autographed. Little Miss here is all fancy these days, starring in a Victorian thee-ater show."

"As if." She nudged his elbow at the insinuation she'd ever put on airs. "Welcome back and I hope you enjoyed your visit. The truth is, my best friend connived me into agreeing to do the costuming. When one of the leads dropped out, the cast wanted me to step in. Though they had to convince the director I could handle Oscar Wilde." She twirled her hand in the air. "La-ti-da."

The grin froze on her face. Sheldon's pleasant expression had dimmed. His brows furrowed, deepening the lines on his face. "Which of his plays are you performing?" he bit out, in an unexpected brusque tone.

She'd anticipated a happy reaction. Perhaps congratulations. *"The Importance of Being Earnest,* in LaPorte. Have you seen it?" Maybe the conversation stirred memories of he and his wife attending theater.

He bowed his head to his chest, hands clenched at his sides. An orange glow lit around him, indicating a thrill seeker. She would never have pegged him that way.

"Sheldon…?" She tossed a worried glance at the others.

When he looked up, he appeared controlled, though tension still tightened his lips. "My apologies. I do believe I'm more jet lagged than I thought. If you'll all excuse me."

She frowned in confusion as he strode toward the door, with a firm step that belied his words. The orange aura remained as he stalked down the sidewalk. "Should someone drive him home?" she whispered.

"Nah." Theo continued to watch the older man's progress through the window. "He's walkin' fine. He's a proud man, and I wouldn't want to insult him."

Sherri picked up a saltshaker to refill. "The poor guy. Grief can kick when you least expect. He'll probably swing in here tomorrow for a cinnamon roll. I imagine he was doubly disappointed we'd sold out."

Something more lurked behind his reaction. Marcy's intuition zinged with unusual vigor, but it was simpler to agree with her friends. She'd never shared about her aura abilities with them. "I sure hope so." Yet goose bumps popped on her arms. She rubbed them in silence and returned to the heat of the kitchen. After the supernatural happenings she'd witnessed, she accepted some "coincidences" really were ghostly manipulations.

\*\*\*\*

Tess agreed when she floated the theory later at Divine Vintage. "Maybe Sheldon knew some of the actors personally. Strong reactions open you to become aware of people's auras, right?" She stood cupping a hand under her growing stomach. "Even years-old grief could rouse a level of emotion. You just have to trust yourself. From what you've told me, your intuition has strengthened with your ability."

"My ability. Or my curse." Marcy unplugged the steamer she'd been wielding on new stock and gathered a handful of pressed items to hang on the racks.

Her boss threw a mock glare and followed her into the shop. "Our abilities are a blessing. Unfortunately, they also carry responsibility."

"Which I'm accepting. Though I'd kind of hoped David had maneuvered the whole light glow shtick, despite knowing we'd seen the visions together." The details of discovering him had tumbled out when she first arrived, followed by a dissection of the scene at the deli. She diverted the conversation, holding up a sea-green lace dress. "How kitschy-cute." The contrasting aqua belt featured funky beads and crochet-work. "Late seventies or early eighties, do you think?"

"Don't change the subject. What's your next step?"

She transferred the dresses onto era-appropriate racks to avoid her gaze. "You tell me. If Ellen can't talk to me, how will I be able to help?" Frustration made her edgy. After Sheldon's visit to the deli, baking hadn't soothed her as it usually did.

Tess approached and laid a hand on her arm. "Maybe if I go up with you again, we can see additional details. When Justine comes home, she could be the catalyst to finally connect with her."

Marcy tossed her the side-eye as she moved down the row to hang another dress. "Sure. We can mirror the three sisters in *Charmed*."

"I love that." Her boss clapped her hands. "With the two of us being only children, we missed out on a sister."

Yes, but even sisters kept secrets. Marcy had spilled most of hers but would hold tight to a big one—the confounding encounters with Mike in South Bend, then in the stairwell.

## Chapter Twenty-Five

The rest of the cast expressed shock and concern when they learned of David's discovery in the theater. Bryant had followed through with the case and stood in the center of the group that evening to provide a semi-positive update. "He's in the juvenile center till they find a foster home. The kid's been trying to survive and doesn't seem violent or have any addiction issues. He'll also receive counseling, which should help." His lips twisted. "Rotten shame how some kids have to live. Happens way too often."

Lindsay reached up to pat his broad shoulder. "Poor kid. What did his mom say?"

"I'm the one who called her. She cares, but she's having enough trouble surviving herself. We agreed he'd benefit from foster care." He shoved his hands in his jeans' pockets. "When I shared the domestic violence shelter details and the hotline number, she hung up."

Marcy sat apart from the others, where she could hear and process. The details saddened her, too. Especially the mother's response. "How can we help him?"

His face puckered. "I'm not sure yet—"

Standing next to him, Mike raised a palm to interject. "I had an idea last night when I couldn't sleep. Which may be kind of nuts." He surveyed the actors, who were either standing or sprawled in the theater seats.

"What if we brought him in to help crew the show? I'd take full responsibility for him. Gut feeling, but I don't think he'd be a safety risk."

Mentoring the teen carried much more appeal than being seen as the hard-nosed authority figures who'd turned him in. Marcy joined his appeal, her mind churning. "I think that's an excellent idea. Kind of an atonement for breaking in and spooking us, while teaching responsibility and an appreciation for theater."

While the others murmured agreement, Bryant began to pace in front of the stage. "We'd need to be sure about him and get approvals from the juvenile center and our board. He may not be a threat, but he's got an attitude."

Will leaned his elbows on the seat in front of him, his face alight. "Wouldn't you have a chip on your shoulder in that kind of situation? Let's give him a chance, man. We can all watch out and mentor him."

More exclamations of support followed, and Bryant's demeanor softened. He stopped to face them. "Sorry for sounding like a jerk and questioning the idea. You can get cynical in this work. I do believe he's a decent kid who deserves an opportunity."

Mike offered him a fist bump. "Thanks for reconsidering." He reached for his phone on the director's table. "You work on logistics from your end, and I'll propose the idea to the board president. The rest of you, let's prep to open Act II."

Marcy's lip tugged up. If he wasn't careful, he'd totally erase his grumpy, macho cred. His compassion for the boy, and for her the night before, illuminated him in a new, positive light. Caught in the upbeat spin, she dropped a hand on his arm on her way to the stage. "What a surprise," she whispered toward his ear. "I guess you're still in touch with your nurturing persona, who helped raise his brothers. We might be able to provide a turning point for David's whole life."

He swiveled in her direction. His face loomed inches away, close enough to see the shadow of dark stubble on his jaw. She smelled the familiar clean scent from his shirt, and her chest tightened, flooding back to their close proximity in the stairwell. "Anyway. Thanks for giving the kid a chance." She snatched her hand away before he could comment and continued on, berating herself. *Stop reading so much into every interaction with him.* Yet she felt a telltale blush creep over her cheeks.

And darn it, the upcoming scene required her to play up the instant amore with Chase. She plopped into her chair onstage, striving for mental balance with a brief meditation: *Focus. Focus. Focus.*

Maria settled across from her, and at the go-ahead they bantered through the dialogue, from German lessons to lost manuscripts. Several pages allowed blessed time to prepare for Chase's entrance, and when he jaunted in, she fell into the action with heightened trust and camaraderie. If nothing more came of their relationship, at least the connection had enhanced their stage chemistry.

When they reached the scene where she expressed appreciation for his wavy blond hair, she wove her fingers into the thick strands. "You dear romantic boy. I hope your hair curls naturally, does it?"

"Yes, darling. With a little help from others."

She offered a coy head tilt. "I'm glad."

He inched forward and tipped his mouth onto hers, lips soft and slightly open.

She startled. He'd ignored the specific directive *not* to kiss. His lips teased hers, and his hand grasped near her spine, drawing her closer for a few seconds before releasing her. She half expected Mike to halt them, but they continued without interruption.

Cecily wouldn't jump away, she told herself. Stay in the moment.

His breath feathered over her face. "You'll never break our engagement again, Cecily?"

"I don't think that I could break it off, now that we have finally met." She wanted to kick him for springing the lip-lock and hoped she appeared unfazed. For the next dozen pages she re-immersed in the action, until Lindsay entered, and finally, Will. The comic interplay between the quartet spooled along to the melodramatic close of the act. She didn't hear Mike chuckling below them, as he often did when they nailed the characters.

She caught Chase's arm when he sauntered by at the break. "You're going to get us in trouble," she muttered, only half joking.

"Nah. He'll be cool." He waved off her concern. "I went with my gut. A kiss makes the scene."

She blew out a breath. "Guess we'll have to see if he agrees." They headed down the steps together into the darkened theater.

Mike sent them a probing look but returned attention to his notes.

Chase grabbed her hand and led her toward the green room. "Told you he'd approve."

The narrowed eyes hadn't signaled approval to her, but he'd surely tell them to drop the kiss if he wasn't happy. "I'm going up to the loft for those darn top hats." She broke away from him, also planning to have a serious chat with Ellen. Sheldon's sharp reaction had remained with her throughout the day, and perhaps she could gather some small insight. Thank goodness the bat worry had disappeared.

Inside the room, the glow greeted her from the same corner where they'd left the scripts. Her stomach clenched. Did it brand her a coward that she couldn't fully embrace being a cosmic messenger? Tess and Justine had accepted the role much more willingly.

First the hats, then the questions. She scooted behind the crowded racks and dug deep to unearth additional plastic storage containers. She hooted in approval when she found five of the formal toppers stacked in the second tub. Holding them to her chest, she edged toward the light before leaving. "What do you want from me?" She stretched out a tentative hand. "Is Sheldon mixed up in this in some way?"

The glow sizzled with such potency she gasped and lurched back.

"Hey, Red—"

Her armload flew in the air, and she shrieked, arms flailing.

"No bat, remember." The urgent reminder came from close behind her.

Panting, she cupped her hands to her mouth and whirled around. "Geez. Don't sneak up on me. Especially up here."

Mike stood wide-eyed, hands up in defensive posture. "Whoa. Sorry to spook you. I didn't think you were alone because I could've sworn I heard talking."

She ran her tongue over her top lip. "To myself. I do that sometimes."

He appeared skeptical. "I'm glad you found them."

"Them?" She focused on breathing out slowly through her mouth.

"The hats?"

"Oh. Yeah."

He lifted a brow and walked past her to gather them. The action broke her stupor, and she bent to grab the closest two, brushing off lint from the dusty wooden floor. She could feel the heat rising again in her cheeks.

He halted to stare at her. "Were you thinking about him?"

*Him. Chase?*

"David," he clarified. "He's tough and smart. He'll survive." His lip curved in a reassuring half-grin.

"I sure hope so." Caught by the unexpected sweetness of the smile, she swallowed and focused behind him. "About the…kissing scene tonight. For the record, I'm as surprised as you." Yikes, she'd thrown Chase right under the bus.

"No sweat. He's always been a renegade." His eyes bored into hers. "But if the kiss is uncomfortable for you…" He let the sentence hang.

"No. Totally your call." *This conversation is much more uncomfortable.* Their own almost-kiss reared up, and she dropped her eyes to the hats clutched in her arms. "Though it might be too soon onstage. Somewhat of a distraction." She loosened her death grip before crushing the brims beyond repair. "Would you mind taking these down? I want to check for a lace fan. Maybe I'll swat him with it if he gets too fresh."

His lip quirked up again. "Comic relief to lighten the mood. Might work. Try it next time." He reached to add her armload to his own and paused; a frown replaced all trace of lightness. "Though it also could highlight the true inappropriateness of his actions." His tone had changed to brisk and serious, and he practically wrenched the hats from her. "We'll start in five."

She huffed out a breath and listened to his footsteps pound down the stairs. Of course, the conversation could have been just as awkward for him, she decided. The guy had a surprising depth of feelings, which he'd begun to reveal. Some "macho men" might regret opening up, considering it a weakness.

But she didn't believe that of him. She rolled her eyes, refusing to analyze further, and recalled what she'd been doing when he'd blundered in and scared her silly. She whirled toward the corner, hands fisted at her sides. "We found your script and the plaque. Is there more to discover in there?" She trotted forward, blinking into the intensified light, and forced herself to kneel and rip open the cardboard box they'd discovered.

Ellen's copy remained on top. She poked it with a hesitant finger. No sizzling reaction this time. She drew in a deep breath and dug lower, past years of old discarded scripts. Near the bottom she found another *Importance of Being Earnest*.

Heat singed her fingers when she wrapped them around it. "Ow." She bit off a yelp and released the book. "Would you stop, please?" Her hands trembled as she finally registered the name scrawled on the cover.

*Rod Whitehead.* Sheldon's last name. Could it be possible? She hovered her palm over the copy. The book had cooled. She straightened and stuck both of the scripts under her loose blouse. They might contain notes. Or clues.

Chapter Twenty-Six

At home later, Marcy headed directly to the kitchen with the scripts. She brewed a pot of decaf and grabbed a handful of cookies before sitting to skim the pages.

Before she could choose which one to dive into, her mother entered the room, covering a yawn. "Memorizing? I thought you had your lines down." Her fingers fumbled to tie the belt of her silky red oriental robe. When she couldn't manage the action, she let the garment hang open over the pajamas.

Marcy's heart chipped a little. "I do have my lines. Sorry if I disturbed you." She patted the seat next to her. "Since you're up, I heisted the old scripts from Ellen and Rod, the actor they questioned most after her death."

"Heisted, eh?" Her mother chuckled and sat. "I raised you better."

She shrugged. "Girl detective in action. Tonight, an intense flash appeared to direct me to these scripts. And you know our deli customer, Sheldon Whitehead? In a weird twist, he and Rod may be one and the same."

"How in the heck did that transpire?"

Marcy tried to condense the details into a concise package. She'd shared about David in another late-night conversation the evening before. "The theater stuff keeps getting crazier, but somehow, everything must be interconnected. Would you want to help me search the scripts tonight for notes or clues? No way I can sleep without knowing if there are any clues in them."

Her mom eyed the books spread between them on the table. "I was hoping you'd ask."

"Pick the one you'd prefer to read." She rose to pour them coffee from the simmering pot. When she sat the mugs down, Ellen's script remained on her placemat. Her mom looked engrossed in the other.

Marcy stared at the slim book, unwilling to open the pages. "Tell me if you run into any relevant notes. Not stage directions, or anything, but—well, I don't know what to expect." Stalling, she ate a cookie she didn't really want and drained her coffee, then forced herself to flick open the cover.

Neat, cursive handwriting lined the blank left page. A list of dates and times. *Sept. 20 Rehearse with Rod.* Three subsequent dates were listed. "They rehearsed together," she murmured.

Her mother peered up over her reading glasses. "Hmm?"

She showed her the page. "From our joint vision, we know their scenes needed work. They weren't friendly, and achieving a semblance of intimacy was a huge stretch."

"Instant intimacy." Pat reached for her mug. "What you and Chase have been working toward?"

"Don't distract me. Have you seen anything similar in Rod's script?"

"One date and time, referring to a college study group."

Marcy stood to retrieve the coffee carafe. "Those details could answer some backstory. Full-time students were deferred from the Vietnam draft, allowing Rod to hang around and maybe do a show. From what Glenda said when I spoke to her at the newspaper, the main actors were in their late teens to early twenties. Anything else?"

Her mom riffled through and opened a page. "How 'bout a heart with initials N and R linked together? The writing's different from the notes, though, with lighter ink and curling letters."

"Drawn by Nan, the girlfriend, you think?"

She hung over Pat's shoulder to examine the dainty, ruffled outline with a cupid's arrow dissecting the middle. She topped their mugs and resettled the pot on its base, eager to return to her own pages. Ellen had written meticulous stage directions in a fine hand, slowing Marcy's progress as she skimmed every written entry. A slash of bold black underlining slammed her to a stop at the familiar hair-curling scene.

*Touch*, the writer had emphasized in larger letters. Beneath that, smaller words were scrawled: *Make him FEEL it.*

Yeow. The entry jarred against the clinical tone of the other notes. She nudged the script in front of her mom and pointed.

Pat read the words in silence, her forehead creased with questions. "Did Ellen and Rod have something going on, too?"

"I wish I knew. In our second vision, the two of them shared a little sizzle before Nan interrupted them." Her positive mood plummeted at the thought. "Sheldon's reaction was so pointed today I'm kind of afraid to approach him. But there's no way I can avoid that now."

*Hey Sheldon. I see auras. Ellen's led me to you.* Aaarggh.

"Oh, my." Her mom's exclamation drew her

attention. "Here's another name you mentioned." She pointed to the inside cover page of Rod's script.

A phone number was written in the strong, slanting script, above a name. *Lorna.*

Chapter Twenty-Seven

Marcy waited at the theater on Thursday for Tess and her hubby to arrive. After channeling his ancestor with Tess three years prior, Trey had sworn never to open himself to the visions again. Yet he'd caved at the possibility of leaving another unhappy or wronged soul to languish in grief or guilt.

She snickered, imagining his attempts to dodge and the final, dejected surrender.

"What's so funny?"

She whirled in her seat to see Mike enter through the green room. "Tess is coming tonight to view the costumes in our first run-through." The half-truth flowed without a hitch. "That gives us a week till actual dress rehearsals to tweak them. She said she'd try to convince her husband Trey to come along and check out the set."

"I imagine, with the baby on the way, he's putty in her hands right now."

"Exactly." Their eyes held, and a lightness infused her spirit.

He appeared happier. More free. The emotional wallop of their confusing yet sexy interactions over the past month rushed over her as he crossed the carpet.

She'd always been the aloof one, steering clear of entanglements. How had she allowed herself to become enmeshed with two men? This one was hands-off, unavailable, yet something kept drawing them together.

"There's the instigator." Trey's voice boomed behind her.

She jumped in the seat, assuring herself he hadn't read her mind. He'd just tossed an inside joke about their intention for the evening. The couple reached them, their arms linked, dressed in similar rust-toned sweaters. His honey-toned hair and brown eyes above chiseled cheekbones made her think of a GQ magazine fall centerfold. Despite a one-foot height difference, he and Tess made a gorgeous couple. Marcy stood, her pulse ticking up at the thought that he might be able to channel Rod. *Sheldon.*

"Thanks so much for coming. I'm excited for you to share input on the costumes and the set."

When he grimaced, Tess tugged on his arm, biting her lip to keep from laughing.

Mike reached to shake his hand. "Good to see you both again. We have two weeks till opening, so we're smoothing the edges. I'm really pleased with the progress, though. Including the novice here." He winked at Marcy.

Pleasure spread through her at the unexpected compliment, but she didn't want to shortchange their exploration time. "I'm glad you're happy, Herr Director. We're heading upstairs first, as they might want to borrow some Edwardian stuff later for an open house party at Carver House."

Tess raised a brow but went along with the ruse. "You'll be invited, of course."

Marcy led their trio out of the room, sans the director. "Sorry. I thought I should say something about why we were going to the loft. I know. I'm overthinking." She kept a fast pace through the back hallway and up the stairs to enter the main costume room.

Following behind them, Trey stopped inside the doorway and groaned, sweeping one arm toward the racks of clothes and stacks of boxes and totes. "You expect me to dig through all this junk?"

"No. I've segregated some appropriate suits for the era." Maybe after the show she'd return with Justine to add some order to the place. Marcy held a finger to her lips, indicating the open half wall to the stage below. The light flashed encouragement from the corner, and she smirked. "In fact, I'm sure there are clues to uncover if we can find them."

He shook his head. "I'm glad I don't have your aura skill. But I never want to see what I do, either."

His wife stroked his cheek. "Hon, that's why I promised such memorable…rewards…if you came tonight."

Marcy flung her hands over her ears. "Don't want to hear it." She strode past them toward the handful of garments she'd selected. "Which one of you wants to go first?"

"Her. Please." He jerked a thumb in Tess' direction.

Nobody snickered. The situation unfortunately smacked of tragedy rather than comedy. Marcy drew out the pink gown they'd discovered earlier. "This one sparked our visions twice. We should try again." The slick fabric caressed her arms, the heavy skirt draping toward the floor.

Tess approached, her face determined yet serene, and laid a hand on the dress.

\*\*\*\*

*"Would you please talk to me." Ellen stood outside*

Nan's sprawling, two-story colonial-style home, pleading with her through the screen door. At least she'd opened up after multiple knocks, but her stone-face aimed to send her packing. "Can I come in? Please don't throw away our years of friendship."

The nasty frown deepened. "Some friend. I should rename you Judas."

The barb slashed as intended. Tears welled in Ellen's eyes. She'd never had such a cold, vicious expression aimed at her. Especially from her dearest friend. "Let me explain. Please, I'm begging." She thrust her entwined fingers under her chin, with no attempt at humor. The stakes were too high.

Nan rolled her eyes, lined in the kohl she'd begun using. Several tension-filled seconds later, she kicked the door open with a bare foot. "You've got five minutes."

Ellen let out a shaky breath, praying they'd be able to connect. Her friend hadn't returned to rehearsal after catching her sitting next to Rod the night before, heads bent close together. He'd only been sharing the drawings for his Surveyor 1 moon landing project at school. But maybe there had been a teensy spark between them.

She felt her cheeks flame. She had kind of encouraged—begun to hope for—a spark, but she'd disavow that intention now and forever to get her friend back. Grateful and relieved, she followed through the familiar domed entry into the formal living room. They never spent time in here, preferring the privacy of the fashionable, Laura Ashley-styled bedroom with a turntable and stacks of the latest records. Ellen clutched her hands together and perched on a gold brocade wing chair near the fireplace, her chest rising visibly with each ragged breath.

*Nan flounced onto the stiff ivory sofa and hugged her arms around her drawn-up knees, bare under her shorts. Definite defensive posture. "Well? The clock's ticking."*

*Perspiration trickled under the embroidered peasant blouse she'd chosen—because they'd selected it together. Years of incredible friendship hung in the balance. Her throat worked, and she had to force out the words. "I think you have the wrong idea. About what you saw."*

*"Really?" Ice dripped from her voice as Nan's hands fisted on her tanned skin. "I think I caught my former best friend flirting with my boyfriend. More than once." She unwound her arms and slammed her feet to the floor. "You've always wanted my life. My house, my clothes. I'll share a lot of things, but you can't have him." Heat had replaced the chill.*

*Ellen's heart pounded against her ribs. "We weren't flirting. I promise. Haven't you asked him?"*

*"No. I refused to take his calls last night and this morning. Had my mom tell him I was sleeping. I needed time to calm down."*

*Obviously, she hadn't. Ellen couldn't control a note of hysteria creeping in. "I'm not the problem here. I've been trying to get along with him because of you, and the play. Now that I know what he and Lorna are up to—"*

*"What the hell does that girl have to do with anything?" Nan leaped off the couch and in two steps stood towering over the chair, her face and neck red with anger.*

*On impulse, Ellen threw up her arms to protect her face against a potential slap. She shrank back into the scratchy fabric. "I heard them talking together. Lorna must've told him I called her out, and he's been trying to get on my good side." Her words tripped as she panted out fearful breaths, weaving a web of lies and truth. "I've heard them plotting backstage twice."*

*"Plotting how?" Her friend glared and leaned closer, wafting hot breath over her face.*

*She had one chance to make her understand reason. Ellen forced herself to hold her blazing eyes and finish. "The first time they were in the hallway whispering. I overheard him saying they had to be super careful. He also said, 'if Nan finds out' before they were interrupted."*

*"Why didn't you tell me if you were so worried?" Nan's brow still creased, but thank goodness, the anger appeared to moderate into confusion.*

*"I didn't have proof. You'd have brushed it off. Plus, I didn't want to hurt you by bringing up something that might turn out to be petty." Her breath came easier, the words were working. "The other night I overheard them again, all intense, and he told her, 'We have to do this now. Saturday. She's getting jealous.' "*

*Her friend slumped to the floor to sit, as if her legs had given way. "What did you think they meant?" Her face sagged with worry.*

*She drew a deep breath to force out the condemning words. "Sounded to me like they meant to run off together."*

*"I can't believe...he'd..." She covered her face with her hands, dark hair falling in a curtain around her cheeks.*

*Ellen bit the inside of her lip and resisted the urge to reach out with a hug, to comfort as usual. Would she accept her explanation, or throw her out and call her a liar? If she did, their relationship probably couldn't be salvaged. Tears gathered in her eyes at the unthinkable possibility.*

*Nan scrabbled to her knees, tear tracks smearing the inky eyeliner. "I'll call him right now and ask him." She scooted the two feet to the princess telephone on the end table and punched in the number. "I don't give a damn if some busybody listens in on the party line; I need the truth."*

*Ellen's gut seized, and bile rose in her throat. The bastard would charm her with empty words. She'd be cast as the enemy, not only losing her best friend but the respect of the other actors. Because, of course, the news would trickle out. She'd end up a pariah.*

*She heard the rings, each one piercing her shredded composure. As they neared four, Ellen had to force herself to breathe, on the verge of hyperventilating. They both startled when a voice answered on the other line.*

*"Hello?" His mother.*

*"Is Rod home?" Nan's voice shook, and she swiped her free hand under her eyes.*

*"No, he's working late, right up to rehearsal tonight. Everything okay, sweetie?" An edge of concern laced the kind tone.*

*"Sure. Thanks. We'll connect at the theater." She hung up and stared off across the room, eyes glistening. "One way or another, we'll get the answers tonight."*

\*\*\*\*

Marcy's blurred vision began to refocus. Maybe someday she'd overcome or even get used to the dizzy, disembodied sensation. She wondered fleetingly if the double whammy of auras and visions struck her harder than Tess. Or if she was more of a wimp.

Her friend stood with one eyebrow cocked, exhibiting a bare hint of purple aura. "That was a first. My other visions have always connected to when the person is wearing the clothing or an accessory." She took the dress and smoothed it back into the rack. "Ellen's presence must have provided the pull into this memory at Nan's house."

Trey placed a hand on his wife's back. "Are you both okay?"

"I'm fine," she affirmed. They both turned to Marcy.

She could only nod, overriding the shock of another immersion into the past.

"What were your impressions?" he asked with another fixed look between them.

"Definitely bad vibes existed between those two," Tess concluded. "All of them were at odds, apparently, with the animosity growing. I really want to know Rod's game. Was he playing all of them?"

Her mind and body re-centered, Marcy tiptoed to the half wall to ensure no one lingered below to hear them. "I still can't wrap my head around Sheldon being Rod. These images don't gel at all with what I know about him. He's a very kind man, and he was devoted to his late wife."

Trey pulled up a wooden chair. "People can change. Sometimes, they're remolded by adversity." He laid a palm on his wife's shoulder to urge her to sit. "You're not exactly reassuring me before I dive in, but we definitely should try to see things from his point of view. I don't want you to try again, to avoid any risk to the baby. So bring it on."

The three suits hung next to the gowns. They reflected a pre-1960s era that could've translated for the show, yet none had fit the male cast members. Trey reached a tentative hand to the natty brown stripe, and his expression remained unchanged. His jaw clenched, and he fingered the gray plaid, which mirrored what Rod had worn in their earlier vision. When he grasped the sleeve of the jacket, his eyes glazed and closed, and a cloud of his green aura surrounded him. No wonder he was reluctant to slide under, having rational problem-solver tendencies.

Driven by overwhelming curiosity, Marcy couldn't resist the urge to place her hand upon his arm.

\*\*\*\*

*"Nan," he shouted, his voice echoing as he chased her through the dark back hallway. He careened around a chair to avoid tripping over it. He didn't see her. Couldn't hear any pants or sobs. Where the hell had she gone? What had she thought she'd witnessed? The idea of losing her flooded him with panic. "Nan!" He barreled through the open back door of the theater and glared into the empty street.*

*Defeated, he slumped around to the front entrance. No little blue car sat parked along the road. He slammed through the doors and ran into the theater. Lorna swung in from the green room, picking at her thumbnail. Her eyes widened as he loped up to loom over her. "Did you see Nan?"*

*"Nope, why—"*

*"All hell broke loose. She saw me and Ellen sitting together talking about my school project and must've thought we were flirting." He scoffed. "Talk about going off the wrong rail. That's ludicrous. Before I could explain, she flew crying off the stage."*

*He grabbed her hand and squeezed. "No excuses,*

*Lorna. We have to do this now. Saturday. She's getting crazy jealous." He dragged his fingers over his cheeks in agitation. "She might not believe me when I tell her nothing's going on. Things are weird between us."*

*The girl's dark eyes were cynical, as usual. She covered his hand with hers. "She loves you. She'll buy what you tell her."*

*"Damn cold way to put it." He stepped back to break the contact. "Noon on Saturday, we go."*

****

"Five minutes." Mike's voice floated over the half wall with enough volume to dislodge them from the vision.

Clenching both hands at her sides, Marcy reemerged, feeling murky and off-kilter. Trey remained immobile beside her, with his eyes closed. She glanced at Tess. They stood silently, waiting for him to re-orient.

"Babe." Tess placed the chair against the back of his knees, guiding him to sit. His eyes fluttered open, and she hovered to pat his jeans-clad leg. "Are you okay?"

He caught her worried look and reached for her hand. "A little off, as expected, but don't worry. I'm cool. Here's my take." He spilled the short, tense scene while Marcy estimated the time ticking down until the start of rehearsal. His words supported her own images. Lorna definitely had played a key role in the mystery.

The two linked visions had led Marcy to a sad conclusion. "I do believe Rod and the other girl might have been playing everyone, with plans to run off together. The big question is, did one—or both of them—also have a hand in Ellen's death?" Nausea churned in her stomach. From their serious expressions, she gathered they both agreed with her assessment.

Chapter Twenty-Eight

On Saturday morning, Theo stared out at the rain-drizzled street in front of Northside Deli and scratched his bald head. "I'm starting to get worried about Sheldon. D'ya think he found someplace that makes a better Reuben? Nah," he answered himself. "But I hope he didn't catch a cold or something on the plane and he's laid up in bed."

The day had been unusually slow, probably due to the wet weather. Yet Marcy shared his concern. She wondered if their friend wasn't showing up to avoid her. With his absence, the mystery gnawed even more at her, and she'd run out of patience. She finished adding her fresh-baked brownies to the display case and hit on a brilliant idea. "Maybe I should go to his house for a wellness check. Nothing obvious. Just bring him a care package and tell him we miss him."

Sherri swung by the counter to pick up an order of French toast. A thick braid hung down her back over a vintage Rolling Stones T-shirt. "The police'll do a wellness check if we call."

"A police visit might scare him, or make him mad," Marcy persisted. "Especially if he has found a new favorite restaurant." She peeked at her boss, who narrowed his eyes.

"Ha ha, Miss Wisecracker." Theo grabbed a pastry box from the stack on the counter. "The rush is over.

How about you bring him a couple of the cinnamon rolls I baked earlier." He bent inside the display case to load two of the oversized treats and handed the package to her to close. "Don't stay long, missy, or I'll have to dock your pay." He chuckled at his wit.

She pulled off her apron and tossed it in the kitchen. "Do you know where he lives?"

Sherri rattled off the address as she returned for the coffeepot. "He told me when we were talking about how Michigan City has spruced up neighborhoods in the historic district."

"Thanks. I'll be quick." Marcy repeated the address in her head, took the box, and hurried out the door.

To minimize time away from the deli, she took her car. Within minutes, she was on Manhattan Street, looking for Sheldon's house. She pulled up in front of a brick bungalow with dark green trim but didn't alight. Her hands tensed on the wheel. Faced with the opportunity, she wasn't sure how to approach the man. Her heart pounded as she balanced the box and walked toward the door. She rang the bell, heard the tinny echo inside, but saw no movement.

A curtain twitched in the window beside her. She shifted from foot to foot, thinking he might well blow off her concerns. She'd have to fumble in her purse for a pen to write a brief, cheery note on the box and leave it on the doorstep.

But when the door creaked open, she jumped back in alarm and stuttered, "H-h-hi."

Sheldon Whitehead faced her with an inquisitive look. "Marcy?"

"I…we wanted to drop you some fresh cinnamon rolls. Theo's a big worrywart when his favorite customers don't show for a few days." She extended her fingers over the smooth cardboard and offered the box. "Consider the treat a welcome home package."

From his reserved demeanor, she expected him to snatch the offering and close the door. Her words tumbled faster. "Truth is, I volunteered to come because I was worried. When we discussed my show the other day, you seemed a little upset."

He stared at her.

*Hmmm, he sure wasn't making this easy.* She gathered her courage. "I have kind of a weird story to share, if you have a couple minutes."

His face shuttered further, yet he motioned her to enter. "Come in."

Sheldon led into the compact living room, filled with furniture he'd probably had for thirty years. A picture of him and Pauline sat on a coffee table next to an overstuffed floral sofa. She peered at their happy faces and turned away, unsettled. After only two months, he had to be lonely and readjusting to an empty house. She perched on the edge of the cushion with a stiff, straight-backed posture and balanced the pastry box in her lap.

He chose a wooden chair and lowered into it to sit, clasping his hands in his lap. "Go ahead, young lady."

The situation had pushed her far beyond her comfort zone. She swallowed hard and tried not to squirm beneath the intensity of his gaze. "I guess, really, I have a question for you. Did you ever do *The Importance of Being Earnest* at LaPorte Little Theatre? As Algernon?" She needed to gather the info as quickly as possible, not only to return to work, but in case he shut down.

He rubbed the toe of his house slipper on the worn brown carpet, leaving a ridge in the nap. An orange aura flushed around his chair, and seconds ticked as he avoided looking at her. "Yes. I did play the role. In 1966."

The breath caught in her chest. "Why did they call you Rod?" Her foot tapped a nervous rhythm, bouncing the contents of the box, enough to release a waft of cinnamon.

"I'd almost forgotten that silly nickname, drawing from my middle name of Roderick. Pauline preferred to use my formal name." His lips broke into a small smile before his face became solemn again. Sharp eyes pierced hers from behind the wire-framed bifocals. "What do you know, Marcy?"

Coming off as a bully badgering a reluctant witness, she regretted the rash decision to visit. But the need to discover the truth drove her to stay seated. "Not much. The cast knows a sad accident happened prior to opening."

"How in the world did you connect to me? Lord, we're talking, what, fifty years or more? I haven't thought much about the show in decades." His fingers fidgeted on his lap, and the aura vibrated with energy. He again focused his gaze somewhere beyond her. "For a long time, though, the circumstances haunted me."

*Like they're haunting me.* Yet she couldn't blurt out the wild story of the glow leading her to the script, of her digging at the newspaper office, or the joint visions they'd experienced. None of them had gone public with their abilities to avoid possible ridicule and manipulation. She decided to sugarcoat how she'd linked to him. "Being the exact fifty-year anniversary, I volunteered to do a little research on the 1966 play. After you came into the deli, I made the possible connection with your last name. It seemed like a long shot. But if you had been in the cast, I thought you'd be pleased to know on opening night we plan to commemorate with a small, tasteful memorial tribute. To Ellen and the rest of the cast."

She'd have to convince Mike and the board to go along with the proposal. Yet if she got Sheldon—Rod—in the theater, she might resolve the mystery and Ellen's restless soul could leave. "Would you be willing to attend?"

His eyes squeezed closed. The pulsing orange color nearly overtook him. When he opened his lids, a sheen of moisture gleamed. She wanted to cry herself for bringing him any level of pain or anguish. The poor man had been suspected of murder, and she'd dragged it all up. The tense silence in the room nearly sent her up and running out to her car. She stiffened her knees to plant her sneakers on the floor.

He pushed to his feet, and she startled as he towered over her. "A memorial sounds lovely. I'm not sure I should attend though. Now I'm sure you have to get back." He pivoted and made unsteady progress toward the door.

She swallowed the bitter remorse, left the box on the couch, and followed. "I'm sorry for disturbing your morning."

The door opened wide, and he gestured toward the sidewalk. "Thank Theo roundly for my treats. Tell him I'll be in soon and he'd better load my Reuben with extra kraut for being an old worrier."

"I will. Enjoy your dessert."

A definitive click sounded as she stepped off the stoop. He hadn't slammed the door, but he'd closed it hard enough to make a statement. She got into the Bug and drove down the block, pulling over when her own vision blurred with tears.

****

Later, Tess teared up when Marcy relayed the story to her between customer visits at Divine Vintage. Pre-Halloween traffic had been steady, and they'd had no opportunity to take a break. After three hours they both collapsed onto the stools at the counter, and Marcy shared the details.

Her boss dug into the pocket of her beaded cardigan for a tissue. "The poor man. Not that you shouldn't have visited and asked him," she amended. "But the memories surely aren't pleasant. I can't imagine what he'd have said if you'd told him we'd envisioned some of them."

"I couldn't out you two. Or myself. Believe me, he wasn't in a receptive mood." Marcy rotated her neck in circles to work out the kinks that had built since the morning encounter.

"If you get another chance, you should tell him the full story."

She halted mid-rotation. "You'd be okay with me sharing your and Trey's abilities?"

"Start with me. That's probably enough, don't you think?"

"I imagine he'll try to avoid any further conversation with me." To re-center herself, she left the counter and began to tidy the racks, where customers had riffled for treasures. "I didn't mean to, but I brought him real pain today. I'm hoping someday we'll be able to get past the awkwardness. He's a lovely person, and I consider him a friend."

She looked down and saw she had clutched the

shoulders of a silky, beaded blue dress hard enough to wrinkle the fabric. She hurried to re-smooth it and rehung the garment at the end of the rack.

"I'm sure he's not judging you." Tess joined her in rearranging garments into their era groupings.

She didn't dare glance at her. A tiny droplet slid down her cheek, and she wiped it with the back of her hand. In front of her, a skinny 1960s shift had been slotted with the fifties' full skirts. She nipped the neon-striped garment out and held it against her torso. "Ellen might've worn something similar. I can't help but feel I'm letting her down." Her words dissolved into a sob.

Despite her growing pregnancy, Tess remained light on her feet. She reached her in an instant and enfolded Marcy, and the dress, in her arms. The dark head only reached her shoulder. "You are *not* letting her down," she whispered. "We have more to unravel, and we'll persevere to make it happen."

*We'll* persevere. Marcy appreciated the words more than she could know. They'd lean on each other to solve the puzzle. She detached from her friend's arms. "What more can we do? We open the show in two weeks."

Tess moved down the rack to continue her work. "When's Justine coming home? We'll drag her butt to the loft and hope Ellen materializes for her."

"I doubt we'd have to drag her. The girl's primed to help." Realizing she still held the '60s mini, Marcy relocated it farther down in the rack. "She and Jackson are planning to make the opening Sunday performance. A couple days ago she texted to ask if I'd be willing to stay at their house Friday night to let the cleaning lady in the next morning."

"Ooh. You'll have the place to yourself in case you

invite *company*." Tess didn't allow for an indignant reply, as she walked away, toward the bay window. She retied the silk scarf on a mannequin, adding, "I hope that group of ladies walking down the street will visit our divine shop. If they only knew our other talents, imagine how popular we'd be on the local party circuit. Please, read my aura. Ah, touch my clothes." Her tone teased.

The women ventured toward their doorway, and Marcy escaped toward the back of the shop to gather her composure. Yes, they could joke about the otherworldly happenings, but her mood hadn't brightened. Other people's emotions were entangled in her clumsy efforts, and she'd already bungled the outreach to Sheldon.

Ellen's misfortune evidently had tainted his life, and now had complicated hers.

Chapter Twenty-Nine

On Monday, Mike was determined to tweak, polish, and suggest more nuances to enhance the actors' distinct characters. Tess and Trey had been complimentary and chuckled several times, but their comments seemed reserved. He knew the play hadn't peaked; he didn't want it to. An early peak led to overconfidence and dwindling enthusiasm as days would pass without the fuel of an appreciative audience. He preferred to rev actors up in the final dress week, to enter performances on a prepared adrenaline high.

Marcy had been a little off during the scenes Thursday night, he thought. Late for an entrance and a tad spacy. Afterward, she'd begged off joining the crew for adult night. He hadn't been particularly up for the jollity himself, but he'd gone. The group's time together was drawing to a close, and he wanted to savor the connections.

"Hey, look who tagged along tonight." Bryant entered the theater area with David in tow. The boy wore clean jeans and a long-sleeved T-shirt, his hair combed back off the high forehead.

Mike approached them and stuck out his hand. "Glad you could join us."

The boy hesitated but offered a brief shake. He slid a glance to the burly man beside him before returning to hold his gaze. "Thanks for how you all handled the other night. Sorry for being a jerk."

"I get it." He wondered if Bryant had coached him to apologize, but at least he'd done so. "No harm done. This dude watching out for you?"

A slim shoulder lifted. "Yeah. I guess you all are gonna put me to work."

They talked briefly of the tasks he'd help with, including assisting the lighting designer in the overhead booth during the show. Anticipation began to well in the kid's eyes, though he attempted to mask the emotion. Hopefully therapy sessions could help him work past the anger and fear he must be dealing with. The theater family could help, too. "Would you be interested in learning more about the directing and set building side?"

The kid didn't answer immediately. He'd learned to guard his answers, apparently. When he did reply, he reflected a tiny boost of confidence. "I suppose I should get the whole picture, right?"

"Makes you more valuable when you know how everything works."

A shy grin lifted his lips. "Let's do it."

"You're on." He didn't have a ton of extra time, but he'd be happy to make the kid feel welcome and knowledgeable. Everyone needed a place to fit in and share their talents. He'd certainly found his in the theater.

As other cast members wandered in, introductions were made. Everyone greeted the teen as an equal, Mike noted. They were great people and also would offer a hell of a show. He'd be proud of the outcome despite being coerced into directing through the infamous poker bet. Even the latecomer to the crew excelled. He tried not to watch Marcy as she strode up the aisle on those long legs, but the joy on her face drew him in.

"David. Glad you're joining us." She stopped to grasp both his hands. Smart kid, he didn't try to pull away. In fact, he looked a little dazzled now that they weren't pinning him in the green room. "Have fun, and I'll thank you in advance for my moments in the spotlight."

The boy thrust his shoulders back. "Mike's gonna teach me about directing and set stuff, too."

She released his hands and tilted her head to one side. "Really? Cool. One day you might even replace him as the directing guru. If you want to learn more about painting sets, I'll be happy to share some tips."

She stepped away and caught Mike's eye, one lip lifting before she continued up and across the stage to disappear behind the flats. Had she approved of his offer to work with the boy, or was she mocking him? Not that it mattered. He assumed she had headed to the dressing rooms. Costumes weren't required till tech-dress week, and he hoped she wouldn't wear them until then. His psyche couldn't take seeing that daisy dress with the tiny back buttons.

Chase walked past him, muttered a greeting, and followed the same path toward the backstage. He turned away. Right. They were "a couple." Which reminded him, he needed to call his girlfriend. Both their schedules had remained tight, prohibiting dates, but they should at least talk or text once in a while.

****

The segregated backstage costume rooms already were filled with changes of clothing for each actor. The women's space featured two racks and barely enough square footage for the four of them to either sit at the mirrored table or change their clothes together. They'd probably have to stagger times in order to get ready, Marcy decided, plus help each other handle the back buttons on their gowns. Especially the close-fitting, daisy-sprigged garden ensemble. She brushed a hand across the slick, polished cotton skirt, which would billow out several feet around her ankles due to the volume of the petticoat.

*How about asking Mike?* Her mind taunted. She nearly shivered when recalling his fingers trailing down her exposed back. A dangerous thought. The door burst open, and she yelped and clutched her chest as a man entered. "Geez, Chase. Give a girl a heart attack. I didn't think boys were allowed in here."

He snickered and caught her in his arms, nipping at her lips. "I missed you. And I'm jealous something other than me occupied your time this weekend."

Easing away, she hoped no one would walk in and catch them. She didn't want a rep as an easy chick who made out in dressing rooms. He waited for her to answer. "I worked so I could feel better about taking off weekends during the show run. Caught up on sleep, too. I've been burning the candle too bright."

"To paraphrase Edna St. Vincent Millay." He trailed a finger up her neck. The guy might be a flirt, but he backed the fun with knowledge. The classic combo of brains and beauty.

He leaned closer to nuzzle her neck, lips soft and insistent. "What else is in your head?"

*That you're available and interested and I'm a fool.*

Any semblance of resistance dissolved. Her body melded against his, appreciating the hard contours. Chest. Arms. Legs. Crotch. Oops, a tad too friendly. She disengaged and pretended interest in the clothing hanging beside them. "The costumes were on my mind, too. They look good, don't they?"

"Especially yours." He brushed his hands down her arms. "We'll have a crazy busy week but promise me we'll go out on Saturday." His eyes compelled her to say yes.

"Okay. Maybe Will and Lindsay would join us at the Oktoberfest celebration downtown."

He considered the suggestion. "Sure. Will and Dan love festivals, and Lins is dating that new hunk. We'll have a blast."

No complaint or pouting. He took the relationship as lightly as she did. Perfect. No ties.

After the rehearsal ended, she waved to him and scooted in the opposite direction, yearning to get a good night's sleep for once. She drove home and entered the dimly lit kitchen, surprised to find her mother sitting at the table in front of their bulky, older laptop.

"Hi there," Marcy called and zeroed in on the burbling coffeepot. A splash of decaf wouldn't hurt and could help chill her out.

Her mom jolted with surprise. "I didn't hear you, honey."

"Thought you might be in bed, so I tiptoed in." She halted by the table and gripped the top of the chair, intuition zinging. "Is something wrong?"

"No. Of course, not." The gnarled hand tilted the computer screen downward. "Pour yourself a cup and sit."

"What lured you to stay up?" She ignored her coffee cravings to drop into the chair and delve behind the reason. Something concerning on the medical front?

"Just hear me out, please, before reacting." Her

mom reached to cover her hand on the table. Her aura shone a dazzling sunflower yellow.

Marcy's apprehension grew. The haze of color surely wasn't reflecting the creative, friendly, and fun side today.

Her mom glanced again at the computer and cleared her throat. "I may as well be blunt. You've been approved to receive scholarship assistance for the certificate program residency in Virginia, beginning in the coming semester. You just have to update and finish the application process."

"Wha—" Her head jerked at the words.

"Listen, please. Yes, I applied for you. They still had your earlier application on-file, from three years ago." Her fingers twitched, but she didn't remove them, instead adding her other hand on top. "You will not waste your life any longer staying here. I won't allow it." Her eyes narrowed, and she leaned in closer. "I will be fine, and you will move on as you're destined and complete the book illustration courses."

The words swam heavy between them. Marcy stretched away, beyond her reach. Her mind whirled between delight at having funds to attend the program and indignation at the secretive method. "You had no right," she ground out.

"You're my daughter." Her mother straightened to an I-mean-business stance, affirmed by the pulsing aura. "I love you and have every right to help you pursue your dreams. You have no idea how much guilt I endure standing in your way." She sounded almost pleading. "The scholarship isn't a negative. I'm opening the door for you to fly free. You've wanted your certification for years, but you're burying your ambition to martyr yourself for me."

She flinched. "Martyr?" The word slashed her rattled brain.

Pat appeared stricken. "I didn't mean—"

"Yes, you did." She bit back the hurt clogging her throat and fled to her room, locking the door with a decisive click.

Chapter Thirty

The next morning, Marcy stumbled out of bed after disturbing dreams she couldn't quite recall ruined a good night's sleep. She suspected the conversation with her mom had been a trigger, along with the continuing saga of the aura mystery. Determined not to reengage in the testy scholarship debate, she got ready and snuck out the door for her shift at the deli.

Her mind cleared as she drove the country backroads toward Michigan City. The autumn days were lovely as the leaves changed. Her favorite time of the year. When she'd been a child, she and her father searched their property for leaves to match her rusty hair. He'd stick them into her curls to make his laughing comparisons, teaching her about the exciting variations of the color palette. She admired a vibrant burning bush along the roadside, longing for those carefree times and their once-easy interactions.

At some point after he'd moved, she'd stopped seeking his counsel, but today the urge to vent about her mom's overbearing action drove her to dial his number. Usually, he rose super early to paint southwestern landscapes by a pale filter of early light.

The phone had barely rung when he picked up. "Hey, pumpkin. How's tricks?"

Her lips lifted at the cozy fall nickname but drooped again at remembering the reason for the call. "I'm glad you're up. Mom really crossed a line last night."

The details poured out as she kept a careful eye on the road, knowing squirrels ran crazy in these nut-gathering days. She finished the tale, expecting him to spew similar thoughts about her mom butting in, etc. etc.

Instead, he hesitated. "You know she's got your best interests at heart."

"Ugh. Not you, too. The timing's not right for me to go." An unmarked railroad crossing loomed, and she stopped to look both ways before proceeding. "She's in pain, and I can't leave her with no help. Even walking is becoming more difficult, too."

"The doctor's working on a new med regimen. Marce, she doesn't want you sacrificing your life for hers." His volume had intensified, coming across with a level of exasperation.

She blew out a breath. "I'm not. Please don't gang up on me. And since when are you two talking so much?" After their separation eight years prior, she'd been under the impression communication remained sparse. Had concern at her direction—or lack thereof—opened them to more interactions?

"We're still married. We do talk." His voice lightly chided. "Daughter-o-mine, please take a step back and really think about this opportunity. Your mom is a strong woman, and if she says she'll be fine, she means it."

"Aaarrgh," she wailed. "I called you for sympathy."

"Yep. I know. You've got that one hundred percent. But I wouldn't be doing you any favors if I didn't try to help you work through the realities of the situation, instead of reacting blindly."

"I'm not—well, maybe I am." She rotated her stiff neck, keeping her eyes on the road as she entered the city limits. "Thanks for the little butt kick. I'm almost at the deli, so I'd better sign off."

"How's my Bug running these days?"

"Fab with the new alternator. Also, much thanks for helping us to pay for that."

"The Love Bug was my first baby, but you're my most important baby. I want to take care of both of you." He chuckled. "Have a great day, love."

"You, too. Happy painting." She'd almost called him daddy, but the knowledge he could only care for them long distance locked the word in her mouth.

\*\*\*\*

Along with his chiding, reminders of her mother's troubled face haunted her as she served customers during the morning rush. *You should've talked to her instead of showering and slipping out*, an inner voice scolded.

Yet, her psyche remained too raw to probe. And what conclusion would they've reached with further discussion? She couldn't envision gratefully accepting her placement and moving hours away to Virginia, leaving her mom to struggle physically and financially. Although she'd made it clear she didn't expect—or want—that level of sacrifice.

No, *martyrdom*. Marcy grimaced and cleared a two-top of dishes, caught up enough she barely noticed the small tip. Her mind began to waver with indecision. With the forced blessing of the scholarship, she could give herself fully to the program she'd dreamed of for years, including internship opportunities.

The elderly lady at a window table broke into her reverie. "Miss? My check?"

"Sorry. Right away." She wiped her hands and delivered the bill. An hour later the clock struck noon, and she took off the pocketed apron. Another shift had passed without Sheldon venturing in. Theo had confirmed the older gentleman hadn't returned since her visit to his home.

After goodbyes to her coworkers, she finished the day at Divine Vintage, her mind warring between the theater mystery and her mom's big reveal. Tess had run out as soon as she arrived, taking the afternoon off as select pieces of their furniture would be delivered to Carver House. To gain room for a growing family, they planned to take over the massive Edwardian mansion while Trey's elderly cousin, Esther, moved into the waterfront Craftsman he'd designed and built over the Michigan border. She snickered at how his architect tendencies leaned to a streamlined, modern vibe, yet Trey had given in to the two women and his persuasive mother and agreed to make the switch.

At the end of the day, Marcy found herself driving toward their new home, to check in and help or maybe grab them dinner, she told herself. *Ah hell, she couldn't wait to unload the distressing college news.*

Five blocks later she parked and ran up the steps of the three-story brick mansion, which dwarfed all the neighbors. White wicker furniture still graced the sweeping front porch where she clacked the brass knocker. Man, the square footage would more than double the couple's current living space. Plus, the humongous ballroom spanning the full length of the place would provide an ideal kids' playroom. How crazy to think that her aura ability had been triggered up there, providing her own extra-special tie to the showplace.

The door opened, and her boss greeted her, dressed in maternity jeans with her hair pulled into a high tail.

Tess frowned and tugged her inside. "Something's eating you. Is it more on the mystery? Come sit and tell me. I've been hoping to rest my feet."

Marcy peered around the mahogany-paneled formal living room. They were alone, but she heard faint voices drifting from the second level. "Thanks. I do want to assist you as needed, but I also could benefit from a sounding board."

Footsteps clattered down the carved staircase, and Trey's cousin Esther popped into the room, her white hair coiffed as usual. She immediately approached for a hug, her head barely reaching Marcy's collarbone. "Lovely to see you, my dear. Before you two get settled, there's a room you'll want to see."

Marcy glanced at Tess, who kept a poker face. She followed the older woman out of the room, adjusting her steps behind her on the broad wooden stairs. On the second floor they turned into a bedroom adjacent to the master.

Next to the sweep of windows, Trey knelt to assemble a white crib. He pushed to his feet and offered a greeting, but Marcy was too excited to respond. She squealed and flung her arms around him, then Tess. "The room is pink and lavender. You're having a girl."

Her friend beamed. "We're hoping you'll paint us a mural."

"Of course, I'd love to." Marcy spun in a twitching dance move then halted to frown. "I'd better start soon, though, because in January I *might* be heading off to Virginia."

Trey held up a hand. "Sounds like a pretty monumental change is ahead for you—and your employers. Why don't we all head down to the kitchen and wait for Jake to come back with the Chinese food. I need his help to finish deciphering these darn directions, and he's going to want to hear your big news, too."

"Possible news," she protested. "I'm still considering."

Esther reached up to take her arm. "Coming from a more mature perspective, I advise not to let life pass you by." She led her from the room, eyes twinkling behind rimless trifocals. "Maybe your fortune cookie will be especially prophetic tonight."

Chapter Thirty-One

Marcy arrived early at the theater the next night, determined to paint a few finishing touches on the revolving flats onstage. Analyzing the movable walls from the audience vantage point, she'd decided to pop up the color. The tech crew milled around her, discussing set changes and prop movements. She tuned them out, but she couldn't stop rehashing the interaction with Sheldon and the weighty decision about the college program.

Earlier, her mom had been more forceful in her approach, expressing her pent-up exasperation over dinner. "You could lose the slot if you don't finish the paperwork."

"I didn't ask you to interfere."

The words had flown before she could stop them. She rubbed her fingers across her throbbing forehead, owing to the fact that she was being stubborn. She should complete the application and move on. Her mom made it clear she didn't want her to stay; her dad and friends supported the idea. Yet after years of dreaming about illustrating books, she couldn't cement the decision. Something held her back, and she gave in to procrastination.

She dipped her brush into the can of red paint to add more poppies to the flowing field. A shadow fell over her, and David plopped down to inspect her work. A welcome diversion.

"Keeping busy?" she asked.

He stretched his jeans-clad legs off to the side of the tarp, which had gathered numerous splotches and splatters. "For sure. These old dudes keep me on the run." But his lips curled at the statement. He leaned nearer to the flat, squinting at the impressionist garden. "How do you adjust from doing a regular-sized painting to a wall?"

An insightful question. She flexed her fingers to relax them and contemplated the three backdrop panels. "For smaller works, I have an idea when I sit down and usually let the spirit flow. For the theater, I sketched out a rough plan beforehand due to the size. I did a mural last year on the wall at the deli where I work, so I was comfortable with the scale."

He pushed back a lock of flopping black hair. "Excellent."

"Do you want to try?" She offered one of the brushes.

"Sure." He took it, face scrunched in concentration, and adjusted his grip as she instructed. A yellow lily began to form from his careful strokes, mirroring one she'd painted.

"Good choice," she praised as he picked up a smaller brush to add a deeper shading of gold. The petals were a tad uneven and fuzzy, but in the sea of color the flower would blend right in. "What's your favorite aspect of the theater, now you've been introduced all around?"

He paused, wrinkling his forehead. "Mike's shown me everything, and yesterday I helped gather some props because I know my way around upstairs." He slid her a wry grin at the admission. "Tonight, I'll help work lights. He explains stuff really clear and answers questions, then lets me run. I'm pretty stoked on all of it. We're going to talk directing, too."

She detected a note of hero worship in his voice. The director had given him an incredible experience, treating him as an equal in the fun, yet challenging creative environment. She hadn't realized the two of them had connected so often.

The teen returned his brush to the jar of water and swished it as she had, to prepare for another color. "Now you've got me painting. But no offense, I'm not interested in costumes." His head popped up, and he leaped to his feet. "Mike's here, gotta go."

She watched them walk down the aisle, heads together. David's laughter pealed out, and her lips twitched into a smile. The big guy's softie side finally had blossomed in full view. The dude had a definite sweet, protective gene. Tara was a lucky girl, and she hoped she appreciated him.

****

On Friday night, Mike arrived at Tara's at seven on the dot for their date. She answered the door, looking killer as usual in jeans and a fuzzy sweater. This time, he craved a quiet moment to talk before heading to the trendy, crowded restaurant. "Can we sit here and have a drink first? I want to bounce something off you."

"I guess." She pursed her lips and pointed him toward the couch. "Beer or wine?"

"Whatever you're having."

The conversation was important, not the beverage. An off-the-wall idea had pounced on him the night before when he'd hunkered down to school David in basic directorial techniques. The kid had been attentive and downright enthusiastic, plus insightful in his questions. All he needed, apparently, was a positive environment to thrive in.

*And he could provide that for him.* The thought had slammed him during the first intermission, and he'd immediately balked. Uh-uh. He'd spent too many stressful years steering his younger brothers down the right path.

Then he kicked himself to think beyond the knee-jerk reaction. Why wouldn't he want to help change someone's life for the better? His brothers had become upstanding citizens instead of unruly thugs. David deserved the same chance. By the time he'd driven home, the decision had been cemented in his mind. With everyone's agreement, including the teen's, he'd apply to become a foster parent.

Tara returned with goblets of red wine. For her, the dryer the cabernet the better. He settled his on the end table next to the couch.

She sat next to him and smoothed her long mane of hair back with her free hand. "So bounce away. I don't want to wait a long time for a table."

His brow wrinkled till he realized she had played on his "bounce something off you" comment. Puns weren't usually her forte. He leaned forward and placed his palm on her arm. "I've mentioned to you that I've been mentoring the teenager who'd been hanging around the theater."

Her lips twisted, and she lifted the wineglass to sip, before lounging against the cushions. "The one who broke in and scared the shit out of you with the fake bat."

He withdrew his hand and tried to get comfortable

on the hard-backed couch. "Anyway, turns out he's a really good kid and a fast learner. He wants to absorb everything he can about running a production."

"Mmhmm," she murmured, inspecting her hot pink nail polish.

"Every kid needs a chance to thrive, and the more I've worked with him, I'm convinced I can do that for him."

Her eyes slid to his. "Are you talking about spending extra time with him after the show ends? Babe, we hardly see each other as it is. Add one more *commitment* and we may as well be pen pals."

He searched her face. She wasn't joking. To buy time, he took a long pull of the wine and balanced the delicate crystal on his knee. "Actually, I'm going to apply to give him a foster home."

"What?" She shot up so fast his wine sloshed in the glass. She noticed and plucked it from his fingers. "Are you kidding me? Look, I'm not heartless, but this boy is trouble. I mean, who trespasses in a theater and delights in inciting fear in everyone?"

"Someone who's frickin' desperate and scared." He rubbed a hand through his hair. From the outset he'd anticipated Tara wouldn't be thrilled, but this level of antagonism threw him.

She put his glass on the table in front of them. "No."

He waited, but she didn't continue. "No…?"

"No, I do not agree. If you came here seeking my blessing, you won't get it." She crossed her arms over her chest and glared. "You're busy. I'm busy, this will be way too much for you to handle. You don't always have to be the superhero who solves everybody's messes."

His nostrils flared. "Is that how you see me?"

"Sometimes, yes." Her tone remained matter of fact, as if they were discussing the merits of the wine. "The trait can be commendable, or way overdone. In this case, I think you're jumping the gun. Are you really willing to sacrifice our relationship over this kid?"

Was she giving him an ultimatum? Trying mightily to control his simmering temper, he steepled his fingers and shifted on the couch to give her an answer.

Chapter Thirty-Two

Lindsay caught Marcy in the reception area on Thursday before she could enter the theater, tugging her by the hand into a small alcove. She regained her balance and glanced around them, her skin prickling. "What's going on?"

"Heads up, tonight could be kinda weird."

As if any night had been normal and routine since she'd first walked in the building. "Weird how?"

The girl leaned close. "My older sister is friends with Tara. She told my sis she dumped Mike last night." She leaned a shoulder against the wall, settling in for a dish session.

Marcy's mouth dropped open. "Oh my God. Poor Mike. How devastating."

More juicy details rolled out, but she scarcely tuned in. Her emotions swung between sympathy and a lightness in knowing he wasn't tied to the tyrannical woman. Why in heck would she dump such a great, caring guy? Not to mention smart and attractive.

The sound of male laughter trailed to them, and Will and Chase walked by the alcove. Lindsay leaped out to bring them into the tight circle and gave them the news. The men expressed varying degrees of dismay at the revelation.

"But we can't let on," Lindsay stressed. "Act naturally, and if and when he wants to tell us, he will."

Chase whistled low. "Whew, that sucks big-time."

Sure did, Marcy thought. Their director put on a tough exterior, but she'd seen the soft heart beneath. Rejection always stung, especially if he'd been caught totally unaware.

The quartet trooped into the theater space together, still murmuring. Chase hung back to loop his arm around her shoulder and hug her close. "You look really cute tonight. Good thing I snapped you up."

She narrowed her eyes at him. "Don't worry, Mike has absolutely no interest." Surprisingly, her spirits sank at the words—but they were true. She almost added, "I'm all yours," but the words caught in her throat. They were getting along great, yet she preferred the slow dance, especially with the show's opening looming the next week. Not to mention, the possibility of her leaving.

Rehearsal passed in a blur with thoughts of the breakup clouding her mind at off-moments. Their leader apparently had decided to pursue the stiff-upper-lip approach because he didn't mention the change in status. The four of them followed his lead, and a stilted, faked obliviousness fell over them.

She snuck a peek at Mike as she sat in the darkened theater before her next scene. Broad shoulders hunched forward over his notebook, creating a protective, don't-ask force field. She kicked off her shoes and stretched her legs over the seats beside her, hoping he wasn't hurting too bad. For herself, she'd never gotten close enough to anyone to be dumped, but that wasn't exactly commendable either. After talking to her dad this week, she'd begun to wonder if she'd set up her own force field of protection since he'd left.

Between that heavy topic and the interaction with

Sheldon, her Zen balance had been out of whack for days. She pulled the hood of her knee-length sweater over her head and nestled down to repeat the soothing five-word mantra in her mind: release, peace, tranquility, love, and joy. By the time she returned to the stage, she had regained a measure of calm.

After they wrapped with brief notes, everyone exited quickly. Outside the building, she reconnected with her new friends to buzz about Mike's avoidance of the Tara topic.

Lindsay had donned a jacket in the cooling fall evening. "I don't think anyone else has heard yet. Maria would've cornered me to ask."

The sharp planes of Will's face were shadowed by the streetlight. "My man held it together. I'd probably have come in drunk as a skunk."

Chase's mouth pursed. "What's his option? He didn't want to look pathetic. Anybody who's watched them over time knew the relationship would explode—or implode. She's too full of herself and loves making a guy jump through hoops. Though I can't say I blame him for hanging in there, 'cause she's pretty spicy."

Lindsay swatted his arm. "You're such a tool. What do you think, Marcy? Let's hear from a rational viewpoint."

She peered around at them, contemplating. An inner warning voice told her to choose her words carefully. Besides their creativity, she'd discovered theater people were perceptive. Not that she had anything to hide—about Mike anyway. "I admire the fact he didn't vent or dis her or attempt to gain sympathy," she said. "Some people would've milked the situation."

The others' heads whipped up, and they tossed

startled glances behind her. "Catch you at the bar." Chase squeezed her hand and joined the other two in chorusing goodbyes as they scooted away toward their vehicles. The hair on her neck prickled. She turned slowly, glad the heat flooding her cheeks would be muted in the darkness.

Mike stood behind her. Seconds dragged, and as she held his gaze and fidgeted with her purse, a diversion tactic occurred. "Hey. You remember how I told you about the newspaper clippings? Well, strangest of coincidences, turns out one of our deli customers played a lead in the cast, and he might be willing to come see the show."

"That's pretty random." His jaw and shoulders relaxed. "Which actor?"

"Sheldon Whitehead. Known as Rod at the time. He played Algernon."

"Wait, isn't he the one they questioned?" He tilted his head. "He really said he'd come here? If that was me, I'd probably prefer to let that past life lie."

"Fifty years have passed, and he wasn't charged…" Her voice faltered. "Yeah, he probably said that to humor me." In fact, Sheldon had never indicated any willingness to come. She'd just been scrambling for a topic to cover the embarrassment of Mike catching them talking about him. "Forget I said anything."

"Right. Well, discovering the connection with him is still kind of cool." He glanced toward his parked pickup. "I'm going to head home. Drive safe."

"You, too." Glad to end the conversation, she scrambled toward her car and unlocked the door. Inside, she released a deep breath and wondered if Mike would go home and drink alone.

## Chapter Thirty-Three

The Sunday afternoon tech rehearsal revealed a new facet of the theater to Marcy. They didn't run the show in entirety, and instead started and stopped to focus on lighting and set changes. Costumes weren't required, and everyone took advantage of a final opportunity to relax in jeans or sweats. Without having to immerse herself in lines and character, her mind bounced between Ellen, Sheldon, and the weighty decision about the master's degree illustration program.

Lindsay sent her a concerned glance from across the garden scene table while they waited through a lighting adjustment. "You feel okay? I'm a little hungover myself from last night. What a blast."

"Headache," she mumbled. "I did have fun, though."

"I've got ibuprofen if you want it."

"Thanks. I should have taken one before I left." When her friend spun off to retrieve the pill, Marcy closed her eyes against the glare of the lights and pondered their group date at the Oktoberfest. She'd been able to bury her concerns for a few hours as she and Chase hung out with their young friends. Lindsay had arrived with a hunky man she obviously hoped to get closer to, and Will had brought his partner, Dan.

She and Chase had danced the polka and sat close together to drink dark beers and munch on bratwurst. The overall tone of their relationship remained easygoing, though he'd put extra effort into the good-night kisses at her door, backing her up against the solid wood to skim his tongue through her mouth. Tipsy kisses were the best, she mused, as your head and body overrode sober inhibitions.

But did she really want to get any closer to him with the possibility of leaving? The carefree atmosphere of hanging with friends and enjoying a fun night out had lured her into the casual intimacy. In hindsight, she regretted that she might be giving off the wrong vibes. Yes, she liked him, and she enjoyed kissing him. She didn't burn to sleep with him or be exclusive.

Lindsay returned to hand over two tablets and a cup of water. Marcy swallowed them and caught Mike observing her from his table below. She mock-toasted him with the empty cup and watched his mouth curve. Happy to lift his mood for a moment, she returned the smile. Their eyes held, and a tinge of red outlined his body.

A rush of warmth swept her limbs. *He's not with Tara,* a little voice lilted through her mind. She broke eye contact and thanked Lindsay again, too loudly. Mike's dating status didn't affect her in the least, and his aura must be linked to his desire to hone the tech. She opened the prop fan on the table and flapped it around her face. Darn, she must be having a hangover hot flash.

Her headache finally faded, and after three hours they wrapped, with the tech-focused concentration adding an extra layer of fatigue. Afterward, Mike approached to thank everyone and address the cast and crew. His face appeared a tad drawn, which could be attributed to the stress of the day or the breakup with his girlfriend, Marcy thought.

He consulted his notes and ran through a few small suggestions before flipping the pad shut. "Bryant, if you and David can stick around, I'd like to talk to you two for a few minutes. For everyone else, go home and rest. Be ready tomorrow for full costume and makeup."

Chase sat on the steps below the stage, his legs sprawled before him. He stretched and stood with an impish grin. "Heads up, everyone. Will needs help applying his makeup. He hasn't mastered a smoky eye."

His target snorted. "I heard you're looking for a volunteer to draw on some chest hairs." He addressed the others. "Makes him feel more macho. Any takers?"

Marcy joined in the laughter. Jokes and jabs had been traded freely the night before, illuminating their long, comfortable friendship. She headed toward the dressing room for her purse, more than ready for a relaxing night. Maybe watching a movie and eating popcorn with her mom.

In the darkened back hallway, Chase sauntered up. "Want to grab a bite? I'm starving." He nabbed her hand and nibbled the ends of her fingers.

She giggled at the teasing. "I'll be hangry if I don't eat soon." Not having to cook sounded appealing.

"Great. We'll start with an appetizer." He tugged her into his body.

Off-balance, she fell against him as his lips sought hers. She anchored her hands at his waist, expecting a quick peck. Yet the pressure increased, nuzzling her mouth open. Drawn back to the evening before, she responded, meeting his tongue. Until his hands slid under her sweater, inching up her ribcage and under the edge of her bra. Despite the pleasure of the touch, she wasn't

227

ready for the level of intimacy, especially backstage where anyone could walk by.

"Whoa." She pressed against his chest and shoved, harder than she'd intended. He stumbled back.

Pounding steps intruded from behind her. "What the hell. Chase, back off."

The angry pitch in Mike's voice sliced into her. She whirled toward him. The situation had progressed from touchy to ugly. Waves of red emanated around his face and body. She'd have to defuse the situation and handle the fallout later.

"Sorry. There's no problem." She flung her hands up in a surrender gesture. "I overreacted." Yet the apologetic words and action warred with the recognition she hadn't been in the wrong—and she could damn well handle the issue herself.

His dark gaze narrowed and swept past her. "I knew you two getting together would throw a wrench in the show. Patch it up."

Her nerve-endings sizzled as she glared between the two of them. Chase's lips had flattened, and a tangerine glow surrounded him. Of course, he'd be a risk taker. "Not your business, my man." He flexed his shoulders and widened his stance. "Marce, grab your purse and let's get out of here."

Next, they'd take swings at each other. She clenched her arms around her waist to keep from slapping them both silly. "I'm not your pawn to be ordered around. Either of you." She ground out the words, head swinging between them. "And yes, we'll handle our relationship." She huffed out a frustrated breath. "Though I probably should've been smart and kept my distance since I'll be moving to Virginia in January."

Chase backed off a couple of paces. "Moving?" His tone reflected the disbelief of someone who usually got the girl.

Her eyes widened. She'd committed herself to the program, in public. "I've just been offered a scholarship to attend a certification program for book illustration. For years I've put it off; now is the right time to go." Saying the words, she finally began to believe the possibility herself.

Neither man spoke. Neither one looked excited nor impressed by her decision. A mental image of two bulls pawing the ground reared up in her mind—surrounded by their colorful auras.

Her heart sank. Ignoring Mike, she addressed Chase. "Truly, I only reached this decision today. I haven't been trying to play you. We've only been having some kicks. Right?"

"Until tonight." His narrowed eyes bored into her. He turned on his heel and stalked away.

Marcy itched to run to the dressing room and stay there till she calmed. But she'd have to leave sometime, and the director had the keys to lock up. She forced herself to hold her ground and met his gaze.

He shook his head with a short, dismissive jerk.

Without another word, she fled, too.

****

Funny how she'd been starving before. Now her stomach twisted with acid, and food was the furthest thing from her mind. Marcy gunned her car away from the theater and found herself headed toward Stone Lake's small beachfront. Humiliation warred with irritation at being in the distasteful situation in the first place.

Chase had overstepped. Mike had overreacted. But apparently seeing the shove had convinced him she needed to be rescued. She could've disengaged from the embrace politely. But no, her building frustration over the angst with Sheldon and her mom had stormed out.

She craved time to calm and center herself before having any level of conversation with her mom. Time to determine if she truly was ready to commit to the program, rather than popping off the information in a heated moment. The decision hadn't been an easy one before, and the basic facts hadn't changed. Now, considering the new direction was buried under remorse. Her new friends were angry at her, and the rest of the theater run could be fraught and awkward.

She caught herself rolling through a stop sign in the Bug and forced her attention to the road. In a few minutes she'd reached the lakeshore, likely to be deserted on the cool autumn evening. She pulled into the empty lot, parked, and inclined her head on the backrest. Why did everything in her life have to blow up at once? She preferred to please people, not antagonize them.

Mom. Sheldon. Chase. All were hurt and angry.

Ellen. She couldn't even gratify a ghost.

*Mike.* The delicate balance had upended. The chill would remain between them. He'd be polite, but distant. Wary of her messing up his precious show. She rubbed the heels of her hands against her tired eyes. His impression mattered. Seeing cool disappointment in his face would gut her after they'd reached such a simpatico state.

The memory blazed of his fingers tracing the skin on her back at the costume shop. Of her clutching his muscled torso after the "bat" attack. Of the near kiss in the stairwell.

What kind of woman had she become, to go from dating one guy to semi-lusting for another? Better to let both connections drift. The fewer ties she had to sever, the better. The fewer hurt feelings on all sides if she did decide to leave.

Defying the cool wind gusting across the beach, Marcy opened her door and tromped toward the sand to clear her head. She had a huge stake in the show, too. Not only in the costumes, but in her acting debut. No way would she risk humiliation by messing everything up when she'd finally gained the confidence to believe in herself.

If she pursued the program, the same level of passion would have to be restored toward her artwork. She'd shelved her creativity for too long and would have to dig deep to gain a new momentum. The breeze whipped hair across her face, and she yanked up her hood and stuffed the curls inside as she trudged over the packed sand. The lake rippled before her, a chill blue-gray in the waning light.

Did fear of failure contribute to her refusal to leave? Did she doubt her creative ability?

An immediate conviction rolled through her. No, her art only lay dormant, not extinguished. After the show closed, she could put the drama of the theater behind and pour all her extra time into drawing and painting.

A long, spindly branch had blown off one of the trees rimming the perimeter of the beach. She stepped around it to reach the end of the narrow strip of sand where a grouping of cattails waved. Her hands stung from the wind, and she rubbed her palms together and jammed them into her pockets, increasing the pace as she headed back toward the car. Another concern taunted, having briefly submerged under the others. She couldn't leave the mystery unresolved for Ellen.

She hoped visiting Sheldon's home hadn't ruined the opportunity to gather his input—or their fond relationship—but why would it? If he didn't have anything to hide, a fifty-year-old trauma surely would have dimmed. A shiver ran through her, not just from the cold. She didn't want to believe the kind, gracious old man could've played a part in the accident, but Tess and Trey's visions had shown heightened conflicts and emotions within the cast.

Oh yes, she could relate. She got into her car and cranked the heater to high, not ready to return home with so many unanswered questions swirling around her brain.

Chapter Thirty-Four

Mike always looked forward to the first true dress rehearsal before a show opened, when weeks of hard work transformed toward a creative gem. But after Sunday's backstage blowup, he cringed. Damn Chase for rutting after Marcy.

Damn himself for caring too much. She'd launched the huge bombshell of moving away, which should've made it easier to detach his emotions. But no, he'd paced through his house hours later, fuming, cursing, unable to enjoy the Bears game on TV.

When had she become…important…to him? He stood in front of the stage and eyed the set, smelling the fumes from the last wall they'd painted over the weekend. During the past weeks he'd pounded nails along with the others to create the three distinct Victorian settings of Algernon's apartment, a manor house garden, and the formal drawing room. Marcy had painted some of the best backdrops he'd ever seen, with the floral landscape and dramatic faux wallpaper inside. He couldn't admire the artistry tonight. His mind kept flashing between his own dramatic life scenes.

Sparring with a tall redhead who declared she'd come to take on costuming for the first time—with a demanding period show. Clutching her body, molded to his by fear of the "bat." Fingering the pale, warm skin of her back, bared in the tight gown. If Bryant hadn't interrupted the almost-kiss on the stairs after discovering David...where would they be?

She probably would've tossed him down the steps. He stomped back to the seat where he'd left his notepad, telling himself to focus on the show, which deserved his full attention. He'd groomed a fine cast. If only his two feuding leads could patch up enough not to blow the chemistry they'd developed. He might've been a little jealous of the growing camaraderie before, but now he hoped they'd recapture it. They could both stay shitty with him; the show needed them to sizzle together.

He couldn't force the issue and didn't plan to mention it. Better to allow them to get past the incident without his intervention. He scrubbed a hand over his face. Jumping in yesterday had made the situation worse. In hindsight, he should've turned around and let her handle it. At any sign of distress, he could've leapt in to assist, instead of wedging himself in the middle. Maybe Tara had been right in calling out his hero complex.

The green room door opened, and a wave of apprehension swamped him. His mood improved at seeing Bryant and David. He'd moved straight from the backstage dust-up last night to broach his idea with them. At least somebody in this world was happy with him. "Ready for the real thing tonight?"

David's face shone, yet he attempted to appear cool. "No sweat. Our show is tight."

*Our show.* Mike's lip curved at the casual ownership. The teen felt included, part of a team, and hopefully he'd continue to grow and mature. Life wouldn't always be rosy, but if the application was approved for him to foster, he'd do his best to provide support, guidance, and connection. Thankfully, after he'd pleaded his case, the theater board had declined to take any action in regard to the trespassing issue.

When they'd spoken the night before, and the teen expressed his approval, Bryant had informed them the process would take time. Which it should. A young life was at stake.

Mike clapped a hand on the thin shoulder. "You're my best worker bee. You've really taken a shine to the lights." He couldn't help grinning at the bad pun.

The boy's face wrinkled, but he shot back a retort. "My shop teacher always says I'm the bright one in her class."

Out of the corner of his eye, Mike caught Marcy darting up the aisle. *Don't turn. Give her space.* He made another dumb comment as she tossed the group a quick hello and sped past them, straight up the steps to cross backstage. He itched to talk to her, to ask if she was okay. To apologize for his behavior.

He didn't have the same desire to clear the air with Chase. In fact, he'd prefer to kick his ass. He realized Bryant was staring, waiting for an answer to some unheard question. "Sorry," he bit out.

"No biggie. I was wondering if you plan a pickup rehearsal mid-week? I'll need to give the juvenile center our schedule." He'd been given permission to pick him up and chauffeur him to and from rehearsals and shows.

"Yes, on Thursday. We won't wear costumes or need all the lighting." He watched the youngster's face fall. "Or at least we don't usually," he amended. "This time, I'd prefer we practice the light cues, too. What do you think? Are you happy with the new scene transition?" He addressed the youth directly, as if he was the one to suggest and implement the subtle shading.

"I think the fade lends atmosphere. Designing a whole show would be rad. Maybe I'll do that one day."

"Believe me, expert light techs are in demand. After the show closes, you could come in and experiment—carefully and supervised—and master the board."

The boy no longer tried to hide his pleasure. "Sweet." He stuck out his palm and executed a fancy handshake.

Bryant beamed his appreciation, and they wrapped the conversation and left. Mike sank into his seat, recognizing coming to the theater provided a welcome break from the juvenile center and a sense of normalcy. Theater folks usually weren't known for being "normal" though. His spirits lifted. At least some of his cast and crew were happy and raring to tackle the show.

Other members flowed into the theater, and he greeted them and exchanged small talk. Maria handed over a loaf of homemade pumpkin bread, and he immediately broke off a spicy chunk as he settled at his table.

Chase hadn't shown his face as the start time neared. He suspected he'd go directly backstage and avoid him as much as possible. He'd be glad to oblige.

\*\*\*\*

Marcy hovered in the dressing room, helping the other women with costumes, hair, and makeup as she didn't enter till the second act. She'd gotten help with the buttons of her gown but had plenty of time to wrangle her hair into an updo. The others finished and left her to face the makeup mirror alone. She sat on a folding chair, spread her skirt to avoid wrinkles, and lifted the mascara wand to darken her lashes. Her hand trembled, and she paused. The nerves didn't stem from performing—she knew they'd build to a crescendo peak at Friday's opening night. Today, she dreaded dealing with the two men she couldn't avoid. After much tossing and worrying in her bed, this morning she'd texted Chase.

*—Forgive me?—*

He'd waited hours to respond. Not a good sign. The return message hadn't reassured her.

*—No sweat. We'll talk.—*

He hadn't popped his head in to find her, but he and Bryant did open the first scene. Probably the best option was for them to connect first onstage. They could fall into the characters' attraction and hopefully skim past the real-life awkwardness. She'd probably barely dented his ego. Her hand stilled, and she applied a layer of black mascara, thicker than she'd normally use.

The night before she'd tackled another upheaval to engage in a serious sit-down with her mom. Despite the wishy-washy declaration that she'd consider finishing the school application, her mom jumped to the positive. "You're not humoring me? You do want to go?"

"You know I've always intended to. Timing has been the sticky issue. Just please, don't push." Marcy's eyes had filled with tears. "You're the bravest person in my world. I have to know I can leave, and you'll be able to navigate." With the truce, they'd tried to discuss logistics, which had exhausted and frustrated them both.

She sighed and moved to apply blusher, a pink-bronze tone under her cheekbones. Makeup had to be overdone under the bright lights. She twisted to examine her face and stowed the items in her Hello Kitty case, haunted by thoughts of the hanging relationships with Sheldon, Ellen, and Mike.

From now on, the older man could steer the

direction of their friendship, she decided. If he didn't mention the issue, she wouldn't either. She'd always burn to hear the juicy details, but she could keep her snoopy self in-check. With Justine's assistance, she hoped to help Ellen, if the spirit could manifest in a different form. Not sure of the possibilities, over the past week she'd avoided going upstairs. She personally didn't have anything more to offer; why frustrate them both?

Speaking of frustration, Mike probably hadn't gotten past his peeve at her and Chase for jeopardizing the show. She wasn't sure how to approach him and would just practice good old avoidance. Her feelings were too convoluted at this point. Her shoulders drooped, and she gathered the heavy skirt and petticoat to maneuver out of the chair. The door popped open, startling her into a straight posture.

Hannah, the stage manager, poked her head in and tugged on her ear, lined with a row of studs. "Mike wants everyone out front. You look fab, darling."

"Thanks, doll. Also, for keeping us on track. Especially me." Though only a senior in high school, the girl stayed ahead of every detail of the backstage work. She waved an airy hand and backed out of the doorway.

Marcy hoisted the skirt to her knees and rustled out of the chair to navigate the narrow, wooden steps. Onstage, Lindsay skipped up in her rose-colored taffeta day-dress with the high neckline, appropriate for visiting society friends. In contrast, her own country garden gown featured a simpler style and fabric, plus a rounded neck. She'd considered adding a cotton handkerchief over her cleavage, but when she'd texted photos, Justine had assured her the fashion choice complemented Cecily's independent nature. The look wasn't tacky, just more than her comfort level. She tugged at the bodice and caught Chase watching her. He darted his eyes away.

Her stomach rolled with a queasy sensation at the blatant distancing. Beside her, Lindsay whispered words she couldn't make out. "What?" she asked.

Her friend leaned close, wafting a floral perfume. "Mike's kind of in a mood. Not bad, but testy."

*Gee, wonder why?* "I'm sure he is. Fill you in later," she muttered. She avoided looking at him, but her skin prickled as if his eyes were glued on her.

"All right, people, let's get started." His voice boomed across the room, and she jumped and tuned in. "When you're not on tonight, please stay backstage or in the green room and get used to lowering your voices if you have to talk."

She trained her eyes on the canvases she'd painted, afraid to meet his gaze. After the brief comments, she returned to the dressing room. If she didn't detach herself from all the crazy in her life, she might lose focus onstage. In the small, cluttered sanctuary she closed her eyes for a few minutes of meditation, murmuring confidence-building phrases aloud.

"You've got this. You *are* Cecily. You've worked hard and memorized every line."

In a more Zen mood, she ran her opening lines in her head as she worked on her hair, wielding a brush and lots of bobby pins. When she finished and peeked out the door, the first act neared the end. She gathered the skirt and tiptoed through the dark to wait for the scene change. They'd enter in the dark, and she reminded herself not to squint when the lights rose on the set.

Maria appeared at her side and squeezed her arm in encouragement. She'd grown to really enjoy her company, especially the insights on serving as a Spanish medical interpreter at the local hospital. They'd giggled at the irony of her serving as a German tutor in the play. When the lights dimmed, they waited for the stage crew to complete set changes before finding their way to the table.

They sat, and the lights snapped up. As their dialogue progressed, Marcy eased into the familiarity and ignored all the taunting outside influences. Despite her initial fears, she loved immersing herself in a character. Acting required a different type of creativity than illustration, yet both thrived in collaboration with fellow artists.

After five pages, Chase arrived with his usual swagger. Her fingers tightened around the lace fan she'd been using. To her relief, he greeted her with the usual cheerful manner. She relaxed into the scene, discussing Algernon's "wickedness" and building the level of absurdity and flirtation. When they reached the curly hair scene, he kissed her hand instead of her cheek. They'd reached a cheek peck compromise with Mike, but he'd added further separation.

They progressed to becoming an engaged couple, followed by an immediate breakup. Other characters joined them, and at the end, she and Lindsay departed in a snit, leaving Chase and Will behind. Outside the door, her friend linked arms and tugged her away, urging, "You left me hanging in suspense earlier. Dish, girl."

They had the intermission to switch costumes. Marcy followed her to the dressing room and closed the door tight. "Chase surprised me backstage by sticking his hands up my shirt. As I was pushing him away, Mike walked up and went off on both of us."

Lindsay's mouth flew open. "WTF."

"Definitely. He overreacted. Well, I guess we all did." She spilled the bare details as Lindsay sank onto the step to listen, alternately wincing and rolling her eyes.

"You're shitting me?" she finally interjected. "I'm going to have to whack them both upside the head. *Men.* Or should I say, boys."

"Yeah, they're both annoying. Shook me up for sure. Oh, and I'd rather not say anything about my leaving to the rest of the cast yet. I'm still wrapping my head around the details." She'd decided not to backtrack publicly on the decision, which could only confuse matters further.

"What an awesome opportunity." Lindsay threw her arms around her for a quick hug. "I wish you all the luck."

"Thanks. I'm hoping the program will jumpstart me into a great, fulfilling career." Marcy caught sight of the clock. "We'd better get changed. I'll undo you." Her fingers flew over the traveling gown's buttons and slick fabric before she presented her own backside.

A gust of breath tickled over her skin as Lindsay revived the conversation. "Have you talked to the guys since the blowup?"

"Nope. I'm kind of afraid to." She shrugged out of the gown as her friend did the same. "Chase wouldn't look at me before we started, but I couldn't tell a difference in our scene. Except he moved from pecking my cheek to a hand."

"He's too professional to carry the baggage onstage. Maybe he decided to finally follow the director's preference for the scene." Lindsay offered her back to be rebuttoned, now wearing the simple yellow cotton gown for the country manor morning room. "How's the vibe with our man Mike?"

"I've avoided him." She finished and turned for her own rebuttoning process of the ice-blue gown. "I suppose I won't be able to through the entire run of the show." The attempt at humor fell flat.

"Don't let him rattle you. He's more bark than bite. I bet he's ticked at Chase rather than you." She grasped her by the shoulders and tilted her head in an appraising glance. "Stay focused on the show. You're downright gorgeous and doing an awesome job."

"Thanks. You, too. The color's wicked hot against your skin. As for the clash the other night, the whole situation feels super weird." Marcy peered in the mirror to smooth her upswept curls. "Like being caught by the principal in the high school maintenance closet."

She giggled. "You know from experience?"

A knock sounded on the door, breaking their laughter. "Five minutes."

Grateful for the vent session, Marcy enjoyed the last act, which reunited the young lovers. The cast filtered out at the end for notes, sharing appreciative comments on each other's performances.

Mike approached with his notebook in hand. "Nicely done, everyone. Not much to tweak tonight."

She sat on the settee next to Lindsay, praying he wouldn't call her name. Though she knew he wouldn't pick on her, she didn't want to hear a strain in his voice or have the rest of the group pick up on any tension. While Chase might have confided in Will, she doubted he'd told anyone else—and she sure didn't plan to spread the gossip.

The director offered brief instructions and praise to certain actors and crew members but didn't mention her. She crossed her arms over her chest, annoyed by her flip-flopping emotions. Being excluded stung.

The comments completed, he shut his notebook. His gaze skimmed, not stopping on her, but she registered the brief contact and burrowed farther into the couch. "Any questions or additions?" He paused, hearing none. "Thursday we'll practice after-show bows before we start. A few board members will attend to get you used to holding for laughter."

Thursday, the night before their first live audience. She shivered, surprised at the whisper of nerves through her system.

"One more thing." He held up a finger. "You probably all know I'm not with Tara anymore. You don't have to tiptoe around the issue. Don't expect me to discuss it, either."

She chewed the inside of her lip and shaded her eyes against the bright lights to finally examine his shadowed face. He didn't appear tense or disturbed. More matter of fact. Yet he could be hiding his true feelings. She recalled Chase's words of not wanting to look "pathetic." No one else dared to comment.

"Enough said." He stepped away into the darkness.

Mulling his delivery of the bombshell, she passed through the garden doorway. A hand grasped her arm. She gasped and nearly leaped out of her shoes.

Chase stood in the darkness. "Can we talk?"

She rolled her lips together and looked around them. They were alone. "Of course."

He took her arm to propel her toward the corner. Her pulse continued to hammer, and when his arms enfolded her, she jolted, unsure of the intent.

At her involuntary jerk, he released her and stepped away. His face appeared contrite in the shadows, with the only light spilling over the onstage flats. "I'm sorry for being a jerk last night," he muttered. "I aimed to be playful, not an ass. Guess we weren't there yet." He seemed to read her hesitation and settled a finger on her lips. "And we probably won't be with you moving away. Am I right?" He withdrew the hand and cocked his head.

What a relief. She should've thought through possible responses; now she'd have to wing it. "I really am having fun with you," she ventured, watching his expression. "I do think we should keep it...friendly, because of the circumstances."

His face didn't change. "Got it. We could go out as friends. Maybe with benefits." He grinned to show he was kidding. *Or probably not.*

"Ah, no." She chuckled and tucked her head into the crook of his neck, appreciating his understanding. They'd be fine. Maybe not close friends, but happy companions.

Footsteps sounded behind them, and she peeked around. Mike strode across the darkened area, stopping to flip on the lights. The large open area flooded with illumination. Her blood chilled as his face registered surprise and hardened, brows flattening into a stormy line. Without a word, he disappeared through the hallway door.

Chapter Thirty-Five

Tuesday morning Marcy reset tables during the lull between the deli's breakfast and lunch traffic. The shift had been busy enough to keep her mind occupied, so she didn't have to dwell on the recent theater encounters.

Well, one encounter in particular. She and Chase were fine. As far as Mike was concerned—they needed to talk, because she couldn't bear the dismissive look on his face. She'd have thought he'd be happy the two of them had made nice.

The front door opened behind her. With dirty dishes balanced on her arm, she said, "Good morning. Please have a seat, and we'll be right with you." She turned, and her pulse thumped a rapid rhythm.

Sheldon stood in the doorway. He locked eyes for a moment before swiveling his toward the window. "I'll sit over here."

She dumped the dishes in the kitchen, motioning to Sherri to stay seated with her sandwich. "Sheldon's here. I've got him."

As she washed and dried her hands, she pondered her approach. Apologize? Ignore her gaffe and say nothing? Demand answers? She tamped down her apprehension and strode out with the coffee pot and a mock-cheerful smile. Years of easy restaurant patter smoothed her through the opening. She tilted the pot toward his empty cup. "Are you set on an old favorite or determined to be adventurous today?"

His face remained solemn. "I'm thinking a cheese omelet with a side of crow."

She sputtered a laugh and halted to keep from sloshing coffee over the rim. "You have a taste for some today?" She resumed filling the mug, leaving a margin for creamer.

"I don't imagine I'll enjoy the meal, but I earned the privilege by being rude to you the other day. Can you sit?" He patted the chair next to him with a veined hand.

The handful of remaining customers were engaged in deep conversation. She sank down and poured herself a mug, hoping he didn't notice the tremble in her movements. He sipped and stared out the window. She did the same, hoping for a few uninterrupted moments alone. Sherri veered past, saying a cheery hello, but the looks on their faces must have cued her to give them space.

He cleared his throat and paused, seeming to share her struggle for words. "In regard to the memorial. I'm sorry I overreacted." He edged his empty sugar packet away with a finger. "The idea's quite kind, and Ellen should be memorialized."

"I'm glad you agree." A neutral, friendly comment. She didn't wish to offend him further, but she had to push to achieve a resolution. "Will you be able to join us?"

He shook his head with slow deliberation. "I don't believe she'd want me there."

The words popped out before she could weigh them. "Actually, I'm sure she would."

His face creased, and he leaned away to regard her. "Would you care to elaborate? You came off a tad too invested the other day. Marcy, is there something else you plan to tell me?"

He'd probably believe she was crazy. Yet he needed to hear the truth. She laid a hand over his, registering the sharp edges of his knuckles, keeping her eyes on his. "Please keep an open mind for an off-the-wall story."

"Go on."

She'd deliver the words in snippets to gauge his acceptance. "You remember how I said I first went to the theater to costume this show, before being drafted onstage?" Her throat dried, but she persevered while her courage lasted. "Every time I've gone into the upper loft, I've seen a blazing glow of light."

His white brows drew together again. "All right."

Now for the first big leap of faith. "I should preface by saying I have an...ability. To see auras of color around people when their emotions run high."

"You see auras." The word sounded as grudging as he looked. He disengaged his hand and straightened in the chair.

Alarmed at the distancing, she plunged ahead. "The glow isn't from any connected light source. I've checked every possibility. At times, the intensity changes, reminding me of a beacon. That's how we found your and Ellen's old scripts."

He visibly jolted. His orange aura emerged and glimmered. "You have my script?"

"Yes. I also have permission from my boss at Divine Vintage to share something else incredible." She lowered her voice and sped up the pace, hoping he wouldn't get up and walk out. "Tess has an especially acute ability, to link visions to vintage clothing." She stopped to determine how he'd react.

*Stone-faced and silent, but he hadn't run.* "I had her

join me in the loft on three separate occasions. We've seen images of Ellen with Nan, Lorna, and you."

His jaw clenched. A deeper aura color pulsed around him. "Are you playing with me? If this is some kind of sick joke—"

"No. I swear it." She plastered a hand over her heart. The trembling had returned, rippling through her body. "If you need to hear this from other people who are aware of what we can do, I can arrange that. But in the meantime, as proof, here are a few insights you may recall."

"I think I should go—"

"The director wasn't happy with the onstage love connection between you and Ellen, so she made you rehearse alone. Ellen baked you cookies, and you talked about *The King and I*."

His skin paled, and he flinched away. "I don't remember all the fine details, but we were asked to rehearse together for that reason. How could you know that?"

"Another time, Nan was upset and ran from you." She mustered every ounce of bravery to continue. "You told Lorna she was getting jealous, and you had to go do… something…on a Saturday."

His eyes fluttered closed; the aura rolled and darkened. The deli's front door swung open, and two chatting women entered. Marcy spun in her chair to look for Sherri.

Sheldon stood, his eyes filmed with moisture. "I need time to take this in."

"Of course." She jumped up to join him. Her conscience twisted at the distress she read on his face. "Could we talk more? Either today or soon?" Guilt kicked at her for again dredging up painful memories he'd probably buried decades ago. Yet how deep did his own guilt go?

"I'm not sure that's wise, but I'll consider attending the opening night of your play." He walked with a slow gait to the door, digging a handkerchief out of his pants pocket. He wiped his eyes as she forced her feet to move toward the new visitors.

When the door banged shut, the impact slammed into her, physically and mentally.

**** 

She couldn't wait to share the story with Tess. The retelling further ripped her shredded composure. "Am I horrible for talking to him?" she asked, thankful they were in the office where no one else could wonder about her reddened eyes. She sniffed and pulled a tissue from a nearby box. She'd held in the threat of tears through the rest of her deli shift, murmuring a vague excuse to her co-workers on why Sheldon had left without ordering.

"No, hon. You had to." Her friend stood in the doorway, ready to offer assistance to the browsing customers. "He can't be too upset. He said he'd try to attend the memorial." She turned back inside to whisper. "Something else is nagging at me. After our visions and two conversations with him, we still don't know whether he played a part in what happened."

"Much as I hate to, I've thought the same thing. In my stress at the time, I didn't ask why he said, 'I don't believe she'd want me there.' But why would he say that?"

A voice floated across the room to them as one of the customers asked a question. Tess lifted her voice to respond. "Yes, those are marvelous 1950s cocktail dresses. They'd make an elegant statement for a special occasion."

Marcy stood and composed herself—even though their previous conversation had chilled her. "Go and help them. I'm okay. I'll finish the packaging for the next post office run."

"Don't beat yourself up. Until we get a clearer picture, from the visions or Justine's encounter, we have to keep digging." Tess' face softened. "Ellen hasn't gone away, indicating we haven't discovered all the depths to the story." She held her eyes for a moment before retreating to the shop floor and closing the floor-length drape. Her voice lilted with enthusiasm as she engaged the women in a conversation to pair accessories with their dresses.

Cocooned back in the storeroom, Marcy busied herself rolling garments in tissue paper. Despite her shiver at recognizing that Sheldon wasn't "in the clear," she found she couldn't allow herself to assume the worst. Her angst over the situation had begun to settle when her phone rang on the table, startling her. She didn't feel up to talking to anyone but couldn't resist checking the details.

*The Herald-Argus* popped across the screen. Renewed tension frittered through her body, and she tapped the icon and identified herself.

"Hello again. This is Glenda from the newspaper," the twangy voice said. "You won't believe who I ran into today at Kroger."

She crushed a piece of tissue paper in her free hand and waited. "Um, who?"

"Nanette Goins. Well, Peterson now. I nearly

dropped a gallon of milk on my foot when I saw her." Her tone sounded triumphant, as if she'd landed a scoop. "She'd moved away and has only been back a couple of years. Isn't that something, after we'd just discussed her and the fiftieth anniversary for the show?"

"Sure is." Too shocked at the revelation, Marcy couldn't match Glenda's enthusiasm. She started to smooth the crumpled paper but found it too smushed to salvage.

"I told her how you all are planning a little memorial to Ellen on opening night, and I knew you'd love to have her attend."

Marcy stiffened. "How'd she react?"

"Surprised." Glenda paused. "And a little sad. Ellen was her best friend after all."

The question had come off callous. "I hope the news didn't upset her too much. The poor thing."

"Five decades is a long time. Emotions and memories dim, my dear. Yet we can't downplay the tragedy of the situation." Glenda sounded matter of fact. "Oh, I also asked if I could have her number so you could share more information. Ease her mind that she won't have to speak or anything."

The hair rose on Marcy's arms. "I'd be glad to call." Though at the moment she couldn't bear the thought of hurting—or irritating—another person.

"Do you have paper and a pen?" At the assurance, the woman rattled off the digits. "My goodness, such an interesting story," she continued. "I'll plan to attend opening night to take some photos and notes for a nice little feature."

"That would be great. Thanks so much."

Marcy clicked off, then sat staring at the piece of

tissue paper with the scrawled number. Now she'd have to call Nan. But first she'd have to approach Mike about the possibility of more unexpected visitors and hoopla.

One more reason for him to stay upset with her.

Chapter Thirty-Six

Not wanting to stumble around or blurt too many details, Marcy planned her approach to Mike while she dashed the completed packages to the post office. Later during dinner, she filled her mom in on Sheldon's visit, concluding, "I wonder if he's aware Nan has returned to the area?" She twirled fettucine on her fork as a new realization slammed her. "We have no clue how things resolved between them. What if they're upset and don't want to go anywhere near each other? The situation could turn even nastier and more painful."

Pat dished up more green beans, balancing the spoon in her twisted fingers to dribble them onto her plate. "Don't jump to any conclusions. You'll find out how Nan feels when you call her and go from there."

"I don't want to call her." She dangled the fork, pasta unspooling into an untidy pile. "I already wish I hadn't approached Sheldon. Here's another option: avoid the costume loft till the show's done or keep my back to the corner if I have to go up. Ellen will have to understand I can't help her." She pushed her plate aside, no longer hungry.

"That's not what you want to do. Yes, Sheldon's unsettled, but he'll get past it. Your dad says…" Her mom's voice trailed off, and she averted her eyes.

"Dad? I didn't think you two communicated unless some big issue forced the interaction." Marcy knew better after talking to him, but she crossed her arms and pinned her with the question. What would she reveal?

Her mom didn't look up; a flush of color stained her cheeks. "We've been talking more over the past months, on your future and my condition. Your play and when he can come to see it. His upcoming painting exhibit. Your acceptance into the program. Lots of stuff."

Was she *blushing*? Marcy's eyes widened. "I love to hear you're getting along better, but I'm not crazy about being the pressing topic of your conversations." At least they weren't arguing again.

Her mother snickered, and her body seemed to relax. "Don't worry, sweetie. Our world doesn't only revolve around you."

"I'm glad. My track record for pleasing people hasn't been stellar lately." She tried to eat a few more bites but soon rose to clear her plate. The upcoming conversation with the director had filled her stomach with new dread.

\*\*\*\*

"Two of the leads from fifty years ago are in town, and they're possibly willing to come on opening night." Marcy feigned enthusiasm in her voice and face, though she would've preferred to slink past Mike and hide in the dressing room. "Isn't that super exciting? We can acknowledge them being here." She'd leaped into the explanation to ward off any mention of her hugging Chase. If they never discussed the topic, they could pretend everything was fine. Or she could anyway.

He positioned his hands on his hips and emitted a ripple of red aura. "Wait. What? We open in three nights. Rather short notice to pull off an event."

Of course, he wouldn't make this easy for her. "Not

an event. I'm not suggesting anything big," she stammered, shifting from foot to foot. "Maybe we seat them up front and you recognize them in the director's welcome speech. Glenda wants to come from the paper and take a photo afterward and write up a feature, which gives us added publicity. I could also give them a VIP tour before or after the show. Or you could."

If she got the two former lovers together in the loft, would Ellen be pleased or upset? How would she know the difference?

His face crinkled as if she'd eaten too much garlic for dinner. Miffed at having to convince him, she stood her ground. He might be jerking her around because he was pissed from the night before. Well too darn bad.

Before leaving for the theater, her mom had nudged her to acknowledge she wasn't ready to let go of the mystery. Strong women didn't bail when they stumbled over obstacles. They got up and ran faster. "When you leave the area, you might never do another show here," she'd said, attempting to be helpful.

Never acting, costuming, or hanging out with her new friends again—including Mike—had made her wince.

"Earth to Marcy."

"Huh?" She blinked as the director waved a hand in front of her face.

His features had softened, along with the aura. "I said I'm okay with what you suggested. Sometimes, I admit I can be rigid and too grounded in the details." He chuckled. "I bet you're surprised to hear me being all touchy-feely, but the sentiment and the plan are solid."

She firmed her lips to keep her mouth from dropping open in amazement as he continued, "You can tell them to come early to meet us and settle in. Tomorrow I'll touch base with the board. One of the members has been putting together a tabletop display with a few things from the show, including Ellen and Rod's scripts."

"Sheldon."

"What?"

"He's gone by his real name for decades. Rod was a nickname he adopted for coolness."

"I get that. Sheldon isn't exactly a studly name." He rubbed his chin, dotted with black stubble. Apparently, he hadn't shaved. Which was super studly in her book.

She shook herself internally and focused her eyes on the carpet. "The name suits him now," she said. "He's a really sweet gentleman."

"I'll enjoy meeting him." He clapped his hands together, indicating a close to the conversation. "Okay. Why don't you jot a few notes for me since you did the newspaper research. I also could include a line on where they've both been, and about their families. I don't know yet. You caught me off guard."

She tried not to stare at the stubble on his face. "I am sorry to dump on you without warning. Everything tumbled into my lap when Glenda told me she'd seen Nan. I'll try to call her tomorrow and report back to you on her intentions."

Hopefully, the woman wouldn't hang up.

****

Through the morning hours at the deli, Marcy worked up her courage to make the call. For privacy, she decided to phone from her car. Tess wouldn't mind her doing it at the shop, but she'd been flaky enough lately. They'd become good friends over the past three years, but she was an employee who should present a professional persona.

She'd slipped in that capacity while handling all the show biz-related drama, pouring out her worries and craving constant support. Tess only laughed in her good-natured way and said she enjoyed living on the edge vicariously. Marriage, the baby, the move, and the business kept her settled and adulting instead of "flirting with boys and solving mysteries."

Marcy tucked into the Bug and stretched her legs under the dash. People sometimes marveled at why someone as tall as her would drive such a tiny car. She told them the VW had been her dad's first vehicle, but she didn't share the underlying reason she refused to part with it. He didn't live with them anymore, but when she drove, she imagined her equally tall father sitting in the same seat, shifting the manual transmission, peering up into the rearview mirror. Nostalgia usually cheered her. Today, she was too preoccupied by the present challenges.

She groaned, realizing she'd procrastinated away another five minutes, and finally tapped the number in her phone. Her eyes remained glued to the screen as the first ring spiked her blood pressure. She gritted her teeth at the second ring, debating whether to leave a message. No, probably best to try again later.

"Hello."

She jerked at hearing the unexpected voice. "H-hi. I'm Marcy Alexander. Glenda from the paper gave me your contact info—"

"Yes. I've been expecting your call." The woman sounded smooth and polished. If she'd ever had a Midwest drawl, she'd overcome it.

Marcy attempted to mirror her composure. "We

were very pleased to hear you're in town. The cast would love to be able to recognize you during opening night remarks on Friday, if you're free. Being exactly fifty years and all." She bit her tongue before she babbled too much.

Silence hung. She waited, clenching and loosening her fingers.

"I've mulled over the situation." The voice had slowed and quieted. "I'm not sure we should commemorate such a tragic anniversary. People may interpret the gesture as callous. Or manipulative."

Yeow. No minced words. "True." She drew out the word, buying time to present a compelling explanation. "But I—we—see the opportunity to memorialize Ellen. Not ignore or gloss past the fact that five decades ago she did the same show. And sadly, suffered a tragic accident." *Did the statement sound uncaring?* She stumbled on. "You all suffered and grieved. Yet you persevered and put on the play. Your efforts should be applauded." *Yes, good, keep building on the praise…* "Patrons over the years probably noticed the plaque in the theater entry, and they'd think us remiss for not making any mention." The piece had returned there after Lindsay's discovery in the loft.

"My parents purchased the plaque." Nan said the words without inflection.

"What a kind gesture to commemorate your friend." *Friend.* According to their visions, she'd been jealous at catching her flirting with her lover.

"They also made a donation to the theater in her name." She again uttered the words without evident emotion. "But I haven't stepped foot in the theater since our show closed." Nan stopped and cleared her throat, pausing for a few seconds. "When I look back, I can't fathom how I got through the performances. Pure numb shock, I suppose. Afterward, my parents reacted to how broken up I was. I wasn't getting better. They decided to move us out of the area."

A quiver of emotion drifted over the admission. Fifty years later she'd buried the bulk of her grief, but she had of course been devastated. Marcy pursed her lips, knowing if she'd been entangled in a similar situation, the fallout would've nearly taken her down. Yet similar to Sheldon, Nan seemed to have overridden the impact. Or at least made peace with it.

*Until she came along and dredged up the details.* She wasn't sure how to respond to the woman's blunt confession.

"Are you inviting anyone else?" Nan asked.

"We aren't aware how to find everyone, and don't have the time to, really." She took a deep breath, forced to plunge into another touchy subject. "But in a strange coincidence, I know Sheldon—Rod—through my work. He may be attending."

"Rod." The name whispered through the air and hung between them.

The sense of loss and longing in the word pierced straight through her. Marcy couldn't probe further. Her energy had drained in the stuffy car, in dredging up the sad old story. She needed the few minutes before her Divine Vintage shift to pull herself back together.

She could only imagine how the older woman must feel. Guilt again gnawed at her conscience. "I'm very sorry to drop the idea on you out of the blue, or to raise painful memories. But Glenda called to say she talked to you, and I wanted to follow up. I understand how you might feel blindsided, or not want to go back after all these years."

"No. I believe I'll try to come." Nan's voice had regained the initial solemn strength. "I believe your calling is a sign. I should put these ghosts behind me forever."

Marcy's hand clenched around the phone. Suspicion shouldn't only fall on Sheldon. Nan had been a huge player in the drama.

Chapter Thirty-Seven

Opening night had arrived, and Marcy sat in front of the dressing room mirror trying to immerse herself in a Zen space. Multiple anxieties had plagued her over the past two days, but she was determined to submerge them during the show. Their final tech the evening before had gone well despite minor glitches, and the board members who attended had laughed often. She closed her eyes to meditate and registered the wispy curls escaping from the updo to caress her cheeks. The smooth daisy-patterned cotton slid beneath her fingers.

*Would Sheldon and Nan really attend tonight? How—or would—they interact?*

She batted away the thought, focusing on the weight of the skirt and petticoat as an anchor to transport her toward a Victorian-era mindset. She concentrated on her opening lines, immersing her consciousness into the rhythm of Oscar Wilde's dialogue.

A glance at the wall clock confirmed twenty minutes till curtain. The director planned to give a go-team pep talk in the green room. She hiked up the skirt to stand but stayed rooted at the table, reminded of the peek she'd caught of him earlier. Mike still hadn't shaved. Was it a pre-opening ritual?

Would the dark stubble at his jaw feel soft or wiry? She caught her wide eyes in the mirror, enhanced by extra layers of stage makeup. Nope, she absolutely could not. Go. There.

She wrestled out of the chair and up the steps. Along the darkened backstage corridor, she hefted the dress to her knees to avoid wires, ropes, furniture, and other threatening obstacles. At the green room doorway, she slipped inside to admire her new friends in the period garments she'd pulled together. They'd have to snap more photos to capture the memory of her first solo costuming effort. Her peers had complimented the style statement when they'd taken the full cast and crew photo the night before. Yet the director had not.

Fine. She'd never been a praise seeker and didn't need his affirmation. Justine and Tess were the experts she aimed to impress. She scanned the room. Mike wasn't among them yet.

Lindsay pranced up and grasped her arm. "We'll have a great show tonight, no doubt. I can't wait to celebrate afterward." She improvised a series of funky dance moves, contrasting against the elegant dress and Gibson Girl hairstyle.

Chase walked up and joined in the dance. He twirled her out into the room, ballooning the full skirt. "Watch the hair." She laughed and ducked back under his arm. "If the 'do falls, we won't be able to replicate it easily."

He released her, caught Marcy's eyes, and held them. "You ready for the spotlight?" His voice tipped soft and supportive.

The question sent energy pulsing from her toes to her fingertips. "We have to be, right? No running away now."

He laid his hands on her shoulders and caressed the bared skin with his fingertips. "You're going to rock the stage, especially in our scenes."

She relaxed into the touch, happy they'd gotten past any awkwardness. "I feel pretty confident. You all have been so supportive and welcoming to a newbie."

He pulled her in for a hug. She embraced him back but remained cautious of her hair and makeup.

The door opened behind them. Mike strode in from the theater and stopped on the threshold. His face remained cool and blank as he regarded them and turned away. Yet a rim of red outlined his imposing figure. Her fists clenched as she disengaged, again telling herself it didn't matter what he thought. Not his biz. He should be thrilled to see them make nice.

Chase kept a hand on her arm as they joined the others. She didn't shrug him off. The comfort level and intimacy were critical to their scenes working. She wouldn't change her behavior to appease anyone else.

The director stood in the center of the room, his expression lighter as he surveyed the actors. "You guys clean up nice. If I didn't know better, I'd think I'd time traveled to 1895. And I'd be scrambling for the return portal."

Ah, an indirect compliment to her talents, finally.

"We've got a good house tonight," he said, oblivious to her pique. "Be prepared to wait for the laughs. Believe me, they'll come. Especially with a loose, Friday night audience. You've worked hard, and you're going to kick ass."

The corner of his lip lifted amid the distracting beard stubble. "I didn't exactly take on the show willingly, but your dedication and the top-notch performances make me damn glad I did. I've enjoyed working with every last one of you, and you all should be proud."

He caught Marcy's eye in the mirror before glancing

away. Her pulse kicked up. She turned her attention to her short, buffed nails. No loud nail colors for Victorian ladies.

The director added, "If you go out there and give it the same attention as last night, the show will be a big hit." His voice rose, like a coach prepping his team. "You have it in you to soar higher. Loosen up. Go out and have a blast."

The cast and crew responses were enthusiastic but muted, due to the audience seated beyond the door. Every person wore an expectant, energetic air, ready to unleash weeks of preparation onto the stage. Marcy felt moisture gather in her eyes. Not sadness, but a communal joy. She blinked the tears away to preserve her makeup.

Mike hadn't quite wrapped. He brought forward a vase of multi-hued roses. One by one, he thanked people, offering a firm handshake to the men, and a hug and a rose to the women. She didn't intend to be last, but the others filtered ahead and then left the room. He reached around her to grip Chase's hand. The air was charged between them, but their expressions remained amicable. Her co-star shook and stepped aside but didn't exit.

Mike ignored his presence, focused on her. "Nan and Sheldon are here. I had them seated together front and center."

She swallowed her concerns, wishing she could observe them. They could be stiff and ignoring each other, or quietly reminiscing. Did decades of time erase the high emotions of a tragedy? "How were they getting along?"

He shrugged. "They arrived several minutes apart, so I greeted them separately and an usher seated them.

Both seemed happy enough to be here. Maybe a little nervous, but I assured we wouldn't put them on the spot." He looked up as Hannah popped her head in to relay the "five minutes" warning.

Chase followed the girl out the door and paused to shoot Marcy a thumbs up. She stood rubbing her palms together. The show didn't induce her worry. She dreaded that high drama might unfold in the audience.

Mike zeroed in on her fidgeting hands, and his lips pressed together. "What's wrong?"

She squeezed her eyes shut. "I get the impression Nan and Rod broke up fifty years ago, when she couldn't cope with Ellen's accident and moved away." She dared to peer up at him. "I'm glad they're here, and we should absolutely honor them and the moment. Still, I'm anxious about dredging up the underlying sorrow."

He pushed out an audible breath and squinted in exasperation, but at least he didn't growl. "You're telling me right before I walk out there to make my comments?"

"Sorry. I really didn't consider the point earlier." She wrung her hands again, imagining the expletives flying through his mind. He should be heading onstage now. "Look. Forget I said anything. Your comments will be insightful and appropriate, and the two of them will be fine. Otherwise, they wouldn't have come, right?"

"Let's hope so. We'll talk later." He pointed his index finger at her, resembling a chiding parent. "Everything'll work out. Don't let this affect your performance." He pivoted toward the backstage hallway and disappeared.

She sank onto one of the benches in front of the long wooden counter, glad for the moments alone to compose herself. Within seconds she caught movement on the camera monitor mounted in the corner. He'd reached the stage. She rubbed her arms and leaned forward to hear his remarks. The spotlight illuminated him, poised and smiling. So, he could act, too. She regretted pouncing the last-minute information on him. The words spilled out in her distress, without thinking of his role in introducing tonight's players. Her eyes rose, toward the plaster ceiling. The room was situated under the costume loft. Was Ellen aware of the unfolding dramas?

She tuned in to his voice. "Welcome and thank you for attending our opening night performance. I'm Mike Figueroa, director of *The Importance of Being Earnest*. The show by Oscar Wilde was first produced on our stage fifty years ago this month. Unfortunately, some of you may recall the run was marred by the tragic accidental death of one of the leads, Ellen Sanders."

Leaping up, Marcy positioned herself beneath the screen as he went on. "We'd be remiss not to honor her tonight and the cast who persevered, after a delay, to present the show. Please welcome two of the other leads who have joined us tonight. Sheldon Whitehead and Nanette Goins. Please join us in a moment of silent commemoration."

She grabbed her skirts and sprinted from the room, glad to be wearing soft, quiet slippers. The back hallway remained dark because a light might be seen from the stage. She didn't attempt the stairs but got the confirmation she'd hoped for. A hint of a white glow filtered through the doorway of the upper loft. The intensity must be blinding up there—but only to her.

"I brought them here, Ellen. What more do you want?" she whispered.

Chapter Thirty-Eight

Alone again in the dressing room, Marcy compartmentalized her concerns during the first act. Later, she'd overanalyze the entire night. Now she had to concentrate on her debut performance. Fragments of encouraging mantras swirled in her head. She ran her lines silently until the end of the last scene neared, and she rose to head backstage.

Standing behind the flats she'd painted, she tuned in to the lines being exchanged, accompanied by a burst of laughter from the audience. Her lips curved, and she caught a whiff of paint from the latest touchup to the garden canvas.

Maria reached out to clasp her hand. "You'll rock," the older woman whispered, wearing wire rim glasses and the sizable wig.

"We both will." She returned the palm squeeze, super grateful for the support of the fantastic veteran thespians. In silence, they waited for the lights to dim— the cue to take their places. A spike of tension-fueled adrenaline zipped through her system, and Marcy harnessed the emotion as weeks of rehearsal kicked in. Onstage, she immersed herself in the witty dialogue with heightened animation.

When Chase entered, they played up the romantic sizzle. Algernon's boyish charm and flirtatious ways matched his own real-life personality. As Cecily, she fell under his spell, until discovering his deceptive ways led to their estrangement. She and Lindsay exited in a scornful huff at learning Will and Chase's characters had both been pretending to be named Earnest.

In the dressing room during the intermission break, they released a swell of quiet giggles. Marcy plastered her hand over her mouth and presented her back to be unbuttoned. "What an incredible rush. You all told me how much difference an audience makes. I'm so pumped."

"Please say you'll audition again when you finish the program. Unless you get a big-time job offer to move somewhere rad." Lindsay released the loops with efficiency. "Anyway, I'd love to work with you again. We all would."

Maria opened the door and caught the last words. "Especially Chase," she said.

Apparently, she hadn't heard about the Sunday post-show dust-up. Good to know some secrets could be held at the theater. "You're all so wonderful and welcoming." Marcy ducked toward the rack to grab her next dress while avoiding the older woman's eyes. With the quick change accomplished, she headed toward the door. "If you two don't need me for anything more, I think I'll refill my water bottle."

In the green room, she added cool liquid to the refillable bottle and sipped carefully to preserve her lipstick. Capping it to leave, she spied a lone red rose in the vase on the counter. In their earlier agitation, Mike had forgotten to present it to her. Typical. While she'd helped him out by costuming and acting in the show, she'd also provided a series of distractions. He didn't appreciate distraction.

She sighed and hoisted her skirt to trot back to the dressing room. At the doorway, she nearly collided with another entering person. Mike flung out his hands to grip her shoulders, halting them inches apart. "Slow down to a gallop and save your energy for the stage."

His thumbs rested on her bare collarbones, reminiscent of Chase's earlier grasp. She registered the pressure and the warmth. The dark pool of his eyes. His body was rimmed with crimson. A tingle slid down her chest, and lower.

He stepped back and released her. "They're fine out there."

"Who?" She wrinkled her nose, partly in reaction to her body's unwanted response.

"Nan and Sheldon. I've kept an eye on them. I don't sense any animosity or awkwardness. I spoke to them briefly, and they're enjoying the show and talking to each other." Though his aura had flared, he appeared to have basked in the success of the first two acts.

She flattened a hand over her chest. "Thank goodness. I'm not trying to matchmake between them or anything. I just didn't want to hurt them." Feeling a little awkward herself, she paused. "Your comments at the opening were brilliant. I apologize for spooking you earlier."

*Hmph. He'd truly be spooked if he knew all the backstories.*

He shook his head, the corner of his lip lifting in a now-familiar, self-deprecating expression. "No, I'm sorry. I'm always uptight before a show opens. Apologies, too, for going off on you and Chase. None of my business. Glad you two seem to have made up." The words didn't mirror his expression, as his cheek twitched, and the half-smile flattened. But he'd made the attempt to clear the air.

With no need to rehash the unpleasantness or kick his butt for interfering, she stressed, "We're fine."

"Anyway. My manners have been lacking all around." He strode past to pluck out the lush red rose and returned to hold the stem toward her. "I got distracted earlier and didn't give this to you with the others. Which is a shame because I'm very grateful for all you've brought to our stage."

Ah. Finally. She accepted the bloom, and their fingers brushed, shooting another quiver of awareness through her system. She raised her eyes to his, her heartbeat pounding as he leaned closer. She inhaled the scent of a woodsy aftershave. His lips grazed her cheek, soft and warm, accompanied by a graze of stubble. Bristly stubble.

Marcy hoped her cheeks weren't flushed as crimson as the rose. "Thank you. I promise to do you proud."

His face had mellowed into the tenderness she'd seen on the stairs after they'd found David. To her surprise, a hint of red aura again outlined his body. His mouth opened—

"Five minutes." The stage manager again tossed the words through the door.

They both snapped to attention. His expression cleared. The color faded. "Better let you get settled offstage." His tone reflected business-as-usual. "Do you want to leave the rose here and retrieve it after?"

"Sure, *boss*." She reached around him to plop it in the vase and grimaced at the quick-change of emotions. Both hers and his. She must've imagined any softer tendencies. But why would she want to? She brushed past him to head backstage. For the few remaining minutes, she paced in the darkness.

****

When she and Lindsay launched into the final scene, she harnessed the emotional upheaval into positive energy. The two of them channeled the enthusiasm of actors who know they've captured the fancy of the audience. As the act unwound, the circle of highly coincidental situations and name changes came together until Chase-Algernon-Earnest uttered the last distinctive line, "…I've now realized for the first time in my life the vital importance of being earnest."

The stage lights dimmed to black. Laughing aloud, Marcy leaped to her feet and gripped Chase and Lindsay's hands in the tablcau curtain call. They all beamed along with the others while applause boomed throughout the theater. The spotlight illuminated the supporting characters before reaching the two young couples in the center. Each of them had an individual moment, and she curtsied low, awed to see people standing to honor their efforts. No matter what happened in her creative future, she'd always have this tremendous memory to cherish.

Offstage in the green room, she hugged a squealing Lindsay before Chase swept her up for a quick kiss. She exchanged excited congratulations with the other cast members as they filtered out the side door to greet the fans. Their positive comments reinforced the heady awareness: she'd held her own with more seasoned players.

She followed them into the theater and accepted words of delight from strangers. Her mother waved from the second row, and she sailed into the tight embrace.

"Baby, you were exceptional." Her mom blinked back tears. "I loved every snarky moment."

"Thanks. I admit I can't wait to do it again." She found it difficult to stand still with adrenaline spilling through her body.

"I'll be here tomorrow night with your dad to ensure you hold up the standard."

Marcy searched her face. "You're coming with him? I guess I assumed—"

"We couldn't spend civil time together?" She chuckled. "Actually, he's going to stay at the house. Since you're house-sitting for Justine tonight, we hope you can join us for an early dinner tomorrow."

She appreciated her parents' efforts to make nice, especially to provide a united front and avoid tension during her debut. Someone tapped her shoulder, and she discovered Tess, Trey, and Jake behind her. She bounced into their group hug as they shared congratulations.

Her best-boss-ever handed over a bouquet of bright painted daisies. "You were sooo good. Dialogue, demeanor, comic timing. Everyone excelled. And the costumes." She fanned herself in mock ecstasy. "I'm super proud, and Justine will be speechless at your success."

Her hubby joined in. "You all made me dig the Victorian era, beyond the architecture. Esther and my mom can't wait to see the show next weekend."

Jake nudged past him. "The three of us couldn't miss your opening splash. I don't have anything to compare to, being my first show, but I'm impressed." He twirled one of her curls around his fingers and tugged.

Marcy retaliated by weaving her fingers into his recent, shorter haircut. "Glad we could expand your horizons. Look at you, all spruced up. Mr. Management." She stepped away to admire the pullover sweater and khakis. Usually he wore jeans and T's, though he'd ditched his scuffed boots once he'd upgraded to a mid-level position at a local packaging company. "Seriously, I'm thrilled and thankful you're all here tonight."

He glanced around to ensure they wouldn't be overheard. "Anything new on the spook front? Pretty wild to have two of the main characters here from fifty years ago." He tilted his head to the left. "I'm assuming those folks are Nan and Rod?"

In her excitement she'd forgotten all about them. And Ellen. She whirled to find Sheldon a few yards behind her, talking to a well-dressed woman with straight, bobbed gray hair. He looked up and caught her eye. Without speaking, the couple moved toward their group. The duo didn't appear angry or upset, but an orange aura floated around him. No detectable color emitted around her.

Marcy's own emotions rose, yet she had to act normal and make introductions. "Sheldon, I'm thrilled you joined us. This must be Nan? I'm Marcy Alexander. How wonderful to meet you." Her fingers twitched on the daisy petals. "I hope you enjoyed the show."

He nodded, but she didn't sense his usual engagement. "Absolutely. A few of the lines resonated as familiar."

His companion shook her head. "I didn't remember specifics, sad to say. Such a lovely production, from the costumes to the acting. Thank you for contacting us." The comments appeared to be genuine yet generic, her composure unruffled, yet the play had to be unearthing unpleasant memories.

"Of course. Please let me introduce you to my friends and family." Marcy began with her mother and Tess, who had met Sheldon at the deli a couple of times. She finished with her other two friends, and a strained silence fell.

The older man broke it by taking her hand. "I hope you don't mind. Nanette's aware of the aura glow you mentioned. We've talked the situation over and would appreciate visiting the loft with you. If not tonight, at your convenience."

The interest and request caught Marcy by surprise. Excited to gain new insights, she registered a tug on her elbow. Tess cleared her throat loudly.

Marcy swung around and found Mike standing beside her. From the twist of his lips, he'd heard every word.

Chapter Thirty-Nine

The cheerful crowd began to clear from the theater, and Mike hadn't checked in again with their honored guests. He wove his way through the remaining clusters of family and friends to see the couple talking to Marcy, Tess and her husband, and a guy he didn't recognize. He tried to ignore the burn in his gut as the tall man and Marcy stood close and toyed with each other's hair.

Chase had left the room. Was she angling to replace him with someone new? If it wouldn't have been rude, he'd have pivoted away from the cozy group, but Tess caught his eye as he neared. He heard Sheldon speaking in a low voice. "…Nanette's aware of the aura glow…"

*What the heck?* Marcy spun to face him, blue eyes wide, her mouth a thin line. She projected big-time guilt. He raised his own brows. She held up a finger in a "hold-on" gesture and turned her back to talk to the others. "I'd love to give you a more thorough tour of the theater and all the updates over the years. Maybe after the Sunday matinee?" Her voice wavered, cementing the suspicion he'd missed an important piece of the puzzle.

Tess placed a reassuring hand on her friend's shoulder, reaching up due to the height difference. "Aren't Justine and Jackson attending the matinee? She's more familiar with the costume loft and could be a great reference."

He shifted forward to see both of their faces reflect

a shared, conspiratorial look. Something was up. Maybe she'd planned a special surprise for the two visitors? But why wouldn't she tell him?

*Because he tended to bark at her.* The self-defense mechanism worked, helping him remain aloof, but she had to consider him a grouchy SOB. He regretted not developing better coping mechanisms to deal with his feelings.

And yeah, he had them. They'd come to the fore since the split with Tara. Yet Marcy and Chase had patched it up, and now a new guy stood in the mix. Around his age, he looked confident, good-looking but far from flashy. Maybe she'd decided to date around before she left town and add a whole new type. His gut twisted, and he realized he'd missed the visitors' reply to her offer of a tour.

Tess addressed the two elders with a respectful warmth. "If you'd rather not attend the show again, you might come by the back door around four thirty after the matinee Sunday, allowing Marcy time to change." She trained the pleasant expression on Mike. "Would you wait to lock up? Or do you feel comfortable leaving us with the keys?"

"Don't worry, I can hang around. We'd also comp tickets if you two would care to view the production again." The older couple deserved attention and respect.

Nan exuded the gracious aloofness she'd shown in their brief interactions. "Thank you. We'll decide what works best." She inclined her head. "I very much appreciate your honoring Ellen and our production tonight. You've also done Earnest a great justice. We'll be out of your way so you can wrap up for the after-party."

They likely hadn't celebrated after their own show. The unsaid words hovered, darkening the mood. Sheldon's face sagged. After a few beats he seemed to gather no response might come off as impolite. "You've presented a top-notch performance. Thank you for including us." The two proceeded down the aisle. Goodbyes followed them.

Marcy attempted to appear composed, but her twitchy fingers gave her away. He wasn't fooled. He'd dig later for details on the "aura glow." Unless he'd misheard.

Nah, he couldn't think of a rhyming term to fit the comment. Of anyone he knew, she'd be the one to believe in chakras and mysticism. He stayed at her side to try to learn the backstory.

She clasped her hands in front of her chest, addressing the rest of the group. "I'm so grateful you all came on opening night, but Nan's right. I can't wait to change and go out and work off my energy with the cast. You're welcome to join us for a drink."

He tensed, waiting for the new guy to leap on the offer, but the trio refused. Trey spoke for them. "My babies need their sleep. Along with this blockhead." He cuffed the man's shoulder and included Mike. "You probably haven't met my cousin, Jake."

Cousin. He now noted a trace of family resemblance. He thrust out a hand. "Thanks for coming."

The dude applied pressure to his clasp yet didn't give off territorial vibes. "Great job, man. Can't say I'll come back for every show here, but I enjoyed this one."

"We love converts. I'm one of them." He relaxed in discussing the topic. "If she hasn't already, I'm sure Marcy will fill you in on how I came to direct the show."

After a few parting comments, the three wandered off. He held her eye to keep her from running away. "Fill me in at the bar." Her face scrunched, further confirming his intuition.

A half hour later he entered the local haunt decorated with flashing neon signs. Through the low lighting, he made out the younger cast members angling their necks to slam shots of tequila. Weary after the charged day, he took the empty seat between the saner influences of the older adults. A beer and wings were in order.

Bryant leaned across the table. "Let me buy you a congratulatory beer. You were plenty busy before the show, so I didn't get a chance to let you know your foster parent app is moving forward."

A slow smile curved his lips. "That's great news, man. Did you tell David yet?"

"Nope. I think you should be the one to share the details with him." He thrust his palm across the table. "Congratulations, Dad."

As they shook hands, the others took note. Marcy tilted her head. "Wait. The music's pretty loud in here. Did you offer congrats to 'Dad'?" She swung her gaze between them with a deepening frown.

Before he could comment, Bryant chimed in. "This guy, our awesome director, is going to foster parent our young tech genius. I've been following the application process for them, and everything's swimming right along."

Lindsay squealed from the end of the table. "That's fabulous. What a wonderful thing to do for him, Mike."

Others added a flurry of comments and congratulations. He ducked his head, feeling his face redden. He'd intended to keep the decision under the radar.

A few seats down, Marcy rested her chin on her fist and regarded him. "Congrats," she mouthed through the din around them.

Pleasure flooded his system. Tara hadn't supported the decision, but his theater castmates understood. "Thanks," he mouthed back. The noise in the room faded from his consciousness as their eyes held. She winked slowly, and his heart rate sped up.

Then Chase tugged her arm, and she whirled toward him, giggling at some comment he couldn't hear. The evening wore on, with the "mature" end of the table enjoying pleasant conversation as the rowdies boosted the hilarity. Another round of shots followed before the food landed, with a toast toward his fostering effort.

He declined to join in and gave them a mock stink eye. "I appreciate the sentiment, but you do have a show tomorrow night. Wicked hangovers will take the edge off a performance."

They responded with laughter. When the food orders arrived, he noted they were at least eating, as well as drinking. He kept a check on their actions as he did the same. More than one cast had overindulged at a party, and he'd joined in his own share of excesses. They were adults, but the responsibility of shepherding the group ultimately rested on him as the director. He didn't want to open anyone up to a DUI.

As midnight neared, Chase and Marcy appeared buzzed, if not outright drunk. Probably an intentional move on his part to loosen her inhibitions. Mike tapped tense fingers on the table, contemplating whether to intervene. She'd refused another round. Lindsay and

Will changed to soft drinks, but the bad boy downed a couple more hits of tequila. Had he learned about that Jake guy and decided he should drown his sorrows?

Geez, he needed to get a grip. He usually stayed far away from others' personal drama, but the redhead somehow had slipped past to make him care. Still, he sure as hell shouldn't stoke any emotional investment after her declared plans to leave the area. Plus, if she wanted to pursue the relationship with Chase, he wouldn't interfere. Despite the dude's sometimes-jerky behavior, he was a good man who deserved a relationship with a caring, giving, talented woman.

*I should leave now*, Mike told himself. They wouldn't be foolish enough to get in any real trouble. The noise level also didn't lend itself to having a serious conversation with Marcy on what he'd overheard at the theater. Otherwise, he'd be tempted to corner her.

Yet he couldn't bring himself to walk away from the group. Some impulse kept him in his chair, unable to leave or to get up and join in the laughter at the other end. After another half hour, the older actors around him said their goodbyes. He watched Chase lean his chair back, snorting with laughter, and nearly topple over.

Mike didn't think, just leapt to his feet, and walked over to clap a hand on his shoulder. "You shouldn't be driving, bud. Will, I hope you're taking him home in one piece."

He towered over them, arms crossed over his chest, feeling like a frickin' chaperone. Four sets of eyes peered up at him in surprise. They reminded him of defiant kids breaking curfew. Forcing him to be the killjoy. Marcy's questioning look spilled his emotions into words. "I'll drive you home," he told her. "Your cars will be okay here overnight."

As anticipated, Chase protested. "I'm fine, man." He waved his hands and knocked over the ketchup bottle.

Will righted it. "Nope. You're with me. We live in the same house, remember? And I need to be able to whip your Algernon butt again tomorrow."

Marcy narrowed her eyes and stared down at her purse. "I'm okay. Really. I'll go slow," she mumbled.

"Let him take you." Lindsay, her hair still in the upswept 'do, kicked in support of the safer position. "You don't want to risk an accident or a DUI. I've been drinking pop for the past hour." She projected an angelic smile at him.

"I suppose you're right." Marcy gathered her jacket, but none too quickly.

Her attitude pushed his temper. He counted to ten, attempting to defuse the annoyance while the server collected their payments. "No change." He handed the girl a twenty-dollar bill and followed the crew outside. Will hauled Chase away by the arm and stabilized him when he stumbled over the curb.

"Twit," Mike muttered. He watched Lindsay start her car and turned toward the fourth partier standing next to his truck, as if she belonged there, waiting for him.

Chapter Forty

Grumbling, Mike kicked the crazy thought out of his head and unlocked the doors. She climbed in and slumped in the seat. Not passed out, just shooting sparks of unhappiness with his decision. So be it. They didn't speak as he maneuvered out of the parking lot onto the street, his lips firmed into a thin line.

He could hit her with the "glow" comment now, but in her pissed-off state she probably wouldn't answer. To break the accusing silence, he flipped on a country station and signaled to merge onto the main street intersecting the town.

She straightened to stare out the windshield. "I'm not staying at home. Justine asked me to house-sit tonight on Michigan Avenue." Her voice sounded level and clear. She must not be as buzzed as her horny friend.

"That's more on my way." The avenue featured some of LaPorte's most impressive historical houses. He'd have another fifteen to twenty minutes before he'd reach his house and decompress. If he could sleep with all the adrenaline, questions, and unwanted emotions flooding his body and mind. He turned right at the next intersection and drove down the quiet street. A popular singer crooned his grief on the radio at losing his girl. He stabbed the button to find another station.

She kept her eyes forward as they transitioned into a neighborhood of older, well-maintained homes. "Will could have taken me, too," she finally tossed out.

He grimaced, not mad at her but upset at the situation.

At the stupidity to even consider pursuing any attraction which might—emphasis on *might*—have existed between them.

At Chase being bold enough to make a move first. "I think you're better off letting lover boy cool his heels alone tonight."

She swung to face him, curls flipping around her cheeks. "What's that supposed to mean?" Her face appeared creased and angry in the brief flashes of illumination from the streetlights. He didn't answer as he cruised up the tree-lined street. They were both on edge. No reason to invoke an argument.

His hands clenched on the wheel. "Where's the house?"

"Third on the right. Really, Mike, what are you saying?" Her voice pitched higher, and she glared, finally giving him her full attention, fists balled in her lap.

He signaled into the driveway and stopped, frustration overwhelming his system. "Nothing. None of my business who you date." He didn't add the acid words "or sleep with." The loaded comment would be way out of line. But he wanted to say the words, wanted to push her into explaining if she was wrapping with Chase and taking up with Jake. Or keeping them both on a string. Any answer would hurt. Either way, she'd be leaving in three months.

"You ass." She pushed toward him in an explosion of energy, stretching the seatbelt, close enough her breath blew warm on his face, carrying a tang of tequila.

"I am not, repeat, *not*, sleeping with him. Or even dating him. Though it definitely isn't your business what or who I do." She stopped to fumble with the seatbelt lock. "I'm sorry Tara dumped you, but don't take your hurt out on the rest of us."

He reared back at the unexpected anger. The words swirled in his brain as he reached for her arm. Relief coursed through his system and consumed his senses, yet he'd made a huge, shitty blunder. She wasn't sleeping with Chase, but he'd infuriated her with the comment.

She attempted to shrug off his restraining hand. He held tight, undoing his own seatbelt with the other hand and sliding out from under the steering wheel, toward her. "I'm sorry." The words sounded lame and feeble.

Eyes lit with fire, she jerked her captured left arm. "I'm not easy."

"I know." He backpedaled, frantic. "You've got my system so messed up I can't think straight." It registered he might be hurting her. He released his grip and shoved a hand through his hair, willing her to please stay and listen.

She finally held still. "I've got *your* system messed up?" She slowed the words, as if measuring them in her mouth. "So you go on the attack. How can one man be gooey and thoughtful and awesome one minute and a frustrating ass the next?"

"You think I'm gooey and awesome?" His pulse leaped again. He could continue to hide his feelings—clearly the smart track—or take the leap.

Smart was way overrated. "I didn't mean to attack, and this is in no way connected to Tara. Not that I'm proud of it, but I'm the one who broke up with her. We'd both lost the spark, and hanging on wasn't fair to either of us." He held her eyes, willing her to believe him. "I was okay letting her claim the dump, but then I did something really stupid. I hid behind words with you instead of acting on what I've been fighting."

With a final exasperated tug, he drew her toward him. The soft body collided with his chest as it had in the costume loft. His lips found hers at last, swallowing the brief gasp.

To his relief, she didn't struggle or slap him upside the head. She wrapped her arms around him and met his lips with equal fever. He groaned deep in his throat as she opened her mouth to welcome his tongue.

A blast of want spread through his body, a blaze consuming all doubts and hesitations while he focused on her sweet mouth. Her lips. Her tongue. She reached up to cup his cheeks, molding her mouth to his. One word sighed through his mind—*Yeesss*.

Kissing alone fell far short of the absolute satisfaction he craved. He spanned her waist with his hands, and his body heat flared as she spun to straddle his lap. She broke the kiss and resettled, facing him with those dramatic blue eyes. An unspoken connection sizzled between them, and she glided forward to nibble at his lips.

The gentleness almost undid him. He feared he might lose it, fully clothed, but couldn't resist roaming his hands under her top to caress the silky skin of her stomach, moving upward to her breasts.

"Inside," she panted into his ear, her breath releasing shivers down his body. His shaking fingers obeyed, lowering to the zipper on her jeans. "No. Inside the *house*."

Finally understanding her through the haze of

desire, they untangled their limbs and leaped out onto the sidewalk to trot to the house hand-in-hand. Urgency built into a storm within him as she fumbled in her purse for a key, unlocked and pushed in the heavy door. He followed on her heels and kicked it shut behind them.

As it banged closed, he pulled her toward him, while recognizing the need to slow the pace or explode too soon. Their bodies strained together as the kiss deepened, lips and tongues stirring a fluid ocean of need. His hands smoothed down her back to grasp the firm butt, fitting her body tighter to his.

The memory of her pushing Chase away at the theater flickered. "You okay?" he whispered. If she asked him to stop, he would, but he'd whimper all the way home. Their coupling might be just as unwise, but he'd gone too far to care.

"Mmm." She moaned the answer, pressing her mouth into the thrumming pulse in his neck.

He lifted the clingy top over her head, sailed it into the darkened foyer, and nuzzled his way toward her cleavage, relishing the smooth, heated skin. His teeth nipped at the lace edge of her bra as his hands roamed her back for the clasp.

"Upstairs," she whispered, her voice breathy.

No clarification required. She hit a light switch, and his body sizzled with energy as he grabbed her hand and bounded up first. At the landing, her palms guided his shoulders, pushing him into the first doorway. From the faint stairway illumination, he saw a double bed. They tumbled onto it, and he reached to slip the bra off her shoulders, caressing as he went. The dim light shadowed her torso and the fullness of her breasts. "So, so beautiful." His whispered words were followed by trailing lips.

She gasped again, and he caught her eyes as he explored along her upper body. The open longing on her face imprinted in his mind. Her hand stroked into his hair, and she undulated up toward him. He reached for her zipper again, asking permission. "Yes?"

Eyes closed now, she hesitated then nodded. The jeans rolled down her legs, the long, gorgeous legs he'd admired when she'd approached him the first night at the theater. He couldn't wait to have them wrapped around his back. He broke apart to unbutton his shirt in the streaming moonlight, and she sat up to push his hands aside and flip the buttons one by one.

She splayed her palms over his bare chest, murmuring, "You remember undoing my buttons at the costume shop? I almost swooned."

*Did he remember?* He'd nearly lost it, too. The reminder of the hot moment made him harder, increasing his urgency as her hands lowered to hook on his belt buckle. When they slid inside the zipper to cup and caress, he quivered, taut and ready to explode. But was she? His fingers trailed along her flat stomach, and down. She arched against the exploring hand. "Now, please."

He dug out a condom, happy to oblige. Sheathed, he poised above her and entered, noting an unusual tightness. She stiffened, and her hands gripped his shoulders. Had he moved too quickly? He wanted her to enjoy the experience fully, not see him as an impatient fool concerned only with his own pleasure. He forced himself to slow, as his body shouted otherwise. "You still okay?"

She attempted a smile. "Absolutely."

An implication burst into his brain, distracting his body. "You're a..."

She shifted her palms to cup his cheeks again, holding his eyes, fully engaged. "No. Not a virgin, just rusty by choice. Let's make it memorable."

She fused her lips to his, and their bodies took over.

\*\*\*\*

Sated and content, Marcy spread her limbs under the sheet in the post-midnight hours. Her toes and fingers connected with a solid mass of muscle and warm skin, drawing her nearer till their sides aligned. His arm crept around her, tugging her into him. The man emitted a furnace blast of body heat.

She relaxed into him, without awkwardness, as they lay together in the dark. She'd imagined—hoped for—romance, fun, emotional connection, and loads of passion in her next sensual encounter. They'd discovered each sensation together. He'd been tender yet coaxed incredible sensations from her body, taking time to determine what she liked, to bring her to a climax.

He'd acted surprised at discovering her tightness but had been so sweet to stop and check on her well-being. After a moment of discomfort, her body had eased into the hot, enjoyable rhythm. Yes, she knew other people experimented with a variety of lovers, but she'd wanted more than experimentation and had waited to find it. She traced a finger down his forearm, lightly covered with dark, soft hair.

Realistically, who knew how, or if, the relationship would progress with her murky future plans, but she didn't want to dim their current enjoyment.

He rolled and shifted to face her, and she marveled at how well they fit together. "Close your eyes," he instructed. His voice, low in the darkness, shivered along her skin. The mattress dipped her toward the middle as he pulled away, and she deduced he was reaching for the bedside lamp. She scrunched her eyes closed, comfortable lounging in the dark, tracing fingers along each other's skin, but turning on the lights made her nervous. Made it "real." She grasped the tangled sheet to her chest as illumination spread over them.

He loomed behind her, fingers edging along the smooth cotton. "Uh-uh." Humor laced the comment as he plucked the barrier down to expose her to the cooler air. "I couldn't wait any longer to see your tattoo."

Goose bumps raised on her sensitive flesh even as the sexy tone melted her. She tilted her hips toward him in a teasing invitation. A calloused finger traced the quarter-sized Celtic symbol on her upper butt cheek, followed by a brush of lips. "I can interpret what this says." His tongue followed to flick the skin with a wet rasp.

She shivered as the tendril of desire concentrated heat at her core and revived her excitement. "Really? What do you think?" Her voice sounded all trembly. She felt all trembly. She prepared for either a straight answer or a joke.

His lips skimmed upward to her shoulder, down to her hip, and lower, to fuse on the ink. Her breathing quickened as she waited, reveling in her body's awakened sensations.

"It says Mine."

She twisted to peer up at him. An unexpected shyness softened his face and showed he wasn't being possessive. The words melted her, turning her insides all gooey. By persevering, she'd managed to tunnel through the mock-gruff exterior to the softie beneath. The man dared to open himself and expose his vulnerability.

She sat up and captured his cheeks in her palms, holding his gaze while caressing the dark stubble. Her lips fluttered to his, staking her own possession.

Chapter Forty-One

Lying on her side, Marcy awoke to bright sunlight slanting through the curtains. She winced and flung up a hand to block the glare. A slight headache niggled at her temple. Ouch. Yet she stifled a giggle. No way she'd inform her mom that tequila had indeed made her clothes fall off. Along with ultra-sexy encouragement from her partner.

Their second *encounter* had been, well, pretty darn explosive. She fingered the sheet and tried to roll without awakening him, to snuggle to his side.

He met her eye and his lip curled up. "Morning." He appeared well-rested and relaxed. As he damn well should.

The rough, sexy voice almost made her purr as she recalled their post-tattoo explorations. He didn't have any ink, but she'd found an appendectomy scar, evidence of hidden details she'd be intrigued to dig out. "Good morning. Hope you slept well."

He held her gaze, measuring the reaction as his hand crept over her quivering skin. "Best night in weeks."

With no need to play coy, she shifted to improve his access. "Are you looking for an encore, Mr. Director?"

\*\*\*\*

After another star-worthy performance, they showered, and she whipped up scrambled eggs with cheese and wedges of buttered toast in Justine's kitchen.

The two-story brick home had belonged to Jackson's grandmother; they'd updated the appliances and added granite countertops and tile flooring. The vintage oak cabinets remained, along with an open-shelved country cabinet. She couldn't quite believe she was eating breakfast across from Mike. He seemed to share the emotion and captured her hand, kissing the fingertips before digging into the food.

*Thanks, Tara. You dope.* She sent up a silent message, wondering how the woman could have let him go without a fight. But wouldn't she have to do the same if she confirmed a decision about the program? She nearly choked on her coffee. He already believed she'd be leaving at year-end. Did he consider their time together a fling? Did she? Her appetite waned, and she nudged the plate away.

He forked up his remaining eggs, chewed, and wiped his mouth on a napkin as she shredded hers in her lap. His eyes pinned her. "Before I forget again, I have a big question to ask. I hope you'll answer honestly."

She stiffened. "All right." Would he pose the relationship status question so early? At this moment, she couldn't answer beyond today. Beyond the show anyway.

According to his confession about the breakup, emotional distance had tanked his relationship with Tara. Literal distance would be every bit as difficult. She considered rising to busy herself with cleanup, to deflect any heartache that might come with the discussion. But she remained rooted, wisps of paper drifting onto the floor.

He settled his elbows on the table and paused, appearing to consider his words. "Last night, I heard

Sheldon mention a glow in the costume room. What did he mean?"

Crud. She'd rather discuss the relationship status. He'd asked for honesty, but could he accept the truth? She covered her mouth with her fingertips and pondered. His dark brows began to knit as a lawnmower roared into life outside the window, making her jump. "You might not believe me," she said in a small voice.

Of course, he looked puzzled. He leaned toward her. "Try me."

His tight features told her he was struggling to be patient. Best to have faith and leap in. "Some people, in the world, have um, abilities." She squirmed in her seat, and the rest of the napkin spilled onto the floor.

"Like acting, you mean."

"Nooo. Like seeing things."

A full-force frown emerged.

Her eyes lowered, and she toyed with her fork. "I didn't believe it, either. Some people see the past. Some people, ghosts." She pushed out a long, martyred breath. "I see auras."

"Auras?"

With her credibility tanking, she hurried to explain. "For instance, you might call Tess a vintage-clothing empath. When handling certain items, she gets sensations, and sometimes, visions from the past. After she and Trey came together, they discovered they could both envision past scenes. In fact, their efforts solved a family mystery."

A shadow clouded his face. "Kinda crazy sounding, but I'll hold my judgment. How does their story impact you?"

He wasn't succeeding in hiding his skepticism.

Which kind of ticked her off. She straightened in the chair and drilled her eyes into his. "After I joined them in seeing a vision, I started to pick up auras around people. One dominant color when their emotions heat up." Her voice strengthened. May as well own and finish the craziness. "When I went up to the costume loft, I discovered a white, pulsing glow. An aura. From Ellen Sanders."

He shoved back from the table. "You what? And Sheldon believed you?" His aura now presented in a solid red wall of disbelief.

"He's known me for five years." She crossed her arms over her chest, simmering. "I'm not some loony approaching him on the street. I suppose you and I haven't been acquainted long enough, *well* enough, to dive into something this flaky."

*You know me well enough to sleep with.* The insinuation floated between them.

He held up a hand, his jaw working. "I'm not saying I don't believe you. I just never expected to hear something so…different." He grabbed his coffee mug and drained it, as if seeking courage in the caffeine.

She tried to relax, unwinding her arms into her lap. She could understand his position. Her family embraced nature, the arts, and the mystical. With his personality, he probably came from a more conservative background. She realized she knew very little of his family. Or much about his job, other than the title of lead engineer and a couple of projects he'd mentioned.

He interjected, "What do you intend to do with Sheldon and Nan in the loft?"

"We're hoping to get closure for Ellen." At least he hadn't stormed off. Yet his aura color remained strong.

She'd persevere in hopes he'd reach a tentative acceptance. "Tess, Trey, and I saw visions when they were up there with me recently. Frankly, we're not sure if what happened to her was an accident."

She rubbed a hand over her stomach, which had begun to twist. "I'm hoping Justine will see Ellen's ghost and be able to talk to her."

He stood up from the table, startling her, his face incredulous. "She's part of this circus act, too?"

She couldn't keep the sarcasm from intruding. "Should I conference call her and Tess so they can back up my story?"

"No. I'm sorry. I don't mean to be a jerk." He walked to her side and began to massage her shoulders with gentle hands. "I've always prided myself on being a down-to-earth, grounded kind of guy."

"Typical red aura," she muttered.

"What?"

"Your aura is red dominant. Hard-working, honest, driven. High standards." She left off passionate, which might derail the discussion.

His hands lifted from her shoulders, and he returned to sit in the chair, bracing his forearms on the table. "You all plan to go ghost busting up there Sunday after the show? No offense." Thank goodness, he must be somewhat receptive; the red haze had almost disappeared. "We plan to convene to try to figure out what Ellen wants. Why she's showed herself to us."

He tapped his fingers on the table. "Do you really think somebody hurt her?"

"No." She'd certainly considered and rehashed all the possibilities. "Not intentionally, at least. Sheldon's a wonderful man. He was so good and gentle to his wife, especially after she became ill. I do think there's something he isn't sharing, though. I'm hoping an intervention with all of us will reveal the truth and untether Ellen from the theater." She slumped in the chair and waved her hand. "The story's far-out and woo-woo for your engineer brain. But you asked for honesty. I'd be a skeptic, too, if I hadn't experienced it all firsthand."

His eyes darted away. "Give me time to marinate in the details, okay. In the meantime, this will sound crappy after my stressing honesty, but I think we have to be careful in how we handle…" He gestured between the two of them.

Her stomach flipped again. They were going to pick their way through another conversational landmine. Thank goodness she'd taken aspirin. The smell of the congealed eggs made her queasy. She tried to project openness and calm. Not to appear as if the words might send her running. Or, worse yet, puddling to the floor.

His gaze returned to her. "Much as I want to shout from the rooftops, the rest of the cast probably shouldn't learn about us yet."

She barely kept from asking, *there's an us?* "You mean Chase."

He nodded. "I don't want to be dishonest, but let's not give him a reason to go off on you. Or me."

"Or to mess up the show?" She narrowed her eyes, wanting to believe the nice-guy explanation, but feeling exposed again—and ultra-vulnerable.

His jaw worked under the dark stubble. "Of course, the show's an issue, but my first concern is you."

Her heart reopened at the words. She believed him. For all his attempts to hide behind bluster, he was an honest, upfront man. "One of the reasons I've enjoyed working with you is you care about people though you hide it behind a tough-guy exterior." Her lip lifted in a teasing smile.

He held up his broad palms. "I'll cop to being sort of an ass when we met."

"Sort of?"

Thank goodness she'd taken the time to dive beyond the façade to admire his other qualities. He ticked the list at kind, talented, smart, mature, good-looking, and sexy. But she held those thoughts inside, not wanting to be *too* vulnerable. Because of his prior relationship with Tara and hers with Chase, she'd tamped down her attraction. Now here he was, with her, right after she'd declared her intention to leave and pursue her dream career.

She stood to hide her divided desires and plunked her loaded plate in front of him to finish. "You're right. We should lie low till after the show closes."

Chapter Forty-Two

As promised, Marcy ate dinner at the house with her parents. She couldn't quite wrap her mind around the two of them sitting together, eating together, *laughing* together. The wholesome family scene she'd dreamed of since they'd split after her high school graduation. Their prolonged dance toward division had included shouting matches, hurled pottery, and days of moody silence, the passionate nature of artists.

Tonight, they'd cooked the meal, shooing her out of the kitchen to rest and revitalize before the performance. She'd rarely held back details of her life, good or bad, from them. But she kept her lips zipped about Mike joining her at Justine's house. The news was too overwhelming to share with anyone right now. Another time, she'd have loved their counsel as her mind remained muddled on how she should proceed. *One day at a time*, she told herself as she forked up another bite of her dad's amazing lasagna, ravenous after having ignored her earlier brunch.

When she'd arrived home, she'd found the two of them laughing together in the living room, sitting close on the couch to pore over an old photo album. In the years since he'd left, the desert sun had tanned his skin and scored new fine lines into his face. But the changes only enhanced his strong jaw and hazel eyes under the silvering hair. The old west cowboy vibe suited him nicely. Plenty of cowgirls probably agreed.

She looked up and caught her parents staring at her. Uh-oh, she'd drifted far away. "Your specialty is really great, as usual," she mumbled around the gooey cheese.

He reached to cover her free hand with his palm, his body rimmed with purple. Something was up. She increased her chewing to swallow the large bite as he spoke. "Since I have to leave tomorrow, we wanted to talk to you." He squeezed her knuckles. "Sorry to drop a surprise before your performance, but don't worry. The news is major, but good."

The fork slipped from her hand onto the plate, and she winced at the clatter. "Sorry. Go on." She tried to accept his "good news" descriptor and not panic.

"Yes. We hope you'll be happy," her mom chimed in. "As happy as we are."

Pat aimed a smile at her former partner, and a stream of sunny yellow encompassed her. His aura merged to overlap hers, forming a bonded light-brown border. He placed his other calloused hand gently over her mom's on the table, to link them all in a colorful, familial triangle.

Marcy stared down at their hands, mesmerized. *They couldn't be... They weren't...* "Please elaborate," she managed to squeak. "Before I pass out from the apprehension."

They chuckled toward her. She barely resisted the urge to shout a clichéd question: *What have you done with my parents?* Her dad, always the more playful personality, appeared giddy.

Her mom's eyes hadn't shone for much too long. "I'm moving to New Mexico after Christmas."

The words circled around her brain but didn't quite

land. "You're…reconnecting."

He jiggled her palm, as if willing her to grasp the situation. "We never got divorced you know. Only separated."

"We never stopped loving each other," her mom popped in again. "Just couldn't live together. Everything became too entrenched and volatile. Our stubborn sides ruled, and we couldn't get back on track."

Marcy scanned between them. The emotions seemed legit, but she had to ask. "Tell me the truth. You're not getting together so I can go into the program without regrets?"

Her mom snorted, but her face crinkled with amusement. "Honey, I'd do many, many things to ease your life. This may appear to be a convenient solution, but if I didn't believe we could and should try again, mountains wouldn't move me."

Dad zigzagged a finger between them in the air. "You inherited her independent, questioning nature. Think carefully. Would your mother grit her teeth and live with me to appease you?"

"No way." Marcy's confusion and concern began to lift, opening her to admit a growing realization. She focused on her mother. "I'll override my own stubborn nature to finally admit you'd have been fine on your own."

"I have to be slow and careful, but I'm not helpless." Her mom softened the words with a gentle lifted brow. "I've appreciated your help so much during this transition, sweetheart. But I hope you can go and commit to enjoy your program without worrying about me."

"I'll always worry about you, but only out of love." Marcy's voice cracked, and she leaped to her feet. Her mother stood, and they met at the end of the table to fling their arms around each other, holding tight. Releasing the happy tears.

Her dad's voice floated over them. "Now this is something I've missed seeing. Not the tears, but my two favorite ladies hugging."

Marcy leaned to drag him up. "Then you'd better join in." His eyes watered, too. Strong, tanned arms enfolded her. She warmed in the overlapping embrace, remembering her artsy, laid-back, chaotic childhood when Dad had led her into adventures and Mom had bandaged the minor cuts and scrapes.

After several seconds, they all disentangled to sit, and she voiced surprise at their revelation. "You two did catch me off guard today. In the best way."

"Understandable." Her dad reached for the salad bowl, resuming the meal. "What you weren't aware of—not that we kept it from you—was we've been talking and Facetiming over the past months." He fished for an olive and popped it in his mouth. "The initial topic centered on supporting you to get out of here to pursue your advanced classes. Before long, we started to recall all the things we loved about each other."

Her parents exchanged those syrupy-sweet expressions again. Marcy grinned with them. She couldn't wait to tell Mike.

*Tell him what? That the major obstacle to her leaving had been cleared?* She covered her mouth with the napkin so they wouldn't misinterpret her downturned lips as relating to their news. Tonight's revelation erased a huge hurdle but couldn't clear all of them.

Chapter Forty-Three

Marcy went directly to the dressing room before Saturday's performance—to get ready and to maintain a distance from Chase. She found Lindsay in front of the mirror, primping and prepping.

Her co-star manipulated the mane of thick, dark hair into an updo and greeted, "Hey, girl. What's the status with lover boy since the news has settled in about your leaving?"

*Lover boy?* Oh, she meant Chase. "We're cool again." Iceberg cold, in reality. She couldn't drop a hint of hooking up with Mike. Tongues would wag for sure.

"Your move to Virginia changes everything, I'd imagine." Lindsay kept her eyes peeled to the mirror as she anchored bobby pins into the tresses. "But huge congrats. I was thrilled to hear your news last night. You'd better believe I'll be visiting."

Marcy stood behind her to insert another trio of stabilizing pins into her friend's dark hair. With no need to pretend, she fully embraced the truth of the transition. "Awesome. I'd love to see you. I'll scope out all the best dance bars and restaurants to sample the nightlife in town."

She took the adjacent chair and began to work on her own hair, pleased at the thought of building a true friendship beyond the theater. With all of the cast members. They were creative, fun, and supportive people. The type she preferred to surround herself with.

Wait. She wouldn't be around to grow the relationships beyond the next three months. As she'd reminded herself the night before, new friendships, and relationships, often fell away with distance.

*Especially fragile ones formed in secret.* She stabbed in a bobby pin and stuck her scalp. "Ow," she yelped and flinched.

Her friend swung with concern. "You okay?"

She rubbed her fingers on the tender spot. "Misjudged my strength. Guess I'm a little nervous about the performance."

"A tinge of nerves is a good thing. Overconfidence and second-night swagger can derail a show. I always 'fill up my tank' before I go on, pushing out all the distractions but maintaining the edge." Lindsay stood. "See you on the other side."

Taking the advice, Marcy buried the concerns to give her best for another applauding audience.

****

Apprehension returned a few hours later at the cast celebration. She sat nursing a ginger ale, observing more than participating. Thoughts of her parents' reconciliation bubbled through her head, but she'd determined to wait and share the news with Mike.

She peeked down the table at the Mexican restaurant to observe him in animated conversation with Will. He gestured broadly and threw back his head to chuckle, looking more lively than he'd been in weeks. Of course, they'd engaged in hours of tension-busting activity the night before.

Since they were meeting at a restaurant rather than a bar, David joined them, fitting in among the older theater crowd. He sat next to Mike, who began to praise his efforts. "He's a natural." He clapped a hand on the boy's shoulder. "I told him he should consider getting a degree in theater someday. At least a minor, if he continues to be interested through high school and Little Theatre productions."

The teen tried to look humble but couldn't contain his pride. "I'm interested, for sure. But if I'm helping with shows, they'll reel you in, too. After all, I'll need a ride."

Marcy took in the open, teasing expressions. The boy must be aware, and supportive of, the fostering application. The night before, she'd been stunned to hear the revelation. Her surprise had quickly adjusted to joy when she recalled her conversations with Mike about how he'd guided his brothers' lives. The man had a huge heart, and hers had swelled at the selfless gesture.

Before slamming shut with annoyance at his high-handed order that she shouldn't drive. From the beginning, her emotions had swung the pendulum with him—but last night passion had ruled. She swigged half the ginger ale, hoping to keep the flush of heat at those thoughts from spreading to her cheeks.

The waiter returned, and she declined a refill, noting Mike had stood and begun to say his goodbyes. They'd kept a cool distance, not sitting together or talking more than usual. Although they'd locked eyes for a couple of careful, steamy glances. They'd agreed he'd leave from the gathering, and she'd wait fifteen minutes and meet him in a church parking lot to follow along the route to Fish Lake.

With Justine arriving home tonight, she'd told her parents she might stay at Lindsay's so she could party and not wake them or drive so far. It wasn't an outright fib because she might have if she wanted to. She told herself she'd come clean with them after the show. After all, their earlier bombshell had dominated the dinner conversation.

Plus, her absence would allow them to *reconnect* without the awkwardness of having her in the house. She bit the inside of her lip to suppress a laugh and laid her phone on the table to watch the time. At the allotted interval, she made her excuses and offered hugs and farewells. A silent chuckle did erupt in her chest as she walked away. Oh, how they'd all react to knowing her secret, true destination.

At the darkened church lot, she rolled down her window to wave to Mike. He blew her a kiss, and she followed his pickup out into the night. Along the back roads to his home, she cranked the radio and warred between nervousness and growing lust. This evening she'd given herself permission to admire the strong, attractive features and his toned body in the fitted dress slacks. Nevertheless, the planned rendezvous felt a tad forced compared to last night's spontaneous combustion. Alcohol had helped reduce her inhibitions then, but she'd also been absolutely willing. Tonight, she'd go in stone-cold sober.

They'd take their time and get to know each other. Her pulse thumped in her throat, and in her ears, as he signaled a turn past the Fish Lake town limits. Pushing out slow, calming breaths, she switched off the wailing radio to maneuver around the edge of the namesake body of water. She only glimpsed the dark expanse of lake, as houses of varying sizes filled every available lot.

He hit the brakes and parked in front of a compact

tan cottage with a concrete stoop and an overhang. The property, or what she could make out, appeared neat but no-frill except for a straggling pot of geraniums. He jumped out to unlock the side door of the house. She clutched her purse, moving in slow motion, and wrinkled her nose at the assault of fishy water.

He flipped on an outside light, capturing her in the glow. She smoothed her face and ducked inside in case a neighbor might be peeping out. After hours of pretend disinterest, an awkward silence floated between them. She swiveled to take in the sparse-furnished living room, the black leather couch and large-screen TV.

"Nice," she managed, peering past into the combination kitchen and dining area. Seascapes would add a needed pizzazz to the blank tan walls. Or her dad's landscapes.

He rubbed a hand on the back of the couch and avoided her eyes. "I know it doesn't have the cozy ambiance of your place."

"You mean cluttered." She attempted a light tone, unclenched her fingers, and laid her bag on the end table. In silence, he helped her shrug off her jacket. Geez, it seemed they both could use a little liquid courage.

They could either wallow in the strained situation, or she could make a move. Gathering her moxie, she spun to place her palms on his chest. "Feels a little weird, doesn't it? As if we've skipped the dating step."

His brows crinkled. "Does that bother you?"

"No. Dating's overrated." She skimmed her finger along his collarbone, inching up the chiseled chin.

His face lightened, and he captured the finger in a playful bite, warm lips closing around it. He now held her eyes with sexy intensity. "I agree we skip the formalities."

Heat flooded her center, and she flashed back on their frantic race up the stairs and the tumble to the bed. She fused her lips on his. The unease disintegrated as they deepened the kiss, hands roaming, until he led her giggling to his equally bland bedroom. She barely registered the non-décor as he stripped her of her clothing with his hands. And teeth.

Chapter Forty-Four

Justine texted Marcy on Sunday morning, confirming they'd arrived home.

—*You didn't have to wash the sheets*— Her friend chided.

Umm, yes, she did, but she wasn't ready to elaborate quite yet. Some stories needed to be told in-person.

After Sunday's matinee performance, she waded into the post-show audience to find Jackson and Justine midway back. A light tan tinted her friend's usually pale skin, enhanced by a peach-toned dress. The waving strawberry blonde hair had been tamed into submission with gel and a barrette.

Justine grabbed her in a hug, to dance and squeal in the aisle. "I couldn't have costumed them better," she finally panted out. "And you were marvelous onstage. Sorry for underestimating the full range of your talents."

"Believe me, I cursed you at first for leaving me here alone." Marcy fanned her face with her hand to cool down. "But I've been thrilled with the entire experience." *Both onstage and off.*

"You'll want to take over from me for good." Her friend's mouth fell open. "Oops. I mean, after you finish the program in Virginia."

*If I come back.* Marcy refused to let the thought dampen their reunion. Despite the frequent calls and texts, she'd missed her best friend. "No one can replace your costuming wizardry. But California apparently agreed with you both. I want to hear all about your project."

Jackson had waited in the aisle, and he finally claimed his turn for a hug. "Come over for dinner this week," he invited. "Now that you won't have every night rehearsals." His skin had tanned a couple of shades darker than his wife's, contrasting with the straight, brownish hair streaked with blond and hip, dark-framed glasses.

"Ooh, that's right. I can reclaim my life." Marcy spoke in a chipper tone, but the reality had begun to slam her. Major changes were afoot. She changed the subject. "What did you think of the show? You're the expert scriptwriter who grew up with an actress mother. Or do I dare ask?"

"Truthfully, I wasn't sure what to expect." He smirked. "But you surprised me. Wilde was a genius with words, and the actors have to grip the deadpan comic delivery. The cast did a commendable job and nailed every character."

"We have our director to thank," she said, pleased at the affirmation. "Especially me."

Her bestie gripped her arms again. "Which did you prefer? Costuming or acting?"

A deep male voice broke in from behind. "I'd be interested in hearing the answer, too." A shiver coursed down Marcy's body. She fought the impulse to lean back against Mike. Instead, she shifted to include him in the conversation as he greeted the couple.

She pretended to debate her answer, ignoring his teasing tone. "Hard call. Guess I'd say you've awakened the ham in me." *In addition to other enticing sensations.*

"I knew it." He stood close enough to brush his arm against hers. "The costumes were first-rate, too. You did give me an anxiety attack when you first pranced in here, though."

He threw a mock-stern glance at Justine, who had the grace to look sheepish. "I'm really sorry for bailing on you," she admitted. "The studio offered an incredible opportunity to join in on the film as a period clothing consultant. How could I resist dabbling in early 1920s decadence?" She sent an adoring look toward her spouse. "They're interested in working with me again on my brilliant hubby's next proposal, set in the '60s."

Jackson wrapped his arms around her from the back. "Lucky for her I'm into historical fiction right now."

The gushy display would have niggled a little jealousy before, but with her own secret lover at her side, Marcy relished their devotion. Till she remembered they'd be joined soon by Tess and Trey, plus Sheldon and Nan. "Speaking of the sixties, are you clear to stick around for a while and *assist* in the costume room?"

Justine's gaze shot to Mike. "Absolutely. But I can't guarantee success."

"He's aware," Marcy reassured her. "He didn't have an easy time accepting the situation at first, until I mentioned all of you." She peered around to ensure the theater had emptied. "I do believe he may have expanded his mindset to accept the slim possibility of otherworldly energies."

Mike scrunched his face. "What do you expect from a down-to-earth red aura?" The others burst into laughter as he stared at Jackson. "Are you going to tell me you jumped right in line when you first learned of your wife's ability?"

Jackson mirrored a similar bemused expression. "No way. I feel you, man. But when you love someone, you accept their quirks and eccentricities."

*Love.* Marcy went rigid at the mention of the loaded word. Time to reroute the conversation. "I'll change, and the others will be here soon. Hopefully, combining all our *powers* will provide a solution." With her friends joining in, she'd feel more powerful and in control of the situation. If an answer could be found, they'd discover it tonight.

In the dressing room, Lindsay hadn't left and offered to unbutton her gown. As her nimble fingers worked, she asked, "Will the hunky guy who came on Friday come to see the show again? Or is he in your sights, too?"

"You mean Jake? We tried dating but decided we're meant to be good buds." Marcy swiveled, yanking the fabric from her grasp. "Wait, are you interested?" She bit her lip to contain the excitement. He'd worked hard on his PTSD and addiction issues, and she'd love to see him with a great, open-hearted woman.

"Maybe. Well, hell yeah." Lindsay grimaced. "I've seen a not-so-nice side of the guy I started dating, and your handsome friend grabbed my interest." She resumed unbuttoning the dress. "Doesn't hurt to ask."

"Intriguing." Marcy removed the gown and hung it up, her mind working. "Let me ponder how to maneuver a meet-cute." She put on her jeans, thinking Lindsay and Jake might make a good pair. Her outgoing, entertaining personality would balance his chill, laid-back demeanor.

Opposites attract seemed to have worked for her and Mike.

"Cool." Having posed the important question, Lindsay gathered her purse and headed up the stairs.

"See you at the Thursday pick-up rehearsal, co-star. For our second weekend of performances."

Their final weekend. Marcy would savor every moment, but first she and her friends had a super important task to tackle. She finished dressing and stepped onstage, where the bright lights had been extinguished. Below, four new arrivals had joined the group. Their voices filtered off when they saw her.

Her legs weakened, and she forced herself to descend the steps, while assessing the reactions. Sheldon radiated apprehension, underscored by a cloud of his orange aura. Nan appeared less assured than she had on Friday, yet she didn't exhibit any color. She must have strong control to tamp down her emotions in the weird, stressful situation.

Mike stood frozen next to them, his jaw working as he flared a tinge of red aura. Tess gave an encouraging wave, arm in arm with Trey. They were all waiting for her to take charge.

She cleared her throat, her gaze pivoting between them. "First, thank you all for coming tonight and pursuing this strange intervention. I really do value the support, and I have faith that together we'll be able to help Ellen." She crossed her fingers behind her back, praying she'd be proven correct. Perspiration bloomed on her palms and under her arms.

*Courage.* The word floated in her consciousness. A leader should exude absolute positivity and determination. She'd spent a good deal of time weighing potential strategies and had decided on an approach. "I'll go into the room first to determine the aura is still there. When you all enter, if Justine doesn't see her immediately, Tess could try handling the gown again."

Nan winced at the "seeing" reference. Her first show of emotion. The others appeared intent and focused.

Marcy held up the old scripts they'd found. "I also brought these along."

In front of her, Sheldon crumpled, drawing a collective gasp. He slumped into a theater seat, surrounded by a rim of pulsing orange. She dropped to her knees in front of him. Before anyone could speak, he flapped an agitated hand. "I'm all right. I swear. Just…overwhelmed. Please, go ahead."

Nan hovered beside him, her face flushed with concern. "We should all sit. May I?" She held out a hand, indicating the scripts, and Marcy handed them over.

In somber silence, the others fell in line in the first row. Marcy stood again to address the group, with a close eye on the older couple. She didn't want to overstress them, but they had to proceed. "I…umm…" She straightened her spine and firmed her tone. "As I said, Tess, if you'd try to summon a vision, maybe we can gather another clue of what she's seeking."

"She may want to punish me."

All their heads whipped toward Nan. Tess' brows furrowed. Without a word, she leaned in to place a hand on the older woman's shoulder. Marcy moved to add her own and dropped her second hand onto Sheldon.

## Chapter Forty-Five

*"What's crawled up your butt, Ellen?"*

*Rod squinted at her in the dim back hallway, frustration hardening his voice. He didn't get this girl, constantly flashing hot and cold with him. He'd tried to make nice with her as his girlfriend's pal, but she seemed intent on complicating his life.*

*All he wanted to do was talk to Nan, to buy time and make up with her. But when he'd bolted through the back door, he'd found Ellen lurking in the shadows. Waiting to ambush him? She glared at him and refused to respond to his pointed question.*

*He stepped closer, for emphasis, and privacy. "If you think you're protecting her, buzz off. She doesn't need your smothering friendship anymore. Can't you accept she's happy with me?" His hands fisted at his sides. "What the heck did I ever do to you?"*

*She held her ground. "You're messing around with Lorna behind her back." Her breath hissed past his cheek. "You'll break her again, and this time she might not recover."*

*"Are you kidding me?" A knot of anger clutched his chest and pounded against his head. He grabbed her arms and shook her, whipping the long brown hair off her face. "The only business I have with Lorna is trying to buy a ring I can afford from her uncle's jewelry shop. Since when is that an almighty crime?"*

*Her mouth dropped open. The eyes flew wide. "Oh no…" She wrenched out of his grasp, whirled, and ran toward the stage.*

*Damn it. She'd spill his surprise, maybe to everyone in the tight-knit group. And possibly open him to humiliation if Nan turned him down. With a burst of adrenaline, he darted out of the hallway to see that she'd reached the wall of velvet drapery backstage. He swerved around a curl of rope in the dark, cursing as she neared the opening to the stage. She'd reach Nan first. But he couldn't give up.*

*He'd have to fight the urge to throttle her when he did catch up. Panting with exertion, he watched the curtain part, but from the outside. Nan walked through the opening.*

*He skidded to a halt a few feet away, stumbling to keep from running them over. Ellen was too close to Nan, moving with too much momentum. She plowed straight ahead. He yelled something unintelligible as they collided hard, sending them both reeling. Nan careened back against the curtains and slammed to the ground.*

*Ellen shrieked and stumbled forward headfirst. Her hands grasped for something, anything, to stop her fall, and connected with a thick, hanging rope. She clung, swayed, and stabilized for a few seconds. Until the spotlight anchored above crashed down with a thundering clatter of metal and glass.*

*His scream joined Nan's and ripped into his soul. He dived the few feet to protect her. To wrench her into his arms and cover her eyes from the gruesome scene, the blood he'd never erase from his memory. He swallowed back the vomit crawling up his throat as excited exclamations and unseen footsteps burst out from all directions, heading their way.*

*His love whimpered in his arms, limp and sobbing. He could barely hear her tortured, broken voice. "My fault." She wailed, a high, crooning note that pierced his eardrums and increased his own trembling. Her tear-filled eyes closed, and she became boneless in his arms as the director and cast members flooded in to surround them.*

Chapter Forty-Six

Why was her face wet? Marcy swiped at her cheeks and realized she'd gone from standing to sitting on the floor. Wooziness blurred her vision, along with the…tears? Nan and Sheldon came into focus, still seated before her, their faces mirroring distress and confusion. She moaned and pressed the heels of her hands to her eyes. The others began to speak over each other, and she couldn't quite separate their words.

"What happened?" Mike's raised voice cut through. "You wavered as if your knees were giving out."

She turned her head slowly to discover him kneeling behind her. "I'm okay."

"I helped you to the floor, but I don't think you were aware." His voice shook, and he stared at her with probing intensity.

Continuing the slow, deliberate movement, she lifted her head to seek out Tess' face.

Her friend now stood next to Trey, who placed a protective arm around her waist. Her skin had paled, but she appeared calm with just a hint of aura. "We saw a graphic vision from Rod's point of view. Of the accident." She addressed the others, her voice remarkably level after what they'd witnessed.

Trey interrupted to steer her to the closest seat. "Sit, please. I don't know that we need to hear all the details."

Sheldon's head reared back. "No, we most definitely

do not. I regret that you viewed that terrible scene." He squeezed his eyes shut. "Through the years, when I was under stress, I'd wake screaming from the dreams and scare poor Pauline witless."

Marcy had regained her equilibrium but decided to remain seated on the floor, with Mike now sitting beside her. She resisted the urge to take his hand for comfort and support. The vision had strengthened her resolve, but she'd proceed with a delicate approach. "I'm so sorry you all went through such a tragedy." Her sympathy went out to the older couple. Nan now sat shivering, hands clutched in her lap. Finally, her aura began to glisten in a haze of blue. *Intuitive, sensitive, generous, and expressive. A people person.*

Yet their efforts today would benefit someone who had passed long ago. "Before we went under, you said she might want to punish you?" Marcy persevered in a gentle tone when Nan remained dazed and silent. "Why would she want to do that?"

Sheldon's head drooped again, shielding his face. His companion stirred to lay her hand over his, braced on the chair arm between them. She took the time to survey the entire group before speaking. "If you saw correctly, you know I'm the reason the spotlight fell on her."

At Justine's gasp, she amended, "Not on purpose. My Lord, of course not." She shook her head with a jerking movement. "That night I walked through the stage left curtains, and Ellen barreled into me. She knocked me down, stumbled, and began to fall. I was paralyzed. Couldn't move, as she attempted to right herself and ended up throwing all her weight around a hanging rope. She didn't realize it attached to a spotlight." Nan covered her face with her hands, the aura flaring indigo.

With a firm jaw, Sheldon slipped his arm around her quaking shoulders. "Not your fault. I told you at the time, and I've always believed it. High time you do, too." He shuddered out a breath, his attention riveted on her, as if they were alone in the room. "If anything, I'm to blame. I was upset at Ellen, and she ran from me. I chased her, because I feared she'd tell you about the ring or spout some nonsense about me and Lorna." He peered across at Tess. "Hopefully you two can confirm my memory of being far behind her when she tripped. Believe me, I never intended to harm her. I just wanted to talk some sense into her and try to put the silly spats behind us."

Tess nodded. "Yes, that's what I saw. A sad, terrible accident."

Mike gestured toward him. "You weren't to blame. Either of you. Though we understand how you'd carry the weight of it."

Nan swiped her fingers under her eyes. She appeared to have aged by years, her face and body sagging at the effort of reliving the incident. "I appreciate everyone's absolution. But difficult as this is, I need to finish the story." She dug for a tissue in her purse and continued. "The shock took me down. I fainted before the cast and crew rushed in. Rod, bless him, didn't tell anyone of my direct involvement. He made it sound as if he walked in alone to see her fall and bring the light down, and I entered immediately afterward. He protected me."

"We protected each other," Sheldon interjected. "You were too broken up to answer all their probing questions."

Marcy drew her knees up to hug against her chest. Her eyes filled with tears again at the horrific burden these two had been carrying for years. She remained torn between wanting to keep them from the pain and fascinated to hear the truth. Hopefully talking out the details would be cleansing. "The newspaper articles said the police especially questioned one of the cast members."

"Me." Sheldon faced her, still emitting a faint aura. "As supposedly the only one near her in the moment, they explored the possibility it might not have been an accident. The rest of the cast wasn't trying to pin anything on me, but when questioned, some of them agreed our relationship had been antagonistic."

"You were cleared," Nan reminded with a pointed look. "Nobody ever really believed otherwise." She drew a deep breath. "In the beginning, I was too incoherent to give a statement. Rod—sorry—Sheldon convinced me to repeat his story. He said if we didn't, our actions would look more suspicious. But if they'd tried to pin something on him, I absolutely would have spoken up." Her voice rose with fervor. "I'll always regret my cowardice in hiding behind the explanation. The lie." She paused but no one else spoke, mesmerized by her words. Another visible shudder wracked her body. "I've also agonized over whether my best friend might've died thinking I tripped her on purpose. Because we'd been on the outs."

Her companion laid a comforting hand on her arm. "Not to belabor our teenage drama, but she came to believe Ellen might be making a play for me, out of jealousy. The girl went to her house and accused me of messing around with the stage manager. I did have secret conversations with Lorna, but only because she connected me to her uncle's out-of-state jewelry store to buy a surprise engagement ring."

Marcy and Tess exchanged glances, recalling the scenes they'd channeled with Trey in the loft. He caught their interchange and leaned in to address the older man. "Not to pry, but did you purchase—"

"No, I never bought the ring. After we finally stumbled out of the theater, in shock and horror, I tried to explain everything to Nan. Sadly, we could never get past the enormity of what happened." He sighed, as if the memory cost him.

Nan patted his cheek, her aura dimmed to a pale, cloudy blue. "No. I couldn't move forward. The accident broke me, mentally. The specter of Ellen would always be in the middle of our relationship." Her voice lowered further. "I couldn't handle life in general, and my protective parents moved us away. With my husband passed, when our son relocated here for work two years ago, I decided family ties were more critical than hiding from my guilt." She glanced at the rapt, assembled listeners. "Truthfully, I'd hoped never to revisit the building. Never to dwell on the experience. But we're here, and I accept we need to be." She stood, pushing up from the chair arms for support. "No more delays, we should go to the loft."

****

Upstairs, without further conversation, they initiated Marcy's suggestions. She entered the costume loft alone first. Her chest tightened as the glow beckoned brighter, larger, than before, spanning the entire back wall. With the additional details she'd heard, her heart fluttered at the possible source driving the presence. Did Ellen seek a vessel to hurl accusations to wound her former friends?

Mike trailed in behind her, followed by the others. This time she clasped his hand for courage and spoke toward the corner. "The aura's here. More dominant than before." She raised her voice, not really necessary in the small confines. "Ellen, your friends have come to honor you. My friends and I want to help bring you peace and resolution. But first, we need more information."

Justine came up and shook her head. "Sorry, I don't see her." She gazed around the room again.

Tension poured through Marcy's body, thickening her breathing, ratcheting up her pulse. The group effort had to work. She wouldn't leave the mystery unraveled, or the spirit behind it in further limbo. "Ellen, can you show us what you want, in a vision, or…a more concrete fashion?" She heard the pleading tone in her voice. "Did you catch what Nan and Rod said downstairs?" After a few beats she dropped Mike's hand and spun to face the others.

He looked dubious but attempted to cover the skepticism. Sheldon and Nan shared a tense demeanor, their palms linked. Her two best friends appeared serene and ready, standing around the perimeter, while their spouses' downcast eyes exhibited the usual resignation to the weirdness. She'd brought them here and dragged them through an emotional rollercoaster for—

Justine's expression changed, her eyes widening. She peeled away to approach the corner with a purposeful step, surrounded by a purple wave. "Hello, Ellen. We're so pleased you've joined us. Would you care to share your message with me?"

Marcy clutched her chest with one hand, while Mike reclaimed the other and squeezed it in an almost painful spasm. "Good Lord above," he mumbled under his breath.

Half obscured by the waist-high hanging racks, Justine proceeded into the corner and stood with her head tilted. The glow billowed out to touch her. Marcy fought another wave of dizziness. She gripped Mike for stability, thankful he'd insisted on coming despite obvious cynicism.

For a handful of minutes, Justine asked short questions and occasionally responded back. Finally, she returned to the group with a somber expression. Surrounded by a blue fog, Nan's face blanched, and she swayed. "Chair. Please," Sheldon barked as Nan slumped against him. He grabbed the offered straight chair and settled her onto the seat, holding everyone's attention. "Okay, hon?" he questioned as she settled. With her affirmative nod he instructed, "Go ahead." He moved behind her to grip the chair back.

Justine moved in to focus on the older couple. "The message is positive. She's asking for *your* forgiveness and apologizes for eavesdropping. For, in her words, 'butting in and destroying your relationship.' She feels responsible for breaking you up and keeping you away from a wonderful love." Her lips curved in a gentle arc. "She's wanted to share the information with you for all these years." She paused, letting the words sink in. "Also, she stressed that she doesn't want either of you to feel guilty." With the message relayed, she eased backward to stand next to Jackson.

Nan's face and body relaxed, and the aura disappeared. They all watched in silence, giving her the privilege of responding. She finally regarded them with damp eyes. "Thank you so much for your support and caring. I'm very grateful. This may sound silly, but what did she look like?"

Justine moved forward to respond. "Late teens. Pretty. Straight brown hair. Wearing a bright red mini skirt."

"Oh yes, we loved being daring as those short styles caught on." Again composed, Nan rose and reached for Sheldon's hand to lead him toward the corner. The others fanned back to give them room in the crowded space. She exchanged a questioning glance with the man at her side and began to speak toward the wall, holding up a trembling hand. "We do forgive you, my dear friend. I missed you more than you could know. Or perhaps, you did. The concept is most comforting."

She hesitated, her eyes drifting to the man at her side. "While I did, indeed, love a certain young man, I later found a fulfilling marriage, with a fine, caring husband and family."

Sheldon couldn't seem to bring himself to take his eyes from her. "I loved my Pauline very much, as well. But you were my first true love."

They exchanged another soft look and hugged as the glow burst into a blinding, magnificent white flash and disappeared. Marcy gasped, blinked a few times, and swung toward the group. "She flashed her approval. This resolution is why she's lingered. Right, Justine?"

"Ellen's gone," her friend agreed, her attention on the corner. "I'd say she's at peace." She cupped her hands around her cheeks, as if amazed at the part she'd played.

Tess dug a tissue out of her jacket pocket and blew her nose under reddened eyes. Trey wrapped a reassuring arm around her shoulders.

Marcy sniffed away the tears clouding her own vision. Mission accomplished. She'd stayed with the task and helped fulfill a cosmic desire. "So beautiful," she muttered to Mike, hardly able to get the words out. He gripped her hand and pulled her into a tight embrace, planting a kiss on her head. Over his shoulder, she saw Tess' mouth fall open. Trey responded with an enthusiastic thumbs up.

Chapter Forty-Seven

With the ghostly mystery solved, the show rolled toward a close the following weekend. On the final Saturday, Tess dragged Jake along and maneuvered him to sit next to Lindsay at the after-gathering at the Mexican restaurant. She jogged Marcy's elbow, on her left, to whisper, "Despite a few years age difference, those two appear to be hitting it off. When you and he decided not to pursue anything, Trey and I hoped he'd find someone special."

"She's the best, and I can see them together," Marcy agreed. "He's such a great guy, and he's really put in the work to turn his life around. The two of us unfortunately didn't have the right spark."

Her friend tilted her head toward the end of the table and kept her voice low. "But Mr. Mike has fanned your flame." She tittered. "He's definitely a keeper, if the scenario works out to stay together with your leaving. Both of you being the loyal, steady sort, I bet you could do the long-distance deal with him. Working at Divine Vintage, unfortunately, not so much." She pursed her lips. "I'll miss you bunches, but I'm thrilled you're finally going after your own dreams."

"Me, too. But leaving is bittersweet for so many reasons. Speaking of spark, though, you should see my mom mooning around the house. A literal beam of sunshine with her aura flashing yellow when she talks to or about my dad." She zipped her lips on the aura subject and halted to thank the waiter as he set another margarita down for her, and a ginger ale for Tess. "Oh, and with the mortgage paid off, they're planning to hold onto the house while I finish school and advertise it for vacation rentals." With her earlier approved application still in the system, the Virginia program had accepted the updated information and welcomed her inclusion in the winter-spring 2017 semester.

"Keeping the house gives you a place to stay during any school breaks. Unless you bunk down somewhere else." Tess started to grin then halted to peek down the table. "I suppose you will need a place with David moving in at the Fish Lake house."

"Mike and I haven't discussed the future. I admit I'm skittish about that." Marcy crunched the tortilla chip on her plate into pieces.

"Of course you are. Don't rush the discussion. Enjoy each other, and the right time will reveal itself."

"If you say so." She looked up, and Mike caught her eye, sharing a quick, intimate look. The subterfuge was titillating, but was the secrecy creating a false thrill that would dissolve after the show closed?

No, she wouldn't ask about the future. Much too early to rock the moment with tough questions.

\*\*\*\*

The cast presented another strong Sunday matinee performance, greeted with enthusiastic audience applause. Afterward, the actors and crew tore down the set, put away the props, and cleaned up the dressing rooms and green room. Mike stashed the costumes in his car, as he and Marcy planned to make another trip to South Bend together.

She helped him load them in the trunk, and he placed the daisy dress on top, murmuring, "How about you model this tonight, and I help with the buttons. Or hinder?"

"Meow. Let's get this tear-down finished double-time." She waited till he'd closed the trunk to back him up against the fender, pressing her body into his. The sexy innuendo had sent an arrow of desire straight to her center. "I love when you talk dirty Victorian." She rotated her hips slowly against his, her lip lifting at the rapid response under his jeans. To heighten the tease, she stepped back. "Oh, I forgot. Our friends don't know about us yet. Wouldn't want to be caught in the parking lot."

"Minx." He grabbed her hand. "Come on." He tugged her along at a rapid pace toward the theater's back door.

Her heart rate accelerated. She'd anticipated the moment and now faced it with a mix of apprehension and exhilaration. They burst into the door and through the green room to the theater space, still holding hands.

Oh my gosh. How would he approach the others? What would he say with Chase looking on? She quivered out a breath and glanced around the room. Lindsay wielded a broad broom to sweep the bare stage. Will rolled a vacuum cleaner across an oriental carpet that had graced the final scene in the country manor house. Additional voices and sound filtered in to indicate activity backstage and in the opposite direction, in the lobby.

Mike grasped her hand tighter and led her up the stage steps. He stopped at the perimeter of the wooden floor, watching them. Will turned off the whirring machine. Lindsay paused.

The director nodded. "Thanks for cleaning the floors. I can help you carry the carpet backstage."

No mention of their coupledom. Marcy waited, her pulse thumping. Lindsay dropped the broom with a loud thwack. Her eyes popped wide, riveted on their joined hands. In the silence, she caught Will's gaze and jerked her head, hard, toward the sight.

He began to chuckle, his shoulders shaking. "If you're sending us a message, we're reading it loud and clear. And we're super happy for both of you."

Lindsay rushed forward to throw her arms around them. "Can we spill to the others? I'm assuming this public PDA is a declaration."

"Nope. This is a declaration." When she backed away, Mike turned to plant a smacking kiss on Marcy. He disengaged, leaving her reeling. "I'm a man of few words."

Chapter Forty-Eight

Over the next month, having confessed their involvement to her parents, Marcy spent most nights and every weekend at Mike's home. They packed in alone-time before David's arrival, with the fostering application still lumbering through the system. On this sunny mid-November day, Mike grilled kabobs outside while she prepped the rest of the evening meal. The two of them often cooked together, which pleased her immensely as he broadened his palate beyond what she considered to be typical man-fare.

She loaded the dishwasher, watching him through the window above the sink. Oblivious to her scrutiny, he cleaned the grill with meticulous intensity. They'd established a sync and rhythm she hadn't imagined possible with their differing natures. She delighted in teasing out his playful side, and they'd discovered shared interests in nature hikes and watching old movies, as well as zipping off on the motorcycle. To enhance the house décor, she'd begun painting a seascape for his living room wall as a Christmas present.

Christmas was less than six weeks away. Three weeks later, she'd load up her car and drive to Virginia. Her stomach churned, and she eyed the wall calendar, seeing the notation to get together with their theater friends the coming weekend. They'd endured a handful of harmless joking comments before their couple status had seamlessly integrated within the group. Chase had only raised an eyebrow, as he'd moved on to date an attractive blonde who had slipped him her number after their final show.

She sometimes pondered how they'd handle running into Tara. In their interconnected area, no doubt they'd end up at the same bar or festivity some night. They'd likely exchange cordial words, and on their exit, Marcy would make a point to shove her hand into Mike's back pocket.

Meanwhile, she noted another important calendar date circled in red—the court hearing on the foster parenting process. With the case manager's approval to spend time with David, she was thrilled the two guys connected when she worked weekend shifts. They usually shot hoops and tinkered on an old car Mike had bought to rebuild. She'd been included in initial discussions ranging from how to decorate his room, to his music and food choices.

While having the teen live at the house would change circumstances, they'd make the situation work, though she wouldn't be staying overnight.

She rinsed the last dish, and he shut the grill top. Their eyes met through the glass, and he waved the metal scrub brush at her, his eyes crinkling. A tiny thrill frittered through her chest, yet for all the positivity, she couldn't help but wonder if the two of them would drift. Especially when the teen settled in.

Would it really be fair to build the relationship further when her deadline to leave ticked down? The program would demand the majority of her concentration and commitment, especially in the beginning. The boy rightly would soak up Mike's time and attention.

Or were the emotions between them deeper, real enough to try to withstand the circumstances and physical distance? She hadn't approached the idea, out of fear at hearing a wary or dismissive answer. Yet she craved definition. She placed the bowl in the dishwasher and opened the slider onto the deck, to find Mike lounging in an Adirondack chair. The sunset shifted to gold over the lake, intensifying the ripple of chill in the air.

She shivered and halted next to the chair, torn at owning her expectations. Her feelings were at stake, and she was falling. *Hard.* She'd fought the attraction for weeks, but now the floodgates had opened. His hidden softie center emerged much more often, and his thoughtfulness swamped her with tenderness.

Mike reached up to tug on a curl, drawing her attention. "You're far away. What're you thinking?" When she didn't respond, he gently pulled her down onto his lap.

She snuggled into the warmth of his broad chest and closed her eyes, blocking the display of nighttime color and a family of floating geese. "Truthfully, I'm thinking about you." She kept her voice small, unsure how far to venture.

"Really?"

The pleased tone drew her to look up, to see a smile hovering on his lips. "Only good things, I hope." He brushed a finger across her cheek. "I've been sitting here thinking how easy it is between us. How we can laugh and talk of big things or nothing at all for hours. How we don't care if our hair's messy or we have morning breath when we wake up. How fricking sexy you are wearing my T-shirt to cook breakfast with those long, tasty legs tempting me."

She felt a stirring in his lap, underlying the words, and couldn't help but laugh. "We're going to have to curtail that activity here when David arrives, you know. As a reminder, we almost left the stove on yesterday when you yanked your shirt over my head. You're a fire hazard, mister."

"A hunka hunka burning love." He sang the words in his smooth baritone. "But seriously"—he tightened his hold around her—"we're good together."

"Yes, we are." Her mood soared, and she nuzzled his jawline—but she had one critical unanswered question. She straightened and hesitated. "I know this is early. Probably too early to ask." He lifted his brows in encouragement to continue. "With my leaving, are we…keeping it cool?"

Her heart pounded so hard he probably could feel it thump against his chest. Anxiety snaked through her stomach, and she was tempted to jump off his lap and dive into the cold, numbing water to avoid the answer.

His arms relaxed their hold. "Do you want us to?"

The defensive wall began to rise between them. She could protect herself or tell the truth. She swallowed and spoke around the nerves drying her mouth. "No. I'd prefer to continue enjoying our time together, to grow in it and see where the emotion takes us. But I'm a goofy optimist who believes in lo—" She bit off the word and registered the warmth flushing over her cheeks.

His eyes bored into hers, and his hands tightened around her waist. "I believe in love, too, sweetheart. I've been burned, but not scarred. I'm not worried at your leaving. If the relationship's meant to go the distance, we can weather a few months with Facetime and flights. I'll work out the logistics with David. I imagine he can spend an occasional weekend at a friend's house."

Now she wanted to jump in the water—with him—and splash in the relief and joy, but there were other, more pleasurable ways to celebrate such welcome news. She slipped a hand between her legs to his denim-covered crotch. "Lucky for us, I sure do love the thrill of flying."

**A word about the author…**

Sandra L. Young's appreciation for vintage clothing inspired her to write a series of three cross-genre novels, heavy on the romance, historical mystery and ghostly sizzle. Her debut novel, *Divine Vintage*, published in 2022, was followed by *Divinely Dramatic*. She's had a blast wearing pieces of clothing from her extensive vintage collection for signings, podcasts, and other presentations. For readers outside Northwest Indiana, she'd be happy to zoom in for book clubs. Just reach out through her website: www.SandraYoungAuthor.com

And for the multitude of readers who have left reviews, she extends heartfelt thanks. The kind words inspire her to keep sharing her quirky genre-mix novels. Stay tuned for Justine's story to wrap the trilogy!